ON A
Midnight
Clear

Books by Tracie Peterson

Books by Misty M. Beller

Books by Karen Witemeyer

ON A Midnight Clear

A 3-IN-1

CHRISTMAS NOVELLA

COLLECTION

TRACIE PETERSON, KAREN WITEMEYER, AND MISTY M. BELLER

BETHANYHOUSE

a division of Baker Publishing Group
Minneapolis, Minnesota

The Shepherd's Heart © 2025 by Peterson Ink, Inc.
A Star in the West © 2025 by Karen Witemeyer
No Room at the Inn © 2025 by Misty M. Beller

Published by Bethany House Publishers
Minneapolis, Minnesota
BethanyHouse.com

Bethany House Publishers is a division of
Baker Publishing Group, Grand Rapids, Michigan

Library of Congress Cataloging-in-Publication Data
Names: Peterson, Tracie. Shepherd's heart. | Witemeyer, Karen. Star in the west. | Beller, Misty M. No room at the inn.
Title: On a midnight clear : a 3-in-1 Christmas novella collection / Tracie Peterson, Karen Witemeyer, and Misty M. Beller.
Description: Minneapolis, Minnesota : Bethany House, 2025.
Identifiers: LCCN 2025018383 | ISBN 9780764245725 paperback | ISBN 9780764245732 (casebound) | ISBN 9781493451326 ebook
Subjects: LCSH: Christmas stories, American | Christian fiction, American | LCGFT: Christmas fiction | Christian fiction
Classification: LCC PS648.C45 O46 2025 | DDC 813/.0108334—dc23/eng/20250416
LC record available at https://lccn.loc.gov/2025018383

Scripture quotations are from the King James Version of the Bible.

This book is a work of fiction. Names, characters, places, and incidents are the product of the author's imagination or are used fictitiously. Any resemblance to actual events, locales, or persons, living or dead, is coincidental.

Cover image © Magdalena Russocka / Trevillion Images

Published in association with Books & Such Literary Management, BooksAndSuch.com.

Baker Publishing Group publications use paper produced from sustainable forestry practices and postconsumer waste whenever possible.

25 26 27 28 29 30 31   7 6 5 4 3 2 1

The Shepherd's Heart

TRACIE PETERSON

CHAPTER 1

For a moment that dawn, everything seemed completely perfect. The temperature was just right, chilly but not cold. The routine aroma of coffee suggested that all was well in the world—that Pa was up and preparing to face the day.

Angellyn snuggled down in her quilt and tried to go back to sleep, but then the awful truth seeped into her thoughts. She tried to push the memories aside, but they surged through her mind too fast, like water spilling over a flooded dam.

Yesterday was to have been her wedding day. She was to be Mrs. Cameron Johnson. At twenty-eight, Angel thought Cam was probably her last chance at romance since the war had killed off so many of the men she'd grown up with. And while she hadn't been all that much in love with him, Cam had been someone with whom she thought she could make a future and eventually love.

But Cam had other ideas. While Angel was dressed in bridal white, waiting for her cue to join her father at the back of the church, Cam was already miles away with another woman. A much younger woman. He'd left a note that his best man had been instructed to bring two minutes before the ceremony. He didn't want to give anyone time enough to come after him. Granny Duran was the one to bring it to Angel. The look on her face left Angel no doubt the news wasn't good.

Without any real explanation, Cam penned his farewell, letting Angel know that he'd found someone else and hadn't the courage to tell Angel face-to-face that he was breaking off their engagement.

The embarrassment of having her father go out and let everyone know that the wedding had been canceled was almost more than Angel could bear. It had been hard enough being the one and only spinster of their small Nebraska town, but now this. She pulled the covers over her head with no plan to ever leave her bed again.

Angel hadn't thought going back to sleep even possible, but soon enough found herself dreaming of an open field of new spring grass. She stretched out on the ground as she often loved to do and stared up at the skies. Large white clouds drifted across the expanse, and Angel found it impossible to keep her eyes open. As she lay there, everything seemed so lovely. She was at peace, and it felt so wonderful.

Then she heard someone call her name. Not her full name, but one reserved for family.

"Angel, fear not. You will have a husband by Christmas."

The words caused Angel to come awake immediately. She sat straight up in bed and glanced around the room for the source of the voice. She was alone, and the sun was now streaming in through her window where what seemed only moments ago had barely been light.

She threw back the covers and jumped out of bed. For a moment, she continued to glance around the room as if she might see the person who had spoken, but there was no one there.

The words echoed in her head. *"Angel, fear not. You will have a husband by Christmas."*

Angel shook her head. "It's the twentieth of September. How can I possibly have a husband by Christmas? I mean I know God can do anything He wants, but . . ." She sighed. It was a dream and nothing more. "Wait until I tell Granny."

Granny Duran was their closest neighbor, and while not at all related, she had taken on the role of grandmother to Angel and her brother. She lived on the small farm next to the Lewises' sheep farm with her husband, John Quincy Duran, who still did his best to keep his land planted in wheat despite his rheumatism and lumbago.

These days, Angel spent more time at Granny's than at home. She did what she could to help the older couple with some of the physical chores that were starting to be a problem. Both were over seventy, and there was great concern about them living through another winter unharmed by the cold and snows. But of course they wouldn't admit this to anyone. John Quincy was much too proud to admit he needed help.

Given the situation Cam had put her in, Angel figured her winter would be best spent helping the older couple. After all, there was no one else who really needed her like they did. Her father and oldest brother, Mark, shared ownership of the farm. Mark and his family lived at the house, and Mark's wife, Ruth, was more than capable of keeping her home and children in order. Recently they had purchased some land next door, and their plans were to double the size of their flock of merino sheep.

Angel's nephews Jacob and Jason were quickly coming of age and were already great help to their father and grandfather. Mark and Ruth's two daughters, Sarah and Sharon, ages thirteen and twelve, were their mother's constant shadows. And while Angel had once been quite useful to Ruth in helping with the children, Ruth had very little need of Angel now. In fact, at times Angel felt very much in the way. It was one of the reasons she had agreed to marry Cam. Her heart's desire was to start a family of her own. Unfortunately, that hadn't worked out.

Making her way to Granny and John Quincy's small two-story farmhouse, Angel gave considerable thought to suggesting she move in with the couple for the winter. She could help with housework and laundry, as well as cooking and animal chores. No one would even miss her at home. When she and Cam had talked about the future, they had plans to live in town, where Cam would be close enough to walk to his railroad job. But of course, none of that mattered now. Cam was long gone.

The arrangement with Granny and John Quincy was that their home was Angel's too. She didn't bother to knock as she made her way into the house through the back door. This opened into the kitchen, and there she found Granny already bent over the stove, loading wood.

"Let me do that for you," Angel said, grabbing some of the slender split pieces of cottonwood.

Granny Duran straightened with a hand to her back. "It's gonna come a rain. I feel it in my bones."

Angel continued to put wood in the fire. "Are you about to do some baking?"

"Planned to. Got bread to make." She motioned to the counter, where a dish towel concealed the contents below.

"I'll help." Angel closed the door on the stove and turned to Granny. "Maybe I can make a pie for John Quincy." Even though the man was more than forty years her senior, she'd always called him John Quincy like most everyone else. It was just the way the older man preferred it.

"He'd like that for sure. Lots of apples. I was figuring to get some canned."

"I can help with that too. Fact is, I was thinking on a plan for winter. Maybe I could come and stay with you two. Things are pretty crowded at our place."

"We'd sure have you here in a heartbeat, child. Goodness knows it's getting hard for us to keep up with everything. I think this may be our last year here. John Quincy can't be responsible for planting another year. We've talked of hiring someone to tend it for us and share the crop profits."

"Why not ask Vincent to come back?" Angel's reference to the grandson Granny and John Quincy had raised brought a look of disapproval.

"He's got enough pain and misery. Doesn't need to feel obligated to help us. Wyoming was a dream he shared with his wife, one that he hopes to pass on to his children."

"Well, we should pray about it." Angel pulled on an apron and went to where the bread was rising. She pulled the dish towel from atop four loaf pans. "Say, I have to tell you something funny."

Granny gave her a sympathetic smile. "Are you gonna just avoid talking about what happened yesterday?"

Angel shook her head. "No, but I didn't see any reason to dwell on it. Cam was a cad, and I'm sorry to have so thoroughly misjudged him. It was never a great love, as you know full well. Goodness, Granny, you warned me."

"I just didn't want you marrying someone you really didn't know. I'm not against arranged marriages or even ones of convenience when folks know each other."

"I agree. I'm sure it's easier to fall in love with someone you know than with a stranger."

"And someday you will fall in love and have a great time of it, Angellyn. That is my prayer for you."

"Well, maybe it'll still happen. Right now, I'm embarrassed

by the whole thing. If I were a wealthy woman, I think I'd get on board the train and go as far away from here as possible. Set up housekeeping miles from this place and settle myself on the notion that God has called me to be alone. That way I'd never have to explain what happened to anyone.

"But here's that funny thing I wanted to tell you, Granny. I was asleep in my bed one minute, and the next I heard this strange voice telling me, 'Angel, fear not. You will have a husband by Christmas.' Scared me to pieces. I jumped up out of bed thinking someone had snuck into my room. Maybe one of Mark's boys playing a trick on me. But it wasn't. What do you think of that?" Angel started carrying the pans of dough to the stove.

When Granny said nothing, Angel glanced up before opening the oven door. The look on Granny's face was one of utter surprise.

"What's wrong, Granny?" Angel turned her attention back to the bread and put the loaf pans into the oven, then returned for the last two. Still Granny said nothing.

When the bread was secured, Angel checked the time. It was exactly eight thirty. "These should be ready at the top of the hour. Now tell me why my comment has you so stumped."

"I'm not stumped, child. I'm thinking the Lord Himself has spoken."

"And said what?" Angel asked, laughing.

"That He plans to have a husband for you by Christmas. And I think I know exactly who it is that He has in mind."

Angel could see that Granny was serious. "What are you saying?"

Granny motioned Angel to follow her into the front room. Granny went to her writing desk and pulled out an envelope. She took a letter from inside and looked at Angel.

"Let me read you something." She unfolded the pages and cleared her throat. "'Granny, the truth is I need a wife. I need her by Christmas.'"

It was Angel's turn to be surprised. "Who wrote that?"

"Vincent."

Angel took a seat and considered the words Granny had said. Vincent Duran was Granny's only grandson. His folks had been killed when he was young, and Granny and John Quincy had raised him. Vincent was best friends with Angel's brothers, Mark and Sam. Angel considered him a friend, as well.

Vincent had been a part of her entire life. He was ten years older than she was and had married some years earlier. The guys had another friend, Zed Martin, whose sister had caught Vincent's attention. Elsa had been everything Angel wasn't. Elsa was a dark-haired beauty with deep brown eyes, while Angel was blond and blue-eyed. Elsa had been tall and shapely where Angel was short and rather pudgy, at least in her teen years. Everyone had thought Elsa the most beautiful woman in the entire state, and even Mark had tried to court her. But it was Vincent who captured her heart.

"You know Elsa died last February. The children all took measles, and she caught them herself. She was expecting their fourth child in just a few months." Granny looked up and shook her head. "The two oldest made it through, but little Paul and Elsa were too weak. They passed within days of each other."

"I remember. It made me so sad. I've often prayed for Vincent and his children. That's why I mentioned asking him to come here and help you."

Granny didn't seem to hear her. "Benjamin is nine and Ava seven. It's a bad age to lose a mother . . . not that there is ever a good age." Granny looked back at the letter. "Vincent asked me to help him find a wife . . . one who could relocate to the

Wyoming Territory immediately. One who loved children and preferably knew about—"

"Sheep," Angel spoke before Granny could finish.

Vincent had learned all about sheep farming from her father and grandfather. He had trained with her brothers since he'd been about thirteen. That was why Vincent was such a constant part of her life. She had never really known a time when he wasn't around.

"Oh, Granny . . . I don't know what to say."

"I think the Lord has spoken, Angel. I think you're to marry Vincent. The two of you already know each other and share many common memories. You were close friends, and that's so important in a marriage. Vincent already trusts you and knows that you're capable and worthy of his children."

Angel felt as though someone had taken the air from her lungs. She forced herself to focus on a deep breath, but it was slow coming. Was this indeed what God had planned? She had once fancied herself in love with Vincent. Of course, she'd been quite young . . . maybe fifteen or so. Elsa had been a couple of years older than Angel and was already looking to find a husband. Unfortunately, she chose the one Angel had been considering as well, and from that time on, Angel had pushed aside her fondness for Vincent Duran.

"Oh, Angellyn, I think your dream was a sign from God. It never came to mind yesterday when we learned what Cam had done, but now it seems certain to me."

"What if Vincent doesn't want to marry me? I mean, we are friends, that much is true. But maybe he would feel strange about marrying a friend."

"Nonsense." Granny folded the letter and stuffed it back in the envelope. "Angel, I truly believe this is the answer to Vincent's needs and yours. You want to leave this area and the embarrassment Cam caused you. You are looking for a man to marry and raise a family with. You were ready to wed Cam without love, and he was most undeserving. Why not consider Vincent, who is very deserving of love? You're both bearing burdens of hurt and loss. You could help each other to overcome this. And my goodness, those children need a mother. They are the sweetest children, and I have feared this loss would make them bitter. You are the very kind of mother they need—a woman strong in faith."

"I know very little about children, Granny. I want to be a mother one day, but I don't know how to take on children already half raised. Besides, what will you do if I go away?"

"God will show you what to do. Just as He'll show us what we need to do. We've been doing fine. Look, let's pray about it." Granny held out her hand to Angel. "Pray and consider it for three days. If you are not convinced by then, I won't mention it again."

Angel came and knelt beside Granny. The very idea of leaving the area and going west was appealing. But the thought of helping a grieving man and his children was terrifying. She would always live in the shadow of Elsa Duran. She already felt unworthy of love and affection. How could she marry herself to a man who might never be able to love her?

Vincent Duran looked at the slightly burnt eggs and shrugged. "Breakfast is on," he told his nine-year-old son and seven-year-old daughter. "It's a little scorched, but we can make do."

He dished up eggs for each of them, trying to give them the less burned portions. He dumped the rest onto his own plate, then put the cast-iron skillet aside and took a seat at the table. He handed them each a piece of toast that he'd managed to cook to a golden-brown perfection and then folded his hands.

"Let's say grace."

"Do we have to?" Benjamin asked.

Vincent knew the boy had struggled with God since losing his mother. It seemed no matter how much he had tried to talk to Benjamin, he still blamed God for taking his mother away.

"We do," he murmured, then closed his eyes. "Father, for what You have provided, we are grateful. Even if we don't always understand why You allow the things You do, we know that there are reasons. We ask a blessing on this food, this farm, and family. Amen."

He looked up to find his children staring at him as if he'd said something appalling. He wished he could convince them that God was still a loving Father—a wonderful and generous God who would provide for them in every way. It was hard, however, to even say those words when Vincent felt just as cheated as they did.

For the last seven months, they had all struggled to go on living after Elsa, the baby, and little Paul's deaths. At the last Christmas, they had all been so excited. The new baby would come in a few months, and they'd had a profitable year with the sheep. Christmas was a merry celebration.

By the end of January, everything had changed. Benjamin and Ava took sick at the same time. Measles spread like wildfire in Cheyenne. It was never completely clear as to how they'd caught them. Their attendance at church was sporadic given the distance into town, and Christmas services were the last they'd been there. Vincent and his family had gone into Cheyenne in the middle of January for supplies, and that's when Elsa figured they'd been exposed. The doctor figured it that way too.

Elsa couldn't remember if she'd had measles as a child, but Vincent knew he had and wasn't concerned for his own health.

He remembered Elsa nursing Benjamin and Ava with tender care and did what he could to share the burden so that she, in her delicate condition, could rest. When Paul grew ill, he was much worse than the others. From the start, it was clear that things weren't going well. His fever ran higher, and his consciousness waned. Vincent had gone for the doctor after two days of watching his son deteriorate. By then, Elsa had come down sick as well. She was more than a little worried. Everyone knew measles could cause miscarriage, and she was terrified for their unborn child.

By the time Vincent returned with the doctor in tow, Elsa had collapsed, and Paul was near death. The doctor was there when the life went out of their three-year-old son. Elsa had been inconsolable, and Vincent delayed telling Ava and Benjamin. Within twenty-four hours, it wasn't only Paul's death he had to break to his children. Losing his wife, son, and unborn child had left Vincent in a stupor for weeks afterward. Had Elsa's aunt Mary not heard about the situation from Granny and come to help, they might have all perished from sorrow.

"I want you children to work on your reading primer like you did with Aunt Mary. I'll help you when I can check in. There's food to eat for your lunch, and it's warm enough you don't need to keep the stove going, Benjamin. Just work together, and I'll be back and forth. I have to see to the animals."

"I don't want to stay here," Benjamin protested. "Can't I come and help you?"

"I need you to watch over Ava. What if a snake gets in the house? You're the one who can keep her safe when I'm not around. Since Aunt Mary had to leave, we've only got each other to count on."

Ava looked up from her plate. "I don't like snakes."

"I know." Vincent gave her a smile. "I'm not real fond of

them myself. Do as I ask, and I'll be able to finish up quickly and come back to the house to be with you."

"Are we gonna get another aunt to come and stay with us?" Benjamin's tone wasn't one of hope, but more of resignation.

"No. That's something I need to talk to you children about. I've asked Granny Duran to help us. She's going to find someone who can come and live with us permanently."

"What's *permanently*?" Ava asked.

"It means forever," Benjamin told her. He looked at Vincent with a frown. "Do you mean another mother?"

Vincent knew the news would not be well received by his son. "Yes. I mean to take a new wife. Someone who can be a mother to you children. We'll be a family again."

Benjamin jumped up from the table, his food only half eaten. "I don't want another mother. I want my mama back!" He ran from the table and up the stairs to no doubt seek solace in his room.

Ava met her father's gaze. "What's our new mother's name?"

Vincent shrugged. "I have no idea."

CHAPTER 2

By October it was quite evident to Vincent that he needed to make a trip into Cheyenne for winter supplies. If Elsa had been alive, she would have reminded him. She would have presented him with a list of all the things they needed to get through the winter, on the chance that the weather turned bad and stayed that way, preventing them from getting into town.

With Elsa gone, Vincent found the job of keeping track of things to be almost impossible. He only learned yesterday that Ava's shoes no longer fit. They definitely had to get her a sturdy pair of boots for winter. Benjamin also had needs. All of his pants were a size, maybe two sizes, too small. He probably needed new boots as well. Vincent had no idea if there would be enough money for everything. They'd have to start their trip with a visit to the bank.

And that was exactly where he went first when he pulled into Cheyenne's city limits. He was relieved to find that there was still a decent balance in his account. He'd forgotten about his decision to sell off those older wethers from the flock. The extra money would come in handy with the children having so many unexpected needs.

They left the wagon at the feed and hardware store, as well

as a list of what Vincent needed for the farm. They were to load up everything while Vincent shopped with his children and then took them to lunch. None of them had had a decent meal since Aunt Mary had left two months ago. He had tried to hire a cook and housekeeper, but no one seemed to want to live on a sheep farm nearly ten miles from town.

Vincent settled the children at a table in one of the restaurants near the train depot and motioned the waitress to the table.

"Yes, sir?" she asked, smiling.

"I'd like black coffee, and some milk for the children. I saw the sign you had out front advertising beef stew. Bring us each a bowl, please. We're kind of in a hurry."

"Of course. I'll be right back."

She hurried to the kitchen and returned almost immediately with their drinks. Vincent took a long draw on the steaming liquid. The children did likewise with their milk. It was a matter of minutes before the young woman returned with a tray carrying the stew and a plate with several biscuits. She placed a bowl before each child before setting one in front of Vincent.

"That'll be six bits," she said, holding out her hand.

Vincent reached into his pocket and pulled out his wallet, along with a letter he'd picked up at the post office earlier. He set the letter aside and handed the girl a dollar. "Bring me a piece of that peach pie as well."

"Of course." She tucked the dollar in her pocket and left them to wait on a newly arrived pair of cowboys.

Vincent returned his wallet to his pocket and noticed that the children were already eating. Rather than chide them for not waiting for grace to be said, he lowered his head and thanked God for the food. When he looked back up, both children had paused in respect. At least there was that much.

"Who sent the letter?" Benjamin asked with a nod toward the envelope.

"Granny Duran. She's always good to write us." Vincent sampled the stew and then reached for the missive. "Maybe I should see what she has to say. You go on and eat. We have to leave town right after lunch, or we'll be driving in the dark by the time we get home."

He opened the envelope and pulled out a single sheet of paper. The letter was short and to the point. Granny had found a woman to be his wife. She'd arrive on the thirteenth. Good grief, that was the day after tomorrow. He scanned the rest of the information to see who it was Granny was sending. Then he saw Angellyn's name.

"What's she say, Pa?" Benjamin put his spoon aside and reached for a biscuit.

Vincent knew his son wasn't going to take well to the news that their search for a new mother had been resolved.

"Granny found someone to come and be your new ma."

"I don't want a new ma." Benjamin looked him in the eye. "It won't be the same."

"No, it won't be the same. That's for certain." Vincent refolded the letter. "But I know Angel, and she's a good woman."

"She's an angel?" Ava asked.

"No, but . . . well, she's a really kind person." He easily remembered the little girl who used to follow her brothers around the sheep farm. "Her name is Angellyn, but everybody calls her Angel."

"We don't need her."

"We do." Vincent looked at his boy. "You have no idea how much. Your ma used to keep track of all the supplies we needed. I made a list, but I'm sure I didn't remember half the stuff that a woman would know to include. I grew up with Angel, and

21

we were friends. She's a kind-hearted gal. You'll like her if you give her half a chance." He said this as much for himself as for them. "Her father taught me all about caring for sheep."

"Is she the one who fell in the pond and nearly drowned, but you saved her?"

Vincent smiled. "Yes. That was her." He'd used the story to illustrate to his children the importance of being helpful to those in need, no matter their age. He'd been a few years older than Benjamin when Angel had fallen in the pond. She'd been four years old.

"Did she ever learn how to swim?" Ava questioned.

Vincent chuckled. "She did. Her brothers taught her how. Like I taught the two of you."

Ava paused with the spoon midway to her mouth. "When will she come be our ma?"

"Day after tomorrow."

Benjamin slammed his hand down on the table. "I don't want a new ma."

Vincent noted several of the customers glance their way. "Son, lower your voice. We don't need all of Cheyenne weighing in on the matter. The truth is, I can't take care of you children and run the farm at the same time. If I don't marry and give you a new ma, you may have to go away and live with strangers. Is that what you want?"

Benjamin fixed him with an angry glare. "No, but I don't want another ma either. Why can't we just go live with your granny and granddad?"

"Because Wyoming was my dream. Your ma's too. I'm not ready to let that go. I could, I suppose, send you both back to live with Granny and Granddad."

"I don't want to go away, Papa," Ava said and began to cry.

Vincent reached out to smooth back her hair. "I don't want

anyone to go away. That's why I'm getting someone who can take care of us."

"Why can't she just come and help like Aunt Mary?"

Vincent heaved a sigh. "Because it wouldn't be proper for a single woman to come and stay with us. The only reason it worked with Aunt Mary is because she's an older widow and your mama's aunt. Being family makes it acceptable.

"Look, I don't want any trouble about this. I know it's hard for you, Benjamin, but we don't have a choice. I'm not asking you to call her *mother* or *ma*, but you will at least show her kindness and respect."

"Yes, sir," the boy replied. His expression betrayed his conflicted emotions.

Vincent felt bad for them. They were scared, and the one person who might have offered them the most comfort was the very soul they feared he was trying to replace.

"I promise you, it won't be a bad thing. Angel is fun to be around. You'll see."

Vincent could only hope she hadn't changed too much. Granny's letter said Angellyn had been jilted . . . left at the altar. She might very well be changed because of that. Not only that, but he hadn't seen her or heard much of anything about her in ten years. Granny occasionally wrote about ways that Angel had helped her, but otherwise he'd paid little attention to any news about her. For now, the important thing was to arrange for the justice of the peace to marry them and to get the house in some sort of order for her arrival.

He hurried to finish his food and was drinking the last of his coffee when the waitress brought their piece of pie. Vincent shared it with the children and then hurried them out the door and down the street to claim their wagon. Hopefully all of the stores would have deposited his purchases by now.

It was only when they were on their way home and the children had fallen asleep that the news really hit him. He was going to remarry. Not for love or consolation for his loneliness, but for the purpose of having someone to take care of the children. He'd done all that he could to hold his family together and would have given up the farm altogether before sending the children to someone else. Of course, they didn't know that. He felt guilty for having said otherwise to convince Benjamin of the necessity of accepting that his father would marry again.

Angel had been like a sister to him in so many ways. She'd always been around, helping out or occasionally pestering him and her brothers. As she grew older, Vincent had even considered her as a possible mate, but then Zed Martin's sister had returned from finishing school back east and caught the attention of every male in and out of town.

Vincent had been honored when she'd made her choice known and picked him. She was beautiful and kind, even-tempered and knowledgeable about a number of topics. She even shared his desires to go west. Both of them felt it was their calling to civilize the frontier. They would speak of it almost every night until they finally made the move. Elsa had been about the most perfect woman he'd ever known, and their marriage had been a good one.

Angel would have a lot to live up to.

———— ◦ ⅄ ◦ ————

Angel stepped onto the train platform in Cheyenne and looked around for any sign of Vincent and his two children. She was still apprehensive about this arrangement, but after Granny's suggested three days of prayer, Angel had been unable to come up with any reason to turn Vincent down.

When he first stepped from inside the depot, Angel couldn't help sizing him up. He looked the same as always. Handsome in that casual, country sort of way. There was no pretense to Vincent. He had on a well-worn coat and trousers, black hat, and blue shirt and tie. It wasn't exactly Sunday-go-to-meetin' clothes, but neither was it the expected shepherd's attire. The two children at his side were precious, and immediately her smile broadened. The boy was the spitting image of his father, and the little girl with her braided pigtails appeared younger than her seven years.

It dawned on Angel all over again that she was about to take on the role of mother and wife. Her first words and actions would set the stage for all that was yet to come. She put down her valise and smiled.

"Angel, it's good to see you again." Vincent drew the children forward. "This is my son, Benjamin, and my daughter, Ava."

Angel gave a nod toward each one. "I'm very happy to meet you both."

The children said nothing.

"They're kind of shy, and of course still grieving their ma."

"Of course." Angel sobered and knelt. "That loss will be felt for a long, long time. I know." She looked first at Benjamin and then Ava. "I lost my mama when I was eight years old. It wasn't easy to bear."

"I'd forgotten about that," Vincent murmured.

Angel straightened and stood. "It's a loss you understand better than most."

He looked away as if uncomfortable. "Do you have more luggage than that?" He nodded at the small valise beside her.

"I have a large trunk." She fished into her purse and produced a ticket. "Here's the claim for it."

Vincent took the stub. "Let's get it picked up, then. I have the justice of the peace waiting for us."

Angel hadn't known how things would be arranged. She only knew that Granny had written to Vincent to tell him she was sending Angel for him to marry. Angel had thought maybe there would be a time to get to know each other once again, but instead Vincent declared they were to be married immediately. She swallowed the lump in her throat and followed after him and his children. Could she really do this? The man she knew him to be had been practical and considerate. There was no reason to believe he had changed. Granny would have said as much if he had. Of course, maybe Granny didn't know.

A half hour later, she sealed her fate and replied "I do" as the justice of the peace officiated over their wedding. She wasn't wearing anything at all ceremonial. In fact, her plum-colored traveling suit was stained with soot and Angel was pretty sure she'd worn a hole in her left stocking. She remembered the beautiful white satin wedding dress she'd worn for Cam. She had sewn it herself and later sold it to a local dress shop. She couldn't imagine anyone wanting to buy a dress with such a sad history, but the owner assured her there would come a customer who didn't care in the least and would give the gown a new, brighter history.

"Do you have a ring?" the justice asked.

"I didn't think of one," Vincent said, looking momentarily panicked.

"I have my mother's wedding ring. We can use it." She pulled the gold band off her right hand and handed it to Vincent. "Pa gave it to me to remember her by. Doesn't matter which hand I wear it on. I'll always remember her."

He gave her a sheepish, apologetic smile. "Sorry that I forgot to buy one."

"It's quite all right."

He placed the ring on her left hand and looked to the justice. "Is that all?"

"Just about." The man closed his little black book. "You may kiss your bride."

Vincent looked at Angel for a moment, then bent and gave her a very quick kiss on the lips.

"I pronounce you husband and wife. Sign here." The justice of the peace pushed a piece of paper toward them.

And that was all there was to Angellyn's wedding. No flowers and no music. No church full of friends and family. In all actuality, it reminded her of the time her father had bought a horse from the livery man in town. They met, discussed the horse and the price, signed a paper, and headed home . . . with the horse.

Only this time, she was the horse.

Vincent stopped by the mercantile on the way out of town. He showed her a list of things he'd purchased for winter on the farm.

"We don't get to town very often, so let's go in and get anything else you think we might need that's not on the list. I have two milk cows and a dozen chickens. I'm due a bunch of pork, including hams, in trade for a ram. It'll be delivered in about two weeks. I didn't get the garden planted this year, and there's not much left in the way of canned goods. Elsa always put up vegetables and meats for the winter months, but we'll have to buy what we need this year."

Angel looked over his list. He'd already purchased a great deal of flour, lard, sugar, salt, and coffee. There was also an ample amount of oats and molasses. Seemed he was still practical.

"I should get some baking soda and powder, yeast and vinegar—oh, and a variety of spices." She looked at Vincent to ascertain his reaction to this. "Canned goods too."

"You might find other things once you're inside."

And she did. They shopped for nearly an hour with Vincent commenting on the children's likes and dislikes, and the lack of fruits and vegetables in his pantry. By the time they finished, Angel was satisfied they had a strong start on surviving any lengthy period away from civilization.

However, as they journeyed away from the town and quickly met up with vast prairies of nothingness, Angel couldn't help but wonder at what she'd just gotten herself into. She was now Mrs. Vincent Duran. A married woman with two children to care for.

God had given her a husband by Christmas. Two months early, in fact.

Merry Christmas to me.

CHAPTER 3

The sun was not far from setting when they reached the Duran farm. Angel was weary from the long train trip and then wagon ride. The day had seemed endless, and now all she really wanted was to take a long soaking bath and go to bed. However, that didn't appear possible. She was the mother and wife now and would need to prepare an evening meal and see to the needs of her family.

"Let me show you around," Vincent said, helping her down. "You children take the supplies into the kitchen, and I'll get Angel's trunk when I'm done showing her the farm. Benjamin, you'd also better light a few lamps. Oh, and make a fire in the stove and get several buckets of water for bathing."

The children said nothing but started doing as their father had instructed. Vincent took Angel by the arm and guided her toward the barn.

"You can see we have a large chicken coop and fenced-in yard over there." He pointed to the left, where a dozen or so chickens pecked at the dried grass. "We have a couple of milk cows. They'll have to be brought in and milked. Benjamin usually takes care of that these days, but I may need you to take over. Oh, and there's a donkey. She wanders with the sheep and guards them. Your pa taught me the value of a good donkey or two."

"They are great guardians. So what size is your flock?"

"I have about a hundred twenty sheep in all. Not a lot by most standards. When Elsa died, I sold off a large number. Almost sold them all." He looked away. "I really haven't known what to do. The children require so much time and attention, and so does the farm."

"Well, that's why I'm here." Angel touched his arm. "Look, Vincent, we know each other well enough to make this work. This is a marriage of convenience, and who knows, maybe in time it will be something more. For now, however, it's a working arrangement. I'll take care of the house and children, milk your cows, and take care of the chickens. Whatever you need me to do, I'll do, and that way you can work on rebuilding the flock and deciding what you want to do with the farm. Now, what arrangements do you want regarding you and me?"

Vincent looked at her oddly for a moment, then broke into a smile. "You always were one to just say what you thought."

"I don't see any reason to do otherwise. I know you don't love me, at least not as a husband should. I don't love you either, but I hope to in time. Still, I know that's probably not uppermost on your mind. You found and married the love of your life, and then lost her. You're going to mourn her and the children you lost for a long time.

"We don't have to share a bed or our thoughts, if that will help you to move on with your life. You know my situation. Granny told me she'd explained. I was left at the altar by a man who I thought loved me. Now I see that wasn't true, and frankly, I don't expect to ever be loved." She shrugged. "That isn't me feeling sorry for myself, but I am twenty-eight and long in the tooth for being a bride. However, I'll be faithful and treat you with love and respect. You and I have a long history, Vincent. I've cared about you for most of my life. You were a close friend years ago, and hopefully you'll go on being that now."

"I want to be. I'm sorry for the situation otherwise. I don't know that I'll ever love again. If not for the children, I certainly wouldn't have gone looking for another wife."

"Thank you for your honesty. I think as long as we continue to be straightforward about this, we can at least have a peaceful household. It might help me if you were to tell me what kinds of things you all enjoy eating and how you prefer to have the house kept and your laundry done."

"We're not going to be fussy about anything, Angel. I'm just grateful to have someone to work alongside. We've got a good friendship—or at least we have the foundation of one, like you said. It has been a very long time since we were around each other, and no doubt there have been a lot of changes besides you growing into such an attractive woman."

"Thank you for the compliment. Ten years have made you even more handsome than you were when last I saw you." She laughed. "Of course, I always thought you were a handsome fellow."

He chuckled. "You used to fancy yourself in love with me, as I recall."

"I did. I thought I had a chance to woo you, but then Elsa caught your eye and heart, and that was that. But, Vincent, I'm glad you had that even for a short time. I'll never know that feeling of belonging and being cherished. Treasure it forever." She turned away and pointed to the two-story house. "Now that that's behind us, I want to say I'm more than a little impressed with the house you built here. Look at all those windows."

Vincent said nothing for a few moments, and when Angel looked back at him, he looked sad. She hoped her talk about

Elsa hadn't caused him too much pain. It was important to state her feelings on the matter and let him know that it was all right for him to feel as he did. She didn't want him to think she'd come here for some great romance.

"When we came out here," he finally began, "Elsa's brother Zed came with us, as you know. He got thrown from a horse and killed shortly after we arrived. It was devastating to both of us. Then a letter came with a check. Zed had bought life insurance, and Elsa was his beneficiary. We had plenty of money to make up for what we'd spent on burying him and enough left over to build this house and a few pens. It was like a memorial to him."

"It's beautiful and unexpected."

"The reason for all the windows was Elsa. She loved the light and told me she didn't care what else the house had to offer, but she wanted a lot of windows. So despite the expense of glass, every room got a window. Some got two."

"I'm glad. I love the light as well. What about keeping out the cold?"

"As you can see, there are shutters for each window. They're very efficient and help a great deal with the cold. It's plenty windy around here, too, and can come up a storm without warning. They help with that as well. You just raise the window and can lean out to pull them closed. I'll show you later."

"Anything else I should know about the house?"

"There's one fireplace to heat the house. The upstairs is one big room for the time being, and the children sleep up there. I keep thinking I might put in a stove upstairs, but usually if I build up a fire downstairs, the house stays warm enough. Elsa and I always had plans to build walls and make several rooms. Our bedroom . . . well, yours now, is downstairs off the front room."

"I can't kick you out of your bedroom. What if I put down a bedroll or make a pallet somewhere?"

"No. I won't do that to you. There's a small room off the birthing shed. I'll set myself up there. I promise you, I'll be quite comfortable. I often sleep there during lambing season. There's even a stove in the room, so I'll keep plenty warm. I haven't used the bedroom much since Elsa died there." His frown deepened. "That won't make you too uneasy, will it? I hadn't honestly thought of how it might be for you."

Angel shook her head. He was still most considerate. "It's fine. I'll be all right. But if I don't get in there and start working on supper, we won't be eating until midnight." She forced a smile. "I was thinking we might have some canned chicken, and I'll make dumplings. Will that be all right?"

He nodded. "Sounds wonderful."

Throughout the evening, Vincent thought of Angel's talk earlier. She had given up on ever being loved or truly cared about. She had married a man who had also given up on love. They were quite the pair. Still, as she had pointed out, Vincent had at least known that kind of love and passion. There was a dull ache in his heart at the memory of Elsa and how much he had adored her. Their love had been one for the ages, Granny had once told him. And now it was gone, and he had let go of the hope of ever feeling that way again.

Angel had given up on it, too, and for some reason that made Vincent sadder than he'd expected. He knew even when they exchanged their vows that he had little to give her in the way of love. He cared about her as the little sister of his dear friends. He could honestly say that he even had a type of love for her. Spending the evening with her had even afforded him a great deal of cheer. Something he'd definitely not anticipated.

"Well, the dishes are done," she said, coming into the front room where he sat by the fire, reading the newspaper. The children followed after her.

"I don't like drying dishes," Benjamin said, plopping down in front of the fireplace.

Ava came to her father. She looked at him longingly for a moment and then moved away to sit on the sofa. Angel headed for the rocking chair opposite his cushioned ladder-back chair.

"No!" Benjamin cried out, jumping to his feet. "That's my mama's chair. You can't sit there!"

"Benjamin!" Vincent looked at his son.

The boy scowled. "That's Mama's chair."

"It's all right," Angel said, smiling. She went to sit on the sofa opposite Ava. "I can sit here."

"Benjamin, I know it's been a busy day, but that's no reason to be without manners. If Angel wants to sit in the rocker, that's entirely her choice."

"Actually," Angel countered, "I was wondering if the children would want the rocker upstairs with them. It might make them feel closer to their mother."

"Yes!" Benjamin went to the chair and took hold of it possessively. "Let's put it upstairs."

Vincent knew he could make a point with Benjamin about how the chair was just a chair. But in a way, he completely understood the boy's discomfort. Angel had a presence about her that seemed to fill the room.

He got up and put the newspaper aside. "Very well. I'll take it up, and you children tell Angel good night. It's bedtime."

"Night," Benjamin muttered and hurried from the room to lead the way.

Ava scooted off the sofa and looked at Angel. "Good night, Angel. I like your name."

Angel smiled. "I like your name, too, Ava."

Ava dashed from the room to the stairs as Vincent came and got the rocker. "I'm sorry about the way Benjamin acted. He's had a real hard time of it."

"Of course he has. His mother and brother died, not to mention the expected baby. You have a right to be grieving."

Vincent looked at her for a long moment. She offered no condemnation or ill temper regarding the matter. He supposed he should be grateful for God sending her into their lives. They needed her.

"Thanks." He picked up the chair and headed upstairs.

The children were already in their beds when he reached the top step. He placed the chair at the foot of Benjamin's bed and then stood back.

"I know this isn't easy. It's not what any of us wanted, but Angel's kind, and we will treat her the way the Good Lord would have us treat all people."

"He's not good," Benjamin replied, crossing his arms against his chest. "If God was good, He wouldn't have taken my mama and my brother and the baby."

Ava sat up, nodding. "God is mean."

Vincent wanted to offer correction, but in truth he bore some of the same feelings. He didn't understand either why God had been so cruel.

"God had His reasons for what He allowed. He is a loving Father, and while it's hard to trust Him sometimes, that's what we have to do. We can put our hope in Him or the devil. I still prefer God, and you should too. The devil doesn't care one whit for us. Now, get to sleep. Morning will come soon enough. I'll be out in the birthing shed, and Angel will take my room."

"You could sleep up here with us," Ava offered.

He shook his head. "Might have to do that come winter, but

not right now." He went to Ava and motioned her to lie down. He pulled up the covers and looked back at Benjamin.

"Say your prayers and go to sleep. There will be plenty to do come morning."

Without another word, he blew out the lamp, then headed for the stairs. There had been a time when he might have offered them a hug and kiss, but since their mother's passing, Vincent hadn't had it in him to offer anyone love. How in the world was it going to ever work with a new wife?

But Angel didn't expect love. At least there was that. The only problem was, Vincent felt she more than deserved it. He remembered the carefree, happy child she'd been. Then her mother had died, and it changed everything. It had changed everything for his children as well. Still, somehow Angel had managed to come through the situation with her spirit of joy intact. Maybe she could help his children to do likewise. Maybe he might even find peace of heart and happiness again. But was that even possible without love?

CHAPTER 4

By the first of November, the family had settled into a routine. Angel was up before first light to prepare breakfast for the family. Vincent generally wandered in around six to have breakfast and tell her what his plans were for the day. Around seven, he would go wake up the children, and by eight they were dressed, fed, and ready to sit down with their books.

Angel enjoyed teaching them. This was a role that held little threat to them, even though their mother had been the one to start it. Angel related stories about going to school and how she loved to read. She even spent a little time each day reading to them from the Bible, using a style of story-telling rather than going Scripture by Scripture. She did stress the importance of memorization, however, and gave them a Bible verse each week to memorize.

Church attendance wasn't a regular event, since it took nearly three hours to ready the wagon and drive into Cheyenne. Sunday school started at ten, and church at eleven, so that required being ready to leave the farm by seven. It was a lot to manage, and Vincent told Angel they'd be lucky to go once a month. However, he always set aside Sunday for the Lord. After breakfast, Vincent would open the Bible and teach from it. Benjamin seemed to hold only a passing interest. He still held a lot of anger toward God for taking his mother.

When teaching, Angel only managed to draw him in by asking questions that she thought might interest him. Often, she focused on stories that involved sheep, since such tales were readily available in God's Word and also encompassed Benjamin's world.

Since the day was surprisingly nice, Angel concluded school for the morning and sent the children out to play for a few minutes. They would soon enough be cooped up inside. Vincent had told her about the terrible winters they sometimes had. Snow had been known to drift up to the windows, and blizzards could last for days. Already she was thinking about projects they could do inside. She knew of plenty of things she could keep Ava busy with, but not nearly as many ideas came to mind for Benjamin. Of course, maybe she could leave him to help his father.

Making plans for the winter created its own problems. Angel now had a new list of things she wished she had purchased. She would like to teach Ava to knit and crochet, maybe work with her to make some quilts for the family. All those things would require another trip to town. Angel figured to approach the subject with Vincent later that night.

Angel heard Ava crying before she even reached the back door. Hurrying to see what the problem was, Angel was alarmed to find the child bleeding. Her sleeve was torn, and blood seeped along the tear.

"Whatever happened, Ava?"

"I . . . I caught my sleeve . . . on a nail in the barn. It cut me," she sobbed.

"Well, I know how painful that can be. Come on. Let's clean it up and see how bad it is."

"It's real bad," Ava said, holding her arm as if she were cradling a babe. "I can't use it."

Angel had turned away to get some supplies from the cupboard. She couldn't help but smile at the child's melodramatic tone.

"You know, once I broke my arm. I was not too much older than you. Hurt something terrible."

"How did you break it?" Ava asked.

"Well, let me tell you about it. I was playing in the barn." Angel came to her and lifted her up to sit on the table. She brought a bowl of warm water from the stove, along with the soap. Next, she retrieved her bandages, scissors, and a salve that Granny had taught her to make. It never failed to heal even the nastiest wounds.

Ava watched as Angel went to work and continued explaining how she'd broken her arm. "I wasn't supposed to go up into the loft, but I was hiding from my brothers."

"You have brothers?"

Angel nodded as she began cleaning Ava's wound. It wasn't really much more than a scratch, but scratches could become a problem if not dealt with properly.

"I have three brothers. They're all older than me."

"How old are you?" Ava asked.

Angel couldn't help but smile. "I'm twenty-eight. Anyway, I wanted to hide from them so I could jump out and scare them. They were always doing that to me, so I hid in the barn loft, and when they came into the barn, I jumped off and landed wrong. My oldest brother, Mark, said that he heard my bone snap. I just know it hurt terribly."

"Did you scare them?"

Laughter escaped Angel. "I did. They said they'd never been more frightened. Especially since I was hurt. They were kind to me, and so loving. Mark carried me to the house, and they waited on me after the doctor came and set my arm. I think they felt really bad about it."

Angel finished washing out the wound and then applied the salve. Ava winced in expectation of pain but seemed surprised that it wasn't all that bad. Angel wrapped a strip of cloth around the cut.

"Speaking of brothers, where was yours when this happened?"

"He went to find Papa and tell him I was hurt."

Just then the back door opened, and Angel turned to see a worried-looking Vincent and Benjamin.

"Everything is fine. The cut wasn't very deep, so she doesn't need stitches."

"I'm sure glad about that," Vincent said, shaking his head. "I had to stitch up Benjamin's foot once when he was little. I don't relish the idea of needing to do that job again. It's bad enough if an animal needs that kind of attention."

Angel stood and began gathering her things. "You know what Granny Duran always said was most beneficial when healing from a wound?"

Vincent shook his head, and the children seemed more than a little interested to know what she might have to say.

"Making cookies." She looked down at Ava. "You and I will make some cookies, and of course, you'll get to eat the very first one. I think you'll be surprised how quickly you forget about the pain."

"I seem to remember that remedy as well," Vincent said, smiling.

"Can we . . . all . . . have cookies?" Benjamin asked in a halting voice.

"Of course." It was a small step of progress, but at least

Benjamin was speaking to her. Angel noted the boy's look of concern. "We'll make enough for everyone to have their fill."

A hint of a smile appeared on the boy's face. He looked away quickly and muttered something before heading back out the door.

"I'll get back to what I was doing," Vincent said, the worry easing from his expression. He really was a handsome man. "You ladies let us know when the cookies are ready. I haven't had a warm cookie in some time."

Angel finished putting the medical supplies away and got down the flour and sugar. "What kind of cookies should we make?"

"I don't know." Ava's brows knit together as if she were thinking quite hard of an answer.

"How about some carrot cookies?"

"Carrots? In cookies?" Ava looked confused. "I never had carrots in my cookies."

"Well, Granny Duran gave me a wonderful recipe for them, and since we have some carrots in the cellar, I think it would be perfect."

Ava shrugged. "I don't know if Benjamin will like them."

"They'll have frosting on them, so I'm betting he will. Come on, let's get the carrots and butter."

⁓

Vincent had to admit Angel had taken charge of the house and children as if she were born for it. He'd been so freed up to get his own chores done that he'd actually worked ahead of what he'd hoped he might accomplish.

True to her word, Angel was capable and focused on the tasks at hand. She rarely asked for help and yet constantly seemed to offer it. She'd even managed to take the early morning milking off his hands. Benjamin had been milking in the evening, and she'd offered to do that as well, but the boy wasn't of a mind to be obligated to his stepmother.

He couldn't help but think of his son and the sorrow he still carried. Vincent had tried to talk to him a time or two, but Benjamin refused to bare too much of his soul. He was hurting and missed his mother. What could Vincent possibly say or do to assuage the boy's pain?

Angel seemed not to mind Benjamin's anger toward her. She didn't tolerate bad behavior and had gotten after him more than once, but he wasn't out of control. When he was called out for his actions, the boy was civilized enough to obey. Angel was quite smart in how she handled him, however, and that made a huge difference. She didn't demand love or adoration from Benjamin. She didn't even try to establish a friendship. She simply included him in what he wished to be a part of and occasionally requested help from him in ways that Benjamin found difficult to refuse.

Once Vincent had come upon them splitting wood. She stood to one side while Benjamin explained the best way to split the wood for kindling. Vincent knew that Angel was fully aware of how to cut wood, but she listened, seeming quite appreciative of Benjamin's lecture. By the time he finished, he told her that when she needed more wood, he'd take care of it for her. Vincent couldn't help but smile. She did have a way about her.

Including when she'd lectured him two nights earlier. He still smarted from her observations that he had put up a wall between himself and the children.

"They need you, Vincent. They need their father's hugs and comfort. Ava so often looks at you with longing that I can only surmise that you used to hug her and hold her but stopped after Elsa died. Ava needs that now on occasion."

And she'd been right. He used to hold Ava all the time, but he'd stopped after Elsa died. He hadn't wanted to hold anyone. He felt terrible for robbing his children of his affection. It wasn't right, but it had been so hard to allow such feelings without coming close to a complete breakdown. Vincent knew if that happened, it would cause far more harm than good. Still, Elsa had hugged them all the time and held them too. Even Benjamin would seek her comfort. Angel pointed out the sorry truth that when Elsa died, they had lost more than their mother.

Vincent was determined to change that. He would be a better father to them and see to it that they had hugs and that he held Ava when she needed to be held.

"Papa! Papa!"

It was Ava. Vincent went to the door of the barn and looked out. "What's that hollering about?" he asked, smiling.

"The cookies are done. We put frosting on them, and I ate the first one. We made the cookies with carrots in them."

"Did you like it?" He wondered if Angel had used Granny's recipe. Oh, it had been so long since he'd had one of his grandmother's cookies.

"I did. They're really good. Even Benjamin likes them."

Vincent laughed and scooped Ava up in his arms.

She looked surprised momentarily and then wrapped her arms around his neck. "I bet you'll like them too." The wind picked up, and Ava buried her face against his neck.

Carrying her to the house, Vincent realized how much he'd missed this. There was nothing quite like carrying your child and having them snuggle against you.

He opened the door into the house, and the aroma of carrot cookies immediately filled his head. The smell reminded him of childhood and Granny's cooking. A lot of what Angel made for them was reminiscent of Granny's meals. And why not? Angel had spent a great deal of time with Granny after her mother died. Granny had taught her far more than her mama had time to teach.

"I heard there were carrot cookies to be had," Vincent said, looking down at his son. Benjamin had a half-eaten cookie in one hand and a glass of milk in the other.

"These are really good, Pa."

"I'm sure they are. If I'm not mistaken, these are the same kind of cookies my granny makes."

"You aren't mistaken," Angel said, coming from the pantry. "They're one and the same. Ava was a bit concerned that putting carrots in the cookies would make them taste bad, but she changed her mind."

"I did," Ava admitted. "Angel told me that carrots are sweet and perfect for cookies, and I think she's right."

Vincent put Ava down and took up a cookie. He popped the entire thing in his mouth and began to chew. Memories flooded back of times he'd snuck into Granny's kitchen to snag freshly baked treats. Having Angel here was almost like having Granny in the sense of comfort she offered. Granny had been smart to send Angel. She had known what Vincent and his children needed even if he hadn't.

"Mmm." He swallowed and smiled at Angel. "Perfection. Tastes just like Granny used to make. One day we're gonna have to take a trip back to Granny's farm. You children need to meet her. She's really very special. My grandfather is too."

"Would we get to ride the train?" Benjamin asked.

"Absolutely. It would take far too long to go by wagon." Vincent grabbed another cookie. "I'd have to get someone to come see to the sheep while we were gone. So we probably won't be able to do it anytime soon, but maybe next year."

"Angel could stay here," Benjamin said, looking at her briefly. "Come on, Pa, you said she knew all about taking care of sheep."

"It's true that Angel is quite capable of taking care of the sheep, but this is her first winter in Wyoming, and she isn't even used to the house yet. Besides, she would probably love to go back and see her family. She left everyone to come here and be with us."

"She can go back and stay," Benjamin said before eating another cookie. "We don't need her here."

"That wasn't a very kind thing to say, son. Apologize right now."

Benjamin looked up with a frown. "Sorry." It sounded neither heartfelt nor sincere.

"I apologize that my son doesn't have better manners, Angel. Especially after you so kindly made him cookies and have done so many other things for us—for him, in particular. I don't suppose he realizes it was you who sewed those tears in his clothes and patched his favorite shirt, the last one his ma made him. I don't think he appreciates what you gave up coming to be here with us, but I do." He met her gaze and smiled. "You've been a balm to my soul, and a man couldn't ask for more."

He could of course ask for more, but he wouldn't. There would be a price to pay, and Vincent still wasn't sure he'd ever be able to manage it. To love Angel would mean taking something from the love he held for Elsa. He didn't think that would ever be possible. He had buried his heart with her and the baby and little Paul. How could he give Angel something he no longer had?

With the mood dampened, Vincent took up another couple of cookies and headed for the door. He wanted to say something more to Angel, but he didn't want to further upset Benjamin. He didn't know what in the world it would take for his son to move beyond his grief, but confrontation and anger weren't the answers.

He found himself praying silently. *Lord, we're all still hurting so much, Angel too. She was wronged, and I know she must have suffered a great deal. So I'm asking for healing here. Healing for my children and self as well as Angel. She deserves to be loved. Help me to at least be a friend to her.*

"Glad you stopped by, Hiram. I was planning to ride over to ask a favor," Vincent told his closest neighbor a week later. Hiram Bennett was a dozen years older than Vincent, but the two had formed a fast friendship.

"Figured I'd best bring the water tank I promised. What can I do for you, Vincent?"

"I need to go into town with the family on Saturday, and I wanted to stay over for church. Wondered if one of your boys could come stay here at the farm and tend the animals?"

"Don't see why not."

"I'll pay, of course." They'd traded favors on more than one occasion, and Vincent knew the man wouldn't allow his son to accept money, but he felt it important to offer it.

"No. I know you'd do the same for me. I'll send Zeb over at first light on Saturday. Will that work, or do you need him to come over on Friday?"

"Saturday will work just fine. Are you sure you can't stay for a cup of coffee?"

"Margaret told me to get right back. She wants me to fin- ish cleaning out an area in the barn so that she can store some things."

"Well, let me get that tank and you can be on your way."

They went to the back of the wagon and made short work of unloading. Vincent was more than pleased for the addition.

"This is going to come in real handy. I've been sectioning off another pen for the sheep, and this will supply their water."

"Glad you could use it." Hiram glanced toward the house. "So, how are things going with the new wife?"

Vincent was used to Hiram speaking his mind and wasn't surprised by the question. "It's been an adjustment, especially for the children. But I knew Angel from when she was a little girl. I was best friends with her brothers. She's a hard worker, to be sure, and she knows sheep. She goes out with me every day for a time so that they'll get used to her and know her. She'll be a big asset come lambing season."

"Sounds like you got a real bargain there. I know I couldn't run our chicken farm without Margaret. A good wife can make all the difference."

The wind blew a cold blast across the open yard, and Vincent did up the buttons to his coat. "You're right about that, Hiram."

The older man climbed up onto the wagon seat. "How'd your children take to her?"

"It's been slow. Benjamin is still so angry at losing his mother that he wants nothing to do with Angel. Ava has shown a lot more interest. Little girls need a ma."

Hiram pulled his hat down as the wind picked up even more. "I'd best be heading back. May be due a snow."

"You sure you don't want to come in and warm up first?"

"Nah, I've got a heap of work to tend to. I'll make sure Zeb is here early on Saturday."

"Thanks, Hiram."

True to his word, Zeb arrived on Saturday as the sun crested the horizon. Vincent had just remade the bed he'd been using and still had the old sheets in his hands. Vincent set them aside by the barn door and gave Zeb instructions for what he wanted done and then showed him to the room off the lambing shed.

"You shouldn't have to worry about anything in the house," he told Zeb. "The room off the lambing shed has a stove, and Angel made sure there was plenty of food that you could rewarm."

"Sounds good." The young man always seemed eager to get right down to work.

"You know, I'm still of a mind that if you wanted to learn sheep farming, I'd take you on. Couldn't pay money at first, but we could work it out in animals."

"I like sheep well enough," Zeb said, following Vincent to the house. "Fact is, I like 'em better than chickens, so I just might take you up on that. Pa needs me right now, but we have talked about how things might be come spring."

"I understand. Still, I'm grateful that you can come to help out. Come to the house and meet my new wife. Have you eaten?"

"I had a little before coming your way."

"Well, join us for breakfast. We can discuss anything else we need to address."

Zeb, being eighteen and still seeming to be growing, was happy to have a second meal. He sat down at the table and immediately began joking with Benjamin. To Vincent's surprise, it seemed to lighten his son's mood.

"Zeb, this is my wife."

Zeb rose again and gave her a nod. "Nice to meet you, Mrs. Duran."

Angel smiled. "Nice to mee you, Zeb. Your mother and older brother stopped by a week or so ago to bring us a couple of stewing chickens and fresh bread. She told me that she had another son. You're the youngest, right?"

"Yup. Zach is two years older."

"Well, I'm sure glad you could come over to watch things while we go to town." She put a plate of flapjacks and sausage down in front of him. "I hope I didn't give you too much."

He eyed the plate with a grin. "No, ma'am."

After everyone finished breakfast, they said good-bye to Zeb and headed to town. Thankfully the skies were crystal blue, without a single cloud to be found. Even the wind was fairly calm. It was shaping up to be a nice day.

————◦Y◦————

Cheyenne seemed to have grown even since her arrival a month ago. Angel couldn't help but notice several new hotels were being built, along with a range of other stores, banks, and doctor's offices. Vincent had told her that the town was barely eight years old and showed no signs of slowing down in its development.

They went to the feed store first. Vincent had already told her that he could leave his list and have things loaded for picking up later in the day while they went about other business. Angel had given him a list of things to pick up for her winter projects. Vincent had agreed quickly to whatever she needed. She appreciated that he was so generous. She'd brought very little of her own money and was totally reliant upon her husband's kindness to get what she wanted and needed. Granny had always said Vincent was the most thoughtful of men, and Angel had known it to be so. Watching him now, she felt those thoughts and feelings she'd had for him as a girl come flooding back. He was the kind of man that a gal wanted for a husband.

"We should secure a hotel room," Vincent said, climbing down from the wagon. "Seems like there are an awful lot of people in town. As soon as I square things away here, we can walk over to the Rollins House and get a room." He reached up and took hold of her at the waist and lifted her down.

Just then, someone called out Vincent's name. Angel saw that it was an elderly gentleman who was grinning from ear to ear.

"I thought maybe you'd moved clean out of the territory, Vincent."

"No, I'm still here. How are you, Bert?" Vincent shook his hand and offered a smile. "Good to see you."

"And you too. We need to sit down and have a long talk. It's been far too long."

"I've come to town with the family this time. I'd like you to meet Angellyn Duran, my new wife. Angel, this is Culbert Finnegan, but most folks call him Bert."

The older man looked to Angel and grinned. "'And the LORD God said, It is not good that the man should be alone; I will make him an help meet for him.' Welcome to Cheyenne, Angel." Then he chuckled. "Isn't the first time an angel has appeared to a shepherd."

Angel smiled. "I even brought good tidings of great joy."

Vincent chuckled, and Bert slapped his leg. "And she has a sense of humor. Good for you, Vincent. A woman who is not only pretty but can make you smile is worth her weight in gold."

"I agree."

Angel felt her cheeks grow warm despite the chilled air. She looked away as Benjamin came to stand beside his dad. Ava squeezed in by Angel. The two were getting closer every day. Ava craved a mother's affection and was willing to let Angel fill that need. Benjamin, however, was much harder to win over and even now seemed to distance himself from Angel's presence.

"You children have grown a great deal." Bert fished some coins out of his pocket. "Use this for candy only." He handed them each a dime. He straightened and smiled at Angel and Vincent. "Will you be staying over for church?"

"We are," Vincent answered before Angel could. "We were planning to go secure a hotel room."

"Nonsense. You'll stay with us. My sister Myra will be thrilled to have the company. We have an extra room, although it is small. You and the missus can sleep there, and we'll make pallets for the children. And though we're short on space, we have plenty of delicious food. Myra loves to cook, and lately she's been baking a great deal. Church plans to have a bake sale, and she's put a lot of effort into making sure they have plenty of things to offer."

Vincent looked at Angel. "Would that be all right with you?"

"I think it sounds wonderful." And she did. The idea of staying in someone's home rather than a hotel was more than a little appealing. She had heard horror stories of hotel occupants crashing through doors to rooms other than their own. Of noisy parties and fights that threatened everyone nearby. Staying with an old man and his sister was definitely preferable.

"I guess that will suit us, then, Bert. Thanks for the offer. Can we bring some extra food or anything else?"

"No, sir. You come on over when you're ready. I'll get on home and let Myra know to set extra places for lunch."

Vincent gave a nod and, to Angel's surprise, put his arm around her shoulders. "We'll be there."

Bert took off down the street, and Angel glanced over at Vincent. She met his gaze, then made the mistake of looking down at their closeness. He stepped back almost with a start.

"Let's get our shopping done before the stores close. They won't be open long since it's Saturday."

Angel enjoyed walking from store to store with Vincent and the children. For the first time, she felt like a family. Ava held fast to her hand, while Vincent acted as a shield for them whenever rowdy cowboys or other rough-looking characters approached.

Vincent even surprised her by accompanying her to the fabrics section of the mercantile. He waited patiently, pointing out an occasional material that he liked while the children searched out the toy section of the store.

"Do you remember that ugly quilt that I had on my bed at Granny's house?" Vincent's voice held a note of amusement.

Angel easily remembered the piece. "I do. It was done in browns and grays and greens. Just simple squares sewn together."

"Yes. Did you realize Granny taught me to sew by piecing that together?"

"No!" Angel stepped back in surprise. "You made that quilt?"

"I swore her to secrecy. She said it was important that I learn to sew a straight stitch, and she could think of no better way than to make something useful. She had a lot of old dark scraps of material that she was saving for a crazy quilt but decided they'd work well for me. We cut out six-inch squares, and I spent all winter sewing them together. Then Granny and I tied it. I was mighty proud of my accomplishment, of course, but I couldn't tell anyone that I'd made it. I was too embarrassed."

Angel shook her head. "Granny is an amazing woman. I can't imagine getting Benjamin to do something like that."

"Well, maybe you should. Or I should. It's served me very well knowing how to sew a straight line."

"I suppose we could try." Angel found the idea to be both humorous and terrifying. It was hard enough to teach Benjamin routine things.

Close to noon they approached the small two-story home of Bert and Myra. Myra was a most gracious hostess and ushered them inside and out of the cold.

"Goodness, go warm yourselves by the fire. Lunch is nearly ready." She noted Vincent carried one valise and Benjamin a small bag. "Just put those things there by the door. I'll show you where to take them after a bit."

Angel couldn't help noticing that there wasn't a square inch of the front room wall that didn't have something nailed to it in display. There were dozens of small, framed paintings. Landscapes, mostly, in varying sizes from a few inches square to much larger. Along with these were playbills tacked with pins, framed tintype pictures of various people, and what looked like Christmas ornaments and other knickknacks hanging in between.

"What a beautiful room. Look at all the memories on the walls," Angel said, hoping she wasn't offending.

"Bert painted most of the pictures," Myra told her. "He used to sometimes paint when he was out in the field tending sheep back home."

"Where was home?" Angel asked.

"Ohio. We were born and raised there. Our father was well known for his sheep."

"How wonderful. We raised merinos in Nebraska. I've known Vincent since I was very young. We grew up together. His grandmother helped care for me after my mother died."

"And now here you are married to him. There must be comfort in knowing each other's past," Myra said almost reverently. "I couldn't abide marrying a stranger, so I've never married."

Angel felt a moment of sadness for the woman. She was probably in her fifties, maybe early sixties, and had never known the love of a husband. Would the same hold true for Angel?

She glanced across the room where Vincent was talking to Bert about something. The children were warming up by the fire and pointing to various things on the wall. Angel drew in a deep breath and forced herself to listen to Myra as she explained who the people were in one of the tintypes. A deep sense of longing tried to rear up, but Angel shoved it back down. The homey setting was taking its toll.

"And that is our grandmother sitting in front of our parents," Myra said. "This was taken just before the war began. They died within three months of each other. I tell people not only soldiers died in that war. Other hearts were stopped as well."

Angel nodded. It would seem Myra and Bert had dealt with a great deal of sorrow in their lives.

After a lunch deserving of high praise, Myra led the way up narrow and extremely steep steps to the small single upstairs room where she told Angel and Vincent they would stay.

"The bed is quite comfortable. I slept here once, so I know it's true." She smiled and squeezed past Angel and Vincent to reach the stairs. "It's a very tiny room, as you can see, but I hope you'll be comfortable."

Vincent waited until Myra headed back downstairs before speaking. He gave a most apologetic look Angel's way.

"I'm sorry about this. I figured I could sleep on the floor, but obviously there's not room for either of us to do that."

Angel shook her head. "We are married. There's no problem in sharing a bed."

"No. No problem."

But later that night, neither one of them was quite so sure that was the case. Angel had let down her hair and changed into her nightgown before sliding under the covers. Vincent returned a few moments later from washing up. He glanced for a moment at Angel and seemed unable to look away. She gave a nervous smile and pressed up against the wall on her side. It was easy to see, however, there was no way they could sleep together without touching.

Vincent blew out the lamp. Angel could hear him undressing and wondered if he would rid himself of everything or leave on his long johns. When he got into bed, she was relieved to realize he had done the latter.

He immediately turned on his side, facing Angel. They both realized the mistake of this, as their faces were just inches apart. Without a word, Vincent turned to lie on his back, but so did Angel. She couldn't contain her laughter and immediately put her hand over her mouth, lest they hear it downstairs. She turned to her side, pressing her face into the pillow. The entire situation was too funny.

Vincent let out a snort of laughter and turned on his side once more. "This is an impossible situation. I don't think we have much choice but to accept the matter. Otherwise, we'll never get any sleep."

"Oh, it's all right, Vincent. Honestly. I don't mean to laugh so much." She fought to contain her amusement at their obvious discomfort. "It'll be fine."

He chuckled softly. "I agree. Good night, Angel."

"Good night, Vincent."

She could feel the warmth of his body taking away her chill. Her heart seemed to pound even faster. She was in bed with a man. A very handsome man.

She chided herself in silence. *He's your husband. Stop being such a ninny.*

CHAPTER 6

Angel awoke to find herself warm and wrapped tightly in the blanket. As the fog cleared her senses, she realized it wasn't just the blanket that held her. She was in Vincent's muscular embrace. For a moment, she didn't move. She scarcely dared to breathe.

The rhythmic rising and falling of his chest told her he was still asleep. She had no idea if he was a light or heavy sleeper, but she hoped it was the latter. She knew she had to disengage herself from his arms and get out of bed without disturbing him. The problem was the bed was against the wall, and there was a dresser at the foot that wouldn't allow for her to go out that way. She would have to climb over Vincent, and that wasn't going to be easy.

She decided to test the situation and slowly sat up. He did nothing, and for a moment all Angel did was watch him sleep. She felt a strange sense of something that she didn't understand. She longed to go back into his arms and close her eyes again. She was comfortable there, safe and protected. Happy. She studied his face and found every appealing feature, taking her back in time to those days when she'd fancied herself in love. He was very fine-looking, and she found herself wondering what it would be like to kiss his lips.

Stop it. Stop it. Stop it. This was dangerous territory. She was starting to have feelings for him. Feelings that she knew he couldn't return. At least not yet.

Oh, Lord, help me.

She pushed down the cover and did her best to tuck it in around him. Maybe this would help him to go on sleeping. Angel glanced toward the small window. There was just enough light to see by. She'd left her clothes hanging on a peg by the door. If she could manage to get out of the bed and get to them before Vincent woke up, they'd be better off.

Scooting down a little more, Angel maneuvered her nightgown to be modest, yet give her room to move. She positioned her leg across Vincent's and pushed off. She intended to throw herself over Vincent and off the bed in one quick motion.

But that didn't work. Her legs were somehow bound in the nightgown, and she started to fall over the side headfirst. This wasn't going to be good at all. She had visions of landing on her face.

Instead, she found an ironclad grip on her arm pulling her back until she was face to face with Vincent. He seemed momentarily surprised to find her there, but then recognition dawned.

Angel gazed into his eyes, feeling his arms around her. She swallowed the lump in her throat, unable to speak.

Thankfully, Vincent came fully awake. His hands went to her waist and with one powerful lift moved her to the side where Angel quickly jumped out of the bed. She raced to claim her clothes and then stood holding them against her body, uncertain what to do next. She could hardly leave the room. The stairs led directly into the dining room below.

"I . . . ah . . . oh goodness, this is embarrassing."

Vincent was already grabbing his trousers from the floor. He managed to pull them on under the covers and then reached for his shirt. Angel looked away as he got out of the bed.

"I'm sorry about that, Angel. I didn't mean to frighten you."

"You didn't." She stared at the wall, still clutching her things close. "Well, you did, but . . ." She fell silent, shaking her head. The situation got the best of her, and she started to giggle. "I'm the one . . . I was trying to keep from waking you up." The giggling turned to laughter. "I thought I could sort of jump over you." She looked at him, and that was her undoing. She gasped for air as her laughter spilled out around them. "I . . . my legs got caught up . . . I started to fall and . . . well then . . ." She could barely breathe for laughing so hard. The images that went through her mind were almost more than she could stand. She knew if he hadn't caught her, she probably would have been thoroughly humiliated.

Vincent chuckled and shook his head. "You sure know how to wake a fellow."

She had started to calm down, but this only stirred her amusement again. "You looked pretty shocked." She forced herself to take in deep gulps of air. "I'm so sorry."

"I didn't say it was a bad way to wake up. Although I did think you were falling."

"I was, and believe me, I'm glad you caught me. It would have been pretty embarrassing otherwise." She let out her breath and steadied her nerves. "I suppose I've probably awakened the whole house with my laughter."

"Better than with your tears." He started doing up the buttons on his shirt. "I'll get out of here in a minute so you can dress."

He finished with the shirt and grabbed his boots. He pulled

them on quickly, and then without slowing down, he headed for the door where Angel stood. He paused for a moment and looked down at her. Angel couldn't help but meet his gaze.

"I have a feeling we're going to remember this moment for the rest of our lives." His voice was barely a whisper.

Angel found it impossible to speak. She was fixed once again on his lips and knew she had gotten herself in a terrible bind. She was falling in love with her husband.

———— · Y · ————

After breakfast, Myra led Angel to a small room, where she pointed to a writing desk. "I heard Vincent say something about you wanting to send a letter to his grandmother."

"Yes. I thought since we probably wouldn't be back in town for a while, we should drop her a letter. We had one from her recently, and I've yet to answer it."

"I have plenty of paper and envelopes in the drawer. I could post it for you on Monday since you plan to head home after church."

Angel found the woman's offer to be too good to pass up. "Thank you so much. I'll do that."

"There is a pen and ink on the desk. I'll leave you to it." Myra exited the room without another word.

Angel went to the desk and found what she needed. She wrote to Granny, thanking her for the news from home. Her father had been down with a bad cold, but Angel was relieved to hear he was on the mend.

I'm so glad to hear that everyone else is well. I know Ruth will see Papa nursed back to health. We are doing well here. The sheep are a good lot—healthy and strong. And all of the ewes are expecting. There's some concern

*that the coming months will be harsh. Vincent says he's
never known anything quite like winter out here. I must
say I'm anxious to experience my first Wyoming winter.*

She told Granny about the children and their accomplishments, then found herself speaking of her own loneliness.

*While Ava seems to accept me more and more each day,
Benjamin and Vincent have little to do with me. I can't
help but admit to you alone that I'm lonely sometimes to
the point of heartache. I expected to feel isolated. After
all, the closest farm to ours is still about a thirty-minute
ride by horse, and the woman there is around fifty years
old with two grown sons who work the farm with their
father. But having no friends, and especially not having
you around, has been so hard. I suppose I do speak more
to the Lord, but it would be so nice to have someone to
talk to.*

She thought for a moment of telling Granny about her
growing feelings for Vincent. But how could she possibly explain what she was experiencing? Angel couldn't understand
them herself. She knew that Vincent was still mourning Elsa.
Their marriage had been a good one, and their friendship
and love ran strong. Even in his need for help with the farm
and children, Vincent wasn't going to overcome that easily. And Angel wasn't about to ask him to forget Elsa. She
didn't think that would be fair to the children. They should
remember their mother, even if she took over that woman's
responsibilities. Angel had never come with the thought of
replacing Elsa.

She concluded the letter with messages to her father and

then signed off with love for all. Noting the time, Angel quickly addressed an envelope, then started to fold the letter.

"Myra said you were writing a letter to Granny. Is there room for a postscript?" Vincent asked. "She won't like it if I don't at least scrawl a few lines."

"Of course. You can use the backside if you like or take another piece of paper. Myra said there is plenty. I'll go make sure Ava's hair is fixed for church. Would you seal up the letter when you're done? I've already addressed the envelope."

"Sure thing."

———— ❧ ————

Vincent was acutely aware of Angel's every move. Since their encounter that morning, he couldn't stop thinking about how she had felt in his arms and the way her wavy blond hair fell around her like a cloak. In fact, he hadn't really thought of Elsa until now. He waited for a feeling of guilt to wash over him, but it never came. When he'd first married Angel, he had worried that he was somehow betraying his wife's memory. Even in needing someone to help with the children and farm, he couldn't help but feel that he'd done Elsa wrong.

Of course, he hadn't. She was gone and in a better place. He knew she'd want him to be happy, and the children too. Even as she lay dying, Elsa had urged him to remarry and do so quickly.

He took up Angel's letter and started to turn it over when his gaze fell upon her words.

I can't help but admit to you—and you alone—that I'm lonely sometimes to the point of heartache.

Now the guilt came. Vincent had never given thought to Angel being lonely. He had been so happy to have someone to

64

handle the children that he'd not even considered what Angel's needs might be. She had known coming here that Vincent wasn't looking for a wife to love. Still, she'd said nothing. She'd borne her loneliness in silence. He felt like a cad, the worst of friends. At least he could talk to her. He would have to make a better effort to seek her out.

But what would they talk about? His mind went back to that morning, waking up to find her there in his bed. Thinking at first it was Elsa. Then realizing it was Angel, and she was falling. He couldn't help but confess, at least to himself, that he hadn't been displeased to find her there. They had slept comfortably together. At least he had. In fact, it was probably the best sleep he'd had since losing his wife. Sadly, he hadn't thought to ask how Angel had slept. He'd so closed off his heart and thoughts since losing Elsa that he hadn't even considered she might have suffered.

Vincent realized the time and picked up the pen. He wrote a few lines to Granny, telling her about the children. He concluded with words of love for her and John Quincy, then quickly folded the letter and sealed it in the envelope. He knew he shouldn't have read Angel's words, but he was glad he had. He was going to find a way to be a better husband to her. Or at least a better friend.

Two hours later, they were on their way home from church. Myra had packed them a lunch to take, and the children were busy eating and talking about the friends they'd seen. Benjamin was more like his old self, and Vincent breathed a silent prayer of thanks for this. He worried so much about the boy. His anger toward God for taking his mother had left him difficult to handle at times. Hopefully, God was at work softening the hardened edges of Benjamin's heart. Vincent knew God had certainly been working on his own heart. He hadn't meant to close God off in his grief.

The pastor had talked about the joy of the Lord that morning. Joy was something that had been sorely lacking in their home, but he intended to see things change. They needed more joy in their lives. Angel had done her level best to bring them some happiness and healing. Vincent felt he owed it to her, if not to everyone, to find some way to experience more joy. After all, Christmas was soon to be upon them.

Elsa had always made a big celebration of Christmas. She loved the festivities surrounding the holiday but loved even more the reminder of God's gift in sending His Son, Jesus. It seemed people everywhere were happy to share some Christmas spirit, but not always for the right reason. Elsa, however, had always felt it a hallowed occasion, and along with the fun and laughter, she brought in an equal amount of reverence and awe.

While the children were otherwise occupied, Vincent leaned closer to Angel. "Are you cold?"

"A little." Her teeth clattered a bit as she shivered.

"Why don't you share that with me." He pointed to the wool blanket on her lap.

She scooted a little closer and spread the blanket across them both. Tucking it under her legs, she gave him a nod. "Thank you. That is better."

"Sorry I wasn't thinking about it sooner. I'm not always the most thoughtful of men. But since we are talking about being thoughtful, I wondered what you might like to do in celebration of Christmas."

"Christmas?" She shook her head. "I hadn't really thought about it."

"Well, you should. It'll be here in a little more than a month." He grinned. "We're rather fond of it."

"I supposed I hadn't really thought about it because of . . . well . . . you're still in mourning."

"True, but we've had enough sorrow to last us a lifetime. Elsa loved Christmas. I mean, she really lived to celebrate it. She always worked to make the house a joyful place for the holiday. You don't have to decide right now what you want to do, but think about it."

"How did you usually celebrate?"

"Well, we always tried to go to church, but it would depend on the weather. Last year we made it and had a wonderful time. Church services were beautiful, and there was a little party afterward. The children had fun because there were games and lots of candy."

"I could make candy. I have a bunch of Granny's recipes. She and I used to make a lot of treats for various families during the holidays."

"Perfect. I miss Granny's sugarplums."

"I have that recipe, as well as the recipe for boiled sweets, maple candy, and of course all sorts of cookies. We would probably have to make another trip back to town, however. I don't have the ingredients at home."

Vincent glanced at her and smiled. "I'm sure we can arrange that. Zeb can probably spare us another day or two of help, and we can attend church again. I do find I miss the fellowship." He sobered and looked back at the trail. He could keep his feelings inside or share them with Angel. He thought of her loneliness and knew his own often threatened to overwhelm him.

"Elsa loved church. She said that her faith in God was the foundation of who she was, but that church and the fellowship of the people there were what gave her the daily encouragement she needed. When we came to this territory, we both knew it would be hard to attend church on a regular basis unless we lived in town. Still, we made an effort to go every week."

"That must have been very hard with little ones," Angel said, glancing back at the children. They had curled up together after eating and were buried under several blankets.

"It wasn't ideal, to be certain, but Elsa made it seem so. She was happy to fix things up on Saturday so that it would be an easier time on Sunday. We padded part of the wagon so Benjamin and Ava could play. They always had a lot of fun unless the temperatures dropped too much. If the weather was bad, of course, we didn't even attempt the drive."

"That makes sense." Angel reached under the seat to where they had put their part of the lunch Myra had packed. "Are you hungry?"

"I could stand to eat."

Angel produced a cloth-wrapped bundle and opened it. "Let's see what we have. Looks like ham and cheese, buttered biscuits—oh, and Myra included some of that delicious lemon cake from last night's supper."

"Sounds perfect."

Angel took a biscuit and put a piece of ham between the top and bottom. She handed it to Vincent and then made one for herself. It was a pleasant way to spend an afternoon, but Vincent had noticed that the skies were growing darker. Heavy gray clouds were moving in, and no doubt they would see snowfall by the time they reached home. He just hoped it might hold off until then.

"It would seem you're going to experience your first Wyoming snow," he said, smiling at Angel.

She frowned and gave a look around them. "What do we do if it starts before we get home?"

"I don't think it will, but if it does, we'll keep pushing on. If it comes up a blizzard, then we might have to seek someplace to wait it out. There are plenty of ravines and a few hilly spots that we can tuck into and wait it out."

"That sounds a bit adventurous, maybe more than what I would like to experience." She shook her head. "I would just as soon be inside the house, looking out at the snowfall."

He laughed. "I agree. That does hold more promise." He snapped the lines. "Come on, you two, let's pick up the pace. We don't want Angel losing her halo in the snow."

CHAPTER 7

The snows came, and continued off and on for three days. Angel had certainly experienced heavy snows back in Nebraska, but there was something about Wyoming that made it feel like she was a world away from civilization. Here, the isolation left her feeling abandoned, forgotten. Especially since her husband held her no love and her stepson would just as soon she disappear. Only Ava offered her any comfort at all. Slowly, Angel was winning the child's trust. Perhaps even love. But the rest of them were another story.

Not that Vincent wasn't kind. He was. He was considerate and complimentary of her cooking. He loved the meals because they reminded him of Granny and the way she cooked when he was a boy. He was amazed by her work ethic and abilities. Her knowledge of sheep and the other animals impressed him, and he told her as much. But that was the limit of it. There was never an encouraging word regarding the children, nor a moment of intimate conversation regarding their future.

At least he'd reached out regarding Christmas, but then just as quickly as he'd brought the subject up, it faded into nothing. Angel wasn't at all sure what that meant. Was she supposed to make the plans for their Christmas celebration? Had Vincent any desires for the festivities?

The last few days had been made more difficult by the children's inability to go outside. Benjamin had accompanied his father to help with the sheep. Thankfully they were penned close to the house. Ava didn't care about being outside as much as her brother did, but even she was growing restless with the continued snow.

Angel did her best to help the children focus on their schoolwork, as well as some sewing. As she'd figured, Benjamin balked at learning what he figured was a woman's interest. Vincent chided him, however, telling him about the quilt he and Granny had made together and how learning to sew had helped him to be able to do a number of things for himself. He could mend his clothes and stitch up a sheep. Those two things impressed Benjamin enough to agree to learn.

Book learning took the hours between breakfast and lunch. Then every afternoon, Angel would have them practice sewing. They had both made pillows and stuffed them with washed sheep's wool. Benjamin actually appeared a little impressed with what he'd accomplished and asked if he could make one for his father as a Christmas gift. Angel had readily agreed. Ava had been upset that she had nothing to give her father, so Angel suggested she could make her father a sachet for his clothes drawer. She was content with this.

After sewing, Angel read to them from the Bible and asked them questions regarding the Scriptures. Today, she shared with them from John chapter eight.

"'Then spake Jesus again unto them, saying, I am the light of the world: he that followeth me shall not walk in darkness, but shall have the light of life.'" She paused and looked at Benjamin. "We were talking the other day about another verse in

John chapter one, that called Jesus the Light. Do you remember which verse that was?"

Benjamin looked at her and shrugged. "I don't know. I don't like it when we read the Bible."

Angel closed the book. "Why is that, Benjamin?"

"Because I don't like to read about God. God is mean. He took my mama and Paul and the baby. He let us be sick with the measles. He doesn't care about us."

Ava surprised Angel by coming to sit a little closer to her. It was as if she knew what was coming and wanted no part of it.

"It's really hard to lose the people we love. It hurts a lot, doesn't it?" She kept her gaze fixed on Benjamin, and when he didn't answer, Angel continued. "When I was a little younger than you, Benjamin, my mama took sick and died. It was the worst day of my life."

"How did she die?" Ava braved the question.

"It was December, and she got winter-fever. Some doctors call it pneumonia. It makes fluid fill in your lungs, and you can't breathe right."

"Did you make her sick?"

"No. She was out in the cold air too much. I guess that's how she came down with it." Angel heard something in Ava's voice that drew her attention. It dawned on her that Ava's mother had caught measles after she and Benjamin had been sick. "Ava, do you think that you made your mother sick?"

The seven-year-old nodded. "Benjamin and me got sick, and Mama took care of us. We made her sick, and she died."

Angel glanced a moment at Benjamin to see if he agreed with this. He looked away, but his expression was one that suggested great discomfort.

"Sweetheart, measles is what made you sick, and it's what made your mama sick. You can't blame yourself. Measles has

73

a way of spreading. We don't know why. It gets in the air, and the air gets into us. It isn't your fault that your mother caught measles. Just like it wasn't anyone's fault that my mama caught winter-fever. People sometimes just get sick."

"And die." Ava's voice was barely audible.

Angel nodded. "Yes, and they die, and it hurts us so much to lose them. And we don't understand why they die, and others don't. And that sometimes makes it even worse."

"Maybe God doesn't love us as much as He loved the ones who die." Benjamin surprised her by speaking up.

Angel looked at the boy and could see the pain reflected in his eyes. She considered her words carefully. "So, you think maybe God loved your mother and the baby and little Paul more than He loves you and Ava and your father?"

"Maybe. Pa says that God has control over life and death. He could have made Mama well like He did Ava and me. Mrs. Humphreys at church said God loved Mama so much that He wanted her to be in heaven with Him. Paul and the baby too. But me and Ava loved Mama, and we needed her with us. Pa needed her too."

"And I needed my mama as well." Angel gave a sigh. "Sometimes we don't know why things happen the way they do, Benjamin."

"It was just plain mean of God to take her." He looked at her as if daring her to say he was wrong. She wondered if he'd spoken out on this before only to get reprimanded.

"It does seem plain mean, doesn't it?"

His eyes widened at her comment, and he gave a slow nod. Angel nodded, too, and even Ava joined in. Angel could see he wanted her to say more. She couldn't help but wonder if anyone had allowed him to really talk about how any of this had made him feel. Vincent certainly had pulled away from his children. No doubt there were well-meaning people like Mrs. Humphreys who commented on the situation but only made matters worse.

"But you know, Benjamin, I don't think there was ever any time in the Bible where God did something out of plain meanness. There are a lot of times in the Bible where God punished folks for their behavior. Did your mama do anything wrong so that God would need to punish her? I know mine didn't."

"She never did nothing wrong." Benjamin sounded offended that she should even question the idea.

Ava shook her head. "Never."

"When I was little, my papa told me that sometimes bad things happen, and we have to keep trusting God even when they do."

"Why?" Benjamin asked.

"Because who else would we put our trust in? The devil? Even if I can't understand why God allows things to happen the way they do, I can't put my trust in anyone else. The devil isn't trustworthy. Besides, my mama told me that God was good . . . that He is love. I want to honor my mama by believing that what she told me was true."

"Our mama said the same thing," Benjamin said, his brow scrunching up as he seemed to really think it over.

Ava crawled up on Angel's lap. "Mama said Jesus loved us so much He died for us. But He didn't stay dead."

"No, He didn't. He rose again and sits with God the Father in heaven."

"And if we ask Jesus to come into our hearts, He will," Ava added. "Mama said so."

Angel smiled. "Your mama was absolutely right."

Ava nodded, looking at Angel with such an expression of trust and hope that Angel couldn't help giving her a hug.

"I asked Jesus to be in my heart," Ava said, then pointed to her brother. "Benjamin did too."

Benjamin nodded and then frowned. "Do you think He's still there, even though I've been mad at Him?"

"I'm sure He is, Benjamin. Better still, He knows about how you feel. You can talk to Him and tell Him that you're sorry you've been mad—that it really hurt to lose your mama. Ask Him to help you to trust Him. He loves you, and that's never going to stop."

Benjamin looked at the table. "Mama used to help me pray."

Angel smiled as a rush of love for this boy flooded her heart. "Would you like me to help you pray?"

He didn't look at her, but nodded. Angel looked at Ava, and she nodded as well. Angel could have cried for joy in that moment. Instead, she bowed her head. Accepting Jesus as her Savior was the most important prayer she'd ever prayed, but this one was surely the second.

———•▼•———

Vincent came into the house through the back door to hear Angel praying aloud. He took off his snowy boots and walked in his sock feet to the doorway that led to the dining room. There he found his children bowing in prayer and Angel asking God's blessings upon each one.

Her prayers were so reminiscent of those Elsa had prayed that for a moment he was transported back in time. He could almost see her sitting there as she had on so many occasions, but this was Angel. Angel, who'd given up so much to come to an unknown place and take on this wounded, grieving, even angry family. She had borne the silence and the hostility with such grace, offering nothing but love in return.

Earlier in the week, he had been captivated by her beauty

and the desire to hold her in his arms . . . to kiss her. But in this moment, he found himself loving her.

"And, Father, please bless Vincent. He's had to endure so much. He's a good man, and I know He loves you dearly. Help him to be a good father to these precious children. Guard his heart and mind and lead him as he makes decisions for his family and the future."

Vincent winced at the comment "his family." Angel still didn't feel they were her family as well. She still felt isolated and alone, and that was something he could change. He whispered his own prayer, asking God to help him to figure out how best to make her feel that this was truly her home and family. And he prayed that God would help them to love each other as a husband and wife.

I never thought I'd pray this prayer, Lord, but I want to fall in love again. I want to feel the deep and wonderful feelings that a husband should have for his wife. I want us to be a real family, Lord.

"Vincent, we didn't hear you come in," Angel said, sounding startled.

He looked up. "I didn't want to interrupt such a beautiful prayer. Thank you for praying for my . . . our children."

Her eyes widened, but she said nothing.

"And thank you for praying for me as a wife should for her husband. I've needed those prayers for a long time now."

She glanced down as if embarrassed. "I think it's probably time for me to start working on supper." She got up from the table and started to maneuver past him, but Vincent took hold of her arm and stopped her. He wanted to give her some token of his changed heart, as well as show his children that she truly belonged to them.

He pulled her closer and kissed her cheek. "Thank you for not giving up on us."

CHAPTER 8

As Christmas neared, Angel felt the age-old excitement of celebration. She easily remembered those times when her mother was still alive, and they'd made merry for the holidays. Mama had so loved Christmas. She always made it a point to tell a variety of Bible stories related to Jesus's birth and the excitement that there must have been among the Jewish people. They had waited so very long for their Messiah, and now He had come.

"Remember when we were talking about Jesus being the Light?" she said to the children as they read from the Bible.

Both nodded, and even Benjamin seemed more interested than he had been when Angel had first arrived.

"We talked about the Bible verses in John that spoke about Jesus being the Light of the world. Sin creates a darkness in our souls and leads us to sorrow and separation from God. Jesus says He's the Light, and if we follow Him, we shall not walk in darkness, but shall have the light of life." She turned back to the first chapter in John. "John also says that Jesus was the true Light, which lighteth every man that cometh into the world. There are many references in the Bible that show God associated with light. He says 'Let there be light' in Genesis when He forms the world. The glory of the Lord shone round about when the angels came to announce the birth of Jesus. That must have been a truly brilliant light. And of course when the wise men came to see Jesus, how did they find Him?"

"A star! They followed the star's light," Benjamin said.

Angel nodded. "Jesus is the true Light for us, and we need to be light for others."

"But why?" Benjamin asked.

"To lead them to Jesus." Angel was excited that he was asking questions about the lesson. He had never been quite this interested before. To her, it showed real progress. "When we let the light of Jesus shine out of our hearts, people see it and know we're different."

"But we don't really shine, do we?" the boy questioned. He looked at Angel.

"We shine in love and hope. When we live a life for Jesus, people notice that we're different. When we are forgiving and kind when others deserve our anger, the light shines. Your great-granny Duran is an example of someone shining the light of Jesus. She's always doing acts of kindness and helping folks who need help, but she also lives her life in such a way that the Word of God comes out of her in her everyday conversations. She is able to share what God has done for her and help others to want that same thing for themselves. She's shining the light of Jesus."

"Mama liked the light," Ava offered. "She always liked having the windows open so there would be lots of light."

"I remember your papa telling me that," Angel said, gently touching Ava's cheek. "Light is so important. Psalm 27:1 says, 'The LORD is my light and my salvation; whom shall I fear? the LORD is the strength of my life; of whom shall I be afraid?' That's our memory verse for this week. We need to always remember that we have nothing to fear with God. He is our light, and He will show us the way."

They practiced saying the verse a couple of times, and then Angel instructed them to write it out. Benjamin easily mastered this, but Ava needed help, so Angel carefully worked with her while Benjamin sat in silence.

Angel could see that he was deep in thought. She hoped that maybe he was thinking about God being there to light their way—to keep them from fear. She hoped he might realize that he could still trust God and rest in Him, despite his mother's passing.

After they finished their lessons for the day, Angel got Benjamin busy bringing in wood while she put Ava to work cracking eggs in a bowl for the fruitcake they were going to make. She had to admit that things were going a little better. She'd written a long letter to Granny the night before, hoping that it wouldn't be too long before she could mail it.

"Ava, you can beat the eggs after you get them in the bowl. I'm going to go out to the barn and speak to your father for a moment. Be a good girl."

"I will." Ava smiled at her. "Angel, I'm glad you're here."

Angel paused and looked at the little girl. "I'm glad I am too."

Ava turned her attention back to her work, but the moment was precious to Angel. It seemed as each day passed, her life here in Wyoming was getting better. The children were adapting to her as their new mother, and even Vincent was showing more affection toward them and Angel as well.

She pulled on her coat and headed outside. The air was cold, but not nearly as damp as it would have been in Nebraska. It was the dampness that made it so bone-chilling, Vincent had told her. Here in Wyoming, the ground and the air were much drier. It made heat and cold a little more tolerable.

"Vincent?" she called, coming into the barn.

"I'm back here," he answered.

She made her way past the wagon and stacks of grain. Vincent was quite organized in his work, and the barn was no exception. She smiled at the sight of it, knowing that her father and brothers would have marveled at the meticulous order but also given Vincent a hard time for the effort he gave it. Her father always said that his barn might look like it was a mess, but he knew where everything was, right down to the last nail.

"Your smile lights up the room," Vincent said as she joined him in the milking stall.

"I was just thinking of the complete dishevelment in my father's barn, compared to your order. Mama would give him a hard time for not being organized, but Papa told her he knew where everything was."

"I remember that too." Vincent put aside the hammer he'd been using. "Your pa would tell one of us boys to go get a certain thing, and we couldn't see where it was to save ourselves. Then your father would walk over to a messy pile and pick out the exact thing he was looking for and chide us for not seeing that it had been right there in plain sight."

Angel laughed. "I fell victim to that many times. Mama was much more orderly, and I came to really appreciate it. I think that's one area where you and I are in complete agreement."

"I think we have a lot in common, Angel. I know I haven't said a great deal about it since Granny sent you out here, but I can't imagine any other woman suiting me quite as well as you do."

"That's kind of you to say, Vincent. I was thinking about how things have been falling into place lately. The children don't seem nearly as out of sorts with me. Even Benjamin is talking more, and I think he knows that I just want to help, rather than take his mother's place."

She met Vincent's gaze and saw such tenderness in his eyes. Her heart skipped a beat when he pulled off his glove and reached out to touch her cheek.

"I know it's been hard on you, Angel, but I mean for it to get better. We don't always get much of a chance to talk, but I want you to know that I care a great deal about you . . . about us."

"I do too. I want to make you a good wife, Vincent. I know I can never be to you what Elsa was, but—"

He put his finger to her lips. "I don't want you to be what Elsa was to me. I want us to have something entirely different. Something just as wonderful, if not better. I haven't always thought that might be possible, but I do now."

To her complete surprise, Vincent pulled her close and pressed his lips to hers. For a moment she didn't even know how to respond, but after that she couldn't help but react. She put her arms around his neck and returned the kiss. The moment was all that she had dreamed of when she'd lost her heart to him at fifteen. When he pulled away, she looked him in the eye, pleased to see that he showed no signs of being ashamed or having remorse for what had just taken place.

Instead, he smiled. "We're going to be all right, Angel."

Angel nodded. "Yes. I believe that we will be."

———◦⋎◦———

Vincent was still thinking about that kiss the next day when he was in Cheyenne, shopping for a list of things Angel had given him. She had managed to tell him her thoughts about getting the children some gifts for Christmas. Vincent had never shopped alone for such things, but Angel had listed what she thought might be appropriate for Ava and encouraged him to contemplate what he might have liked as a boy while shopping for Benjamin.

By the time he was headed back to the farm, Vincent felt he'd done a satisfactory job. He'd found a doll for Ava and a folding knife for Benjamin. He got them both a bag of lemon drops, remembering how much they seemed to enjoy them. Angel was making all sorts of goodies for their Christmas Day celebration, but he knew lemon drops weren't among them.

Thoughts of Angel and their shared kiss had prompted him to buy her a couple of presents as well. He remembered little things about her as a girl and hoped that she enjoyed what his granny called "ladies' doodads." He'd purchased a pretty little hand mirror and brush that had carved wooden handles that had been artfully designed with swirled cuts and curlicues. He'd also found a beautiful blue shawl that matched the color of her eyes. Eyes that he couldn't stop thinking about. They always looked so captivated, as if the people around her were the most important in the whole world. He hoped she'd like the gifts. Hoped she realized that with the kiss they'd shared, he was truly ready to move forward in their marriage.

He thought momentarily of Elsa and glanced heavenward. "I know you're somewhere with the Lord, Elsa," he said, smiling. "I don't know if you know what's going on down here on earth, but I want you to know we're doing pretty well now. It was the hardest thing I ever did, burying you and Paul. I wasn't sure I'd ever make it through. Probably wouldn't have, if not for Benjamin and Ava. I knew they needed me. I know, too, that I pushed them away to a point. They needed more tenderness, and I just didn't have it to give. I've been mighty sorry for that. There were times I wasn't sure I could go on."

He looked out across the vast open prairie. "But Angel has changed everything. I love her, Elsa. I hope that's all right." He thought of the brown-haired beauty and nearly laughed aloud. He could almost hear her chiding him for thinking it would be otherwise.

"I know. You told me you wanted me to marry again soon. You said the children needed a mother and that I needed someone to come alongside and love me. And that I needed to love again. I didn't think it was possible, but I promised you just the same. I think I can finally say I've kept my promise. I've started to love again."

He thought of Angel and the joy she'd brought them. Granny had been so wise in sending her, even if it had come in part to get Angel away from her sorrow and embarrassment at having been left at the altar. He had never really allowed himself to consider her pain. She must have been devastated, and yet she'd never spoken of it. Hopefully now, with the growing love he felt for her, she'd never have to even think on it again.

"I think we're going to be all right, Elsa. The children too. You said you were going to pray for us, and I guess I just want you to know that those prayers were answered."

Angel was glad to hear the wagon rumbling along the drive into the barnyard. Vincent was home safe and sound. It was a relief since the western skies looked to be darkening once again with threats of snow. The wind had also picked up, and Angel figured Vincent would be chilled to the bone.

She checked the coffeepot, then added more wood to the stove. Vincent said he'd be bringing back coal so they'd have it to bank up the stove at night, to help with heating the house. She supposed he'd also use it out in the lambing shed, if he continued to sleep out there. She was already thinking, however, of ways to suggest he return to the house and share her bed.

It was a bold thought, she knew, but they were married after all, and it was foolish for him to think of spending the winter in the lambing shed. They were a family and needed to start acting like one. The children needed to see them working together, laughing together, showing affection for each other.

Vincent opened the back door, then picked up a wood crate and entered the house. Angel stood ready to help in any way she could, but he just waved her off.

"This is heavy. I'll just put it on the table."

"You look froze to pieces. I've got hot coffee and freshly baked muffins to get you through to supper. The fire is built up in the front room, and there are blankets by the hearth. You go on and get yourself warmed up. I'll bring you the coffee."

He surprised her instead by turning around and pulling her into his arms. "You could just warm me up instead." He put his cold face against her cheek.

Angel was surprised by his actions, but not put off. She wrapped her arms around him. "I doubt I'll be as helpful as the fire."

"Never underestimate the power of love," he whispered against her ear.

Could he really be having such feelings for her? How she prayed it might be true. She pulled away slowly and studied his face for any sign of teasing. Instead, she found his expression intense and his eyes fixed on hers.

"Love?" she barely whispered.

"Would you mind?"

He still held on to her, and Angel was grateful. Her knees felt rather weak. She shook her head. "I don't mind at all."

Vincent smiled. "Good. Then we're of one mind." He pulled her close and once again kissed her.

Angel felt as if the world had suddenly turned upside down. Her heart was overflowing with feelings that she had never known. Her mind seemed to whir with thoughts until she could hardly hear what was going on around her. Vincent made her feel things that no one had ever made her feel before. It was clear to her that she'd never really known love for a man until that moment. What a gift to be given. Love.

CHAPTER 9

In the days that followed, Angel and Vincent just naturally grew closer. It was almost as if by unspoken agreement. Angel suggested after supper one evening that he bring his things in from the lambing shed and return them to their bedroom. She could still remember the look in his eyes and the slow nod he gave her. After that, things fell into a routine that included him kissing her as they sat down to breakfast. He laughed more and showed the children greater affection. Angel was amazed at what God had done in a few short months. If only Benjamin would learn to trust her and to let go of his anger with God, life might be perfect.

The boy had made great strides, but there was still that bit of doubt. He had trusted God, and God had taken his mother and siblings away. It was hard for Benjamin to have faith in his Heavenly Father. What if He took away someone else?

The day before Christmas Eve, it began to snow as it had done off and on all month. Up until now, the snow had barely left a mark, and the animals were still able to feed from the dried range grass as Vincent rotated them from one area to another in a wide circle around the house and barn area. Things had been going well, and there was only a minimal need for additional feed and salt.

By Christmas Eve morning, however, the winds had picked up considerably and were getting stronger. The snow grew heavier and was accumulating.

"I'm going to bring the sheep in. Benjamin will help me." Vincent motioned to his son. "Put on an extra pair of socks. Not sure how long we'll need to be out." He looked back to Angel. "We'll move them from the north pen to the shelter fold."

She nodded, knowing very well the fold where he'd set up a protective place for them against the rocky indentation of a low hill just beyond the barn. Benjamin jumped to his feet and hurried up the stairs. He returned with his extra work gloves and a second pair of socks. He sat down by his boots while Vincent continued instructing.

"We've run ropes between the building and gates, so we'll be fine if the snow gets worse. Whatever happens, I don't want you and Ava out in the snow. We'll see to the chickens and cows, and of course the horses. You just stay here and keep things nice and warm so we can thaw out when we're done."

"Is it a blizzard?" Ava asked, looking up from her primer.

"Not exactly, but it may be headed that way," Vincent replied. "But don't you worry. We'll be safe and snug. And it's nearly Christmas. Angel has been making all sorts of delicious things to eat, and we'll sing some songs and open presents later tonight."

Ava grinned and nodded.

"You ready, Benjamin?"

The boy was lacing up his boots. "Just about."

The wind picked up and seemed to moan as it moved around the buildings outside. Vincent looked at Angel. "Better get the shutters closed."

She nodded. "Ava and I will see to it. Please be careful."

He smiled and kissed her forehead. "I will. We'll both be back as soon as possible."

Angel knew it was necessary to see to the animals. They were the livelihood that had kept the family well cared for. Vincent had told Angel how each pregnant ewe represented the difference between them being able to remain in the territory or not. She had wondered, if everything fell apart, if he would want to return to Nebraska. Granny and John Quincy would welcome him back with open arms, but how could Vincent return as a failed sheep farmer? His pride would be sorely damaged.

Angel knew if she opened the downstairs windows to secure the shutters, the house would be freezing from the cold. Instead, she chose to put on her boots and coat and tend the lower level from the ground.

"Ava, I want you to stay here in the house. It's really important. I'm going to go outside and get the window shutters closed."

"Papa told me to help."

"I know he did, but you can help me from inside. I'll close the downstairs shutters from the outside, and then you can make sure it's not letting in any snow or wind. All right?"

Ava nodded. "That sounds important."

"It is," Angel assured her. She dug her wool mittens out from her coat pocket. "It won't take much time. It hasn't snowed that much yet. I'll start with this window here in the dining room. You stand here and make sure the shutter closes all the way."

Angel hurried outside and made her way around the house. The wind blew a fierce attack that nearly knocked her to her knees a couple of times. One by one, she wrestled the shutters into place and secured them. Elsa loved her windows and light, but it was quite the task facing the wind and icy snow to ensure they were protected against the storm.

When Angel finally made it inside, she knew there were still the upstairs windows to deal with. If she didn't get them closed, the second floor would be colder, and the wind could even shatter the glass.

Ava faithfully followed her upstairs and went with her from window to window. There were six in total. Angel couldn't imagine what the cost had been to put in six windows, but she was determined to protect them from the storm. One by one, she opened the windows, then had to stick half her body out into the storm to take hold of the shutters. They were fixed in place by a hook, so that was the first part of the job. It was hard to free the hooks with her covered hands. Angel finally gave up and handed the mittens back to Ava.

She worked as quickly as possible, but her hands were stiff and white with cold by the time she managed to secure the last window. She knew from other experiences with cold weather that she would have to warm them slowly using cold water, then tepid. It would be painful, but at least the windows were taken care of.

Angel made her way back downstairs and went to the kitchen, where she had several pails of water set aside for use. She found it almost impossible to ladle the water from the pail to a bowl.

"I can do that," Ava said, reaching for the ladle. "I won't spill a drop."

"That would be so helpful. Thank you, Ava."

Angel sat down at the table, and Ava soon brought her a bowl of water. True to her word, she didn't spill a drop. Soaking her hands was painful at first, but little by little Angel managed. By the time she was ready for warm water, her hands and fingers were working again. She supposed it was foolish to have rid herself of her mittens but wasn't at all sure what else could have been done.

She glanced at the clock, surprised to see that two hours had already gone by. Where were Vincent and Benjamin? It shouldn't have taken this long. Should it?

By the time another hour slipped by, Angel couldn't help but go to the door and look out. The snow was so blinding she couldn't even see the outbuildings across the yard. She took hold of the rope, more to reassure herself than anything else. It was tied securely and held fast. They would be able to follow it to the house once they were able to get back to the barn.

Perhaps they were waiting out the storm in the barn. There was access to the chicken coop, and no doubt the milk cows, rams, and horses were there as well. Vincent might even decide to milk the cows before coming in for the night. That thought gave her at least a small amount of comfort. Milking took time.

But when the clock chimed six and still there was no sign of Vincent or Benjamin, Angel felt certain something was wrong. Ava was worried as well.

"We should pray," Ava said, coming to Angel.

"Yes, we should." She knelt down with Ava by the fireplace and prayed aloud. "Father in Heaven, please be with Vincent and Benjamin. They've been out in the storm for a long time. Please help them to get back home safely. Please let the storm die down. In Jesus's name, amen."

"Can I pray too?" Ava asked.

Angel nodded. "Of course, sweet child." She bowed her head again.

"Please, God, my papa and brother need your help. It's so dark outside. And so cold. Please help them to come home. Give them some light."

Her words struck Angel like a bolt of lightning. *Give them some light.*

It was dark outside. The storm had made it doubly so, and with the shutters against the windows there would be very little light shining from the house. If they'd lost track of the ropes or if they'd gotten separated, they would have no bearing on where they were or how to get back to the house.

"Ava! That's it! The light. We need to shine the light." Angel jumped up and went to the wooden box that held a large supply of candles. "Here, Ava, put the candles on the table. Find the candlestick holders in the pantry. I'll get the lamps. We need to put lights in the windows."

"But the shutters are closed."

Angel nodded. "I know. We'll just have to open them again."

"But you can't go outside. You can't."

Ava was right. "I'll build up the fire in the hearth and stove. We'll just have to open the windows from inside and push back the shutters. Hopefully the house won't get too cold."

The two of them quickly went to work. It wasn't easy to unshutter the windows. Angel had to make sure that each one was hooked back into place, otherwise the wind would blow it shut again. After that, she closed the window and wiped away any excess snow before putting a lamp or candle into place on the sill.

It seemed to take hours to get the windows exposed, but when they were finally ready, Angel took a piece of kindling and used it to light the candles and lamps. The light seemed insignificant at first, but as more and more was added, the glow became quite impressive. Hopefully Vincent would be able to see it and find his way home.

The candles and lamps added warmth to the house. Those, along with the fireplace and stove, made the house quite comfortable. It would be a welcome to the boys when they made it back.

Angel continued to pray as she paced from window to window, looking out into the snow. There was no sign of it letting up, but the wind had seemed to lessen. She sighed. What a way to spend Christmas Eve. Her shepherds were keeping watch over their flocks by night, but were they safe themselves?

She fed Ava and tried to eat something herself, but found it stuck in her throat. She'd worked all week on a variety of treats and let Ava have whatever she wanted. But the poor child wanted only for her father and brother to return safely.

When the clock struck nine, Ava had already nodded off to sleep on the sofa. Angel didn't have the heart to wake her and send her upstairs. Instead, she took out a warm blanket and wrapped it around Ava and prayed for her and the others.

At ten, Angel took new candles and went from window to window to replace those that had burned down too low to be of much use. She knew it would be a cost to replace their supply, but she couldn't help but feel it was the right thing to do.

The wind continued to blow and howl. It was a maddening sound that wearied Angel to the bone. She kept watching and waiting but couldn't help growing sleepy. She sat down on the end of the sofa, adjusted the blanket over Ava, and gazed at the flames in the fireplace. That was her undoing, and she nodded off to sleep without meaning to.

A noise awakened her, but Angel couldn't quite tell where it was coming from. She listened and heard it again. It sounded like someone knocking. She jumped up from the sofa and hurried to the front door. Opening it, she found Vincent, caked in snow and ice. Benjamin was in his arms. She stepped back to let him inside, then closed the door securely.

"Oh, we were so afraid for you both!"

"Benjamin got lost. I think he hit his head; he's unconscious." Vincent could barely speak.

Angel took the boy from his father and carried him to the dining room table. She began pulling off the snow-encrusted coat, then his hat and scarf. There was a goose egg on his forehead. His skin was pale and icy cold.

"We need to get him warmed up." She looked at Vincent. "You need to get warm too. Go sit by the fire."

"No, I'll help you."

"You'll be no help unless you take care of yourself. Get out of your wet clothes. Go. I'm fine. I'll see to Benjamin."

Vincent looked at his son. He seemed unable to move.

Angel gave him a gentle push toward the fire, then went back to working on Benjamin. She rid him of the snowy wet clothes, then wrapped him in one of the blankets she'd been warming by the fireplace. Next, she picked him up and carried him to the fire, settling on the floor with him still in her arms. As gently as possible, she placed him by the hearth and grabbed another blanket. She pulled it around him and began rubbing each of his legs and feet. They were like ice. Next, she did the same for his arms and hands, gently massaging each finger. Once this was done, she started over again. Benjamin gave a bit of a moan, but still didn't awaken.

Angel began to pray as never before. She loved this boy, and like Vincent, she couldn't bear the idea of losing him.

Vincent had managed to rid himself of his wet clothes. Angel wasn't sure how he'd done it so quickly, but he'd already dressed in dry trousers and a flannel shirt. "What can I do?"

"Get me some water and a couple of dish towels. Oh, and get a bowl of snow for his head."

Vincent didn't say a word but went to work quickly retrieving the items. Angel kept rubbing Benjamin's feet and hands.

She could feel that the warmth was returning to his body. She prayed that he wouldn't suffer frostbite and that he'd soon awaken from the blow to his head.

When Vincent returned, Angel dipped one of the dish towels in the water and began wiping Benjamin's face.

"Benjamin, it's time to wake up. It's almost Christmas," she said as she gently cared for him. She put the towel aside and reached for the snow Vincent had packed into another bowl. She formed it into several small balls the size of grapes and put it in one of the dry towels before placing it on his forehead.

"I hate to make him cold again, but we need to get the swelling down. How did this happen?"

"I honestly don't know. We had trouble moving the sheep. They were spooked by the storm. Even Daisy was upset, and it takes a lot to unnerve that little donkey. Finally got them in the shelter fold. I told Benjamin to go secure the gate. The wind was blowing it back and forth. After that, I'm not sure what happened. I think the gate must have hit him in the head and knocked him out. I couldn't find him at first. He'd fallen in a drift, and like I said, I couldn't see much. I felt around and finally found him, and he was like this."

"I'm so glad you found him."

"I wasn't about to come back without him." Vincent's worried gaze met hers. "I can't lose him, Angel."

"You won't. He's going to be fine." She didn't know what else to say, even though in her heart she was more than a little concerned that she was giving him false hope.

Please, God, please bring Benjamin back to us. Wake him up and let him be just fine.

The boy moaned again and moved his arms. Vincent knelt down beside him. "Benjamin. Benjamin, it's Papa. Wake up, son. It's time to wake up." He gently brushed back the boy's hair.

Angel held her breath as Benjamin's eyes fluttered open. He seemed to be unable to focus at first, but then he looked at his father.

"Pa . . . did I . . . did I get the gate closed?"

Vincent laughed and grabbed his son and cradled him close. "You did, but I think the gate got the best of you. You hit your head, or something hit you."

"It hurts."

"I'll bet it does." He held Benjamin close and smiled over him at Angel.

"I'll make him some willow bark tea. That will help with the pain." She got up and hurried to the kitchen. She whispered thanks to God as she made the tea. She also offered petitions for Benjamin's continued healing. They weren't out of the woods yet.

By the time she returned to the fire with the tea, Benjamin was telling his story.

"It was so dark. I couldn't see to grab hold of the gate, and the wind knocked me back. That's all I remember," he was telling his father.

"I think the gate must have hit you in the head. You've got quite the bump."

"Here, drink this. I put some honey in it, so it shouldn't taste too bad." Angel squatted down and handed Benjamin the cup.

"Thanks. Why are all the candles burning?" Benjamin gazed around the room.

Angel smiled and sat down beside them. "Ava prayed for God to give you light in the darkness, and it got me thinking that maybe we could help."

"We needed it," Vincent said, shaking his head. "The two lanterns I had both went out. One I dropped, and the one I hung near the gate probably ran out of oil. There was no light. Things were as black as pitch. When I found Benjamin, I followed the fence for a ways, but I couldn't see much of anything. Then I must have come around the south side of the barn because all of a sudden there was the house, and the windows were lit up. I thought it must be a mirage. You know, like how thirsty folks see water when they're lost in the desert."

"The light saved us," Benjamin murmured. "Just like Jesus is the Light and He saves us."

"Yes," Angel said, taking his hand. "It's just like that."

"So maybe God really does forgive me for being so mad at Him." It was more statement than question. "Maybe He understands how . . . I felt losing Mama. Just like you said He would, Angel." Benjamin's words touched her heart.

"Yes, He knows and understands." Angel touched his cheek, and he didn't flinch away. "He'll always be there for us . . . for each one of us."

Once Benjamin was comfortably resting on a pallet by the fire, Vincent checked on Ava and found her sleeping soundly. She seemed completely free of worry and care. It was actually the best of Christmas gifts. All he had wanted was for his children to be able to go on without their mother . . . to be happy. Angel had made that happen. He could see that even Benjamin was finally coming around.

He went in search of Angel and found her in the bedroom. She had changed into a nightgown and was brushing out her hair. For a long moment, he stood and watched without her being aware. How he loved her. He stepped forward and touched her long blond strands. They were silky and soft.

She turned and stood, smiling at him. "I finally got the candles put away and the lamps too. Since the wind died down and the snow seems to have stopped, I didn't risk opening the windows to close the shutters again."

"Thank you. Thank you for shining the light. Not just tonight, but ever since you came here. You've been such a blessing." He pulled her into his arms and held her close. "I love you, Angel. For so many reasons."

"I love you, Vincent." She lifted her eyes to his. "I've loved you for a long time, even though I set it aside for all those years."

"Never do that again." He took hold of her face. "Love me now and always, and I will love you the same."

She gave a slight nod, just before he captured her mouth with his.

CHAPTER 10

Angel awoke to Vincent softly calling her name. She opened her eyes to find him sitting on the side of the bed, pulling on his clothes.

"What's wrong?" She sat up and brushed the hair from her eyes. "Is it Benjamin? Is he all right?" She threw back the covers and jumped out of bed.

"Benjamin is fine. In fact, he's hungry. Besides that—it's Christmas."

"It was already Christmas when I finally went to bed." She yawned and stretched. "What was that, an hour ago?" She had spent most of the night at Benjamin's side, long after everyone had fallen asleep. She had prayed for him and found it impossible to rest until she was certain he was going to be fine.

He chuckled and stood to finish dressing. "I promise you can go back to bed, but the children are awake and hoping for presents."

"And Benjamin is really doing all right?"

"Seems to be in order. He has a bruise on his forehead, but the bump has gone down considerably. Sorry I fell asleep. I guess I trusted you to see to Benjamin's needs completely."

She smiled, knowing that this action suggested a deep trust that neither had expected so soon.

Angel pulled on her robe. "I'm ready. I'll dress after they get their presents." She reached under her side of the bed. "I have everything here in the bag. You want to play Santa?"

Vincent took the bag. "Feels pretty heavy. More than just the doll and knife and candy I picked up in town."

"Of course there are other goodies." Angel smiled and shrugged. "Might be something in there for you as well."

"Oh really? Well, in that case, let's get to it."

They exited the room to find the children sitting on the sofa. Benjamin looked much better, and Angel immediately went to him and felt his forehead, then surveyed the knot.

"It has gone down quite a bit. Does your head hurt?"

"No. I feel better," Benjamin replied. "I remember you sat up with me for a long time."

"I wanted to make sure you were warm enough and that you didn't have any bad effects." Angel pushed his hair back from his face. "You're gonna need a haircut soon."

"You can cut it," he said, then looked away. "Mama used to."

Angel knew it must have been a concession for the boy to give her permission to take on a personal chore that had once belonged to his mother.

"That's very kind of you, Benjamin. I would be honored to cut your hair."

"Do you have our presents?" Ava asked, jumping up from the sofa.

Vincent laughed and motioned her back. "You know the rules. We'll do this in an orderly fashion. Now retake your seat, and I'll see what we have in the bag."

Ava scrambled back up on the couch while Angel went to add a log to the fireplace. She adjusted it with the poker and smiled when the fire flamed up. It was so good to be safe and warm. After such a fierce storm, she didn't think she would ever take such a thing lightly again.

"This looks like a present for Miss Ava," her father said, pulling a bundle from the bag. Angel had wrapped the doll in a homemade blanket. Ava pulled the covering away and gasped at the sight.

"Oh, she looks like a real baby." Ava cradled the cloth body and gently stroked the porcelain face. "Oh, thank you."

Vincent reached into the bag again and held up a couple of small nightgowns. "These seem a bit small for Ava."

Angel laughed at his confused expression. "Those are for the baby doll."

She had worked to make clothes for everyone, from Vincent to the doll. The two nightgowns were matches for ones she'd made Ava.

Handing the doll's clothes to his daughter, Vincent went into the bag again. This time he pulled out two more nightgowns. These were clearly meant for a child, but Vincent looked to Angel.

"Those are gowns I made for Ava. I thought she might enjoy having ones that matched her dolly."

Ava took the gowns while still holding the doll. "I love this. Oh, I want to go try them on now."

"Well, maybe we can wait and see what else is in the bag," her father suggested. He pulled out the two small sacks of lemon drops. "I think you'll like what's in here." He handed each child a bag.

"Oh, it's my favorite!" Benjamin declared, popping one in his mouth. "Thank you!"

"Don't ruin your appetite. Remember there's a table full of good things to eat in celebration of Christmas. Oh, and I think you might enjoy this gift," Vincent said, handing the boy a small box.

Benjamin opened it and found the knife. He looked at his dad, eyes wide. "You mean I'm responsible enough?"

Vincent laughed and turned to Angel. "I told him he couldn't have a knife until he was responsible enough to take care of it and not get hurt or hurt anyone else with it." He turned back to Benjamin. "You've proven yourself over and over. I think you're ready for it."

"I won't let you down, Papa. I promise."

"I think there are some more things in the bag," Angel said, motioning Vincent to continue.

He reached in and brought out two flannel shirts in Benjamin's size. "Well, will you look at this. I'm thinking these will fit you just right, son."

Benjamin took the shirts, looking far less excited. He glanced over at Angel. "Did you make these?"

She smiled. "I did. I wanted you to have some better-fitting shirts. I know you love the shirts your mama made, but I know they're getting too small. You can put them away as something to remember her by. Maybe one day you can let your son wear them and tell him all the stories you have about your mama."

"And I can save my dresses," Ava joined in.

"I think that would be a wonderful idea." Angel took a seat on the end of the sofa beside Ava. "You must always remember her. She loved you both so much."

"There's something else in the bag," Vincent said, reaching inside. He pulled out two shirts and a stack of handkerchiefs tied together with a piece of twine.

"Those are for you, Vincent. I heard you say you couldn't seem to find any of your handkerchiefs, and I knew you needed new work shirts."

He ran his fingers over the flannel shirts and smiled. "Thank you, Angel. You've been such a blessing to our family. I have something for you as well."

Vincent disappeared for a moment, and when he returned, Angel was surprised to see a long box in his arms. It wasn't that deep, but still she couldn't help but wonder what in the world he'd gotten her.

"Here you go. Open it."

Angel did as instructed and was surprised to find a dressing table set. A mirror and brush with intricately carved handles. These sat atop something beautifully knitted in blue. Angel set the mirror and brush aside in order to retrieve the blue parcel from the box. Shaking it out, she found it to be a shawl.

"Oh, this is lovely," she said, pulling it around her shoulders. "I've never had one quite so pretty . . . and warm." She hugged it to her robe and smiled up at Vincent. "Thank you. This was so very thoughtful."

"I'm glad you like it. I think it's time I go check on the sheep and Daisy. You children can enjoy some of the things Angel made for our celebration. A little later, we'll read the Christmas story from Luke in the Bible."

"First, we've got a present for you, Pa," Benjamin said, looking at Ava. "We made them." He revealed the pillow he'd hidden beside the couch. "Angel taught me how to sew."

"And I made this sachet for you," Ava declared, bringing it out from her apron pocket. "Angel said it will make your clothes smell sweet."

Vincent took the gifts and smiled. "What a surprise." He inspected each piece and nodded. "This is fine work. Thank you, both." The children beamed with pride.

Angel smiled and got to her feet. "I'll get dressed and go milk the cow and get the eggs."

Vincent took hold of her. "No. I'll see to it. I want you to go back to bed. You tended Benjamin most of the night, and I know you're tired. I'll take care of the milking and such."

Benjamin had been looking over his knife. He gave Angel a quick glance, then lowered his head again. "Thank you for taking care of me."

She knew it had taken a lot for him to acknowledge her care. "I was glad to do it, Benjamin. I'm just so happy that you're better this morning. We wouldn't be the same without you."

———— •Y•————

Angel fell back to sleep without any trouble, and when she awoke, she could smell the undeniable scent of ham. She had cooked everything the day before so that all they had to do was warm it up. Vincent must have taken that upon himself to see to.

She got up and dressed in a dark hunter green wool gown. The bodice was trimmed in red-and-green plaid and seemed most festive for Christmas. Normally she would have saved the dress for services at church, but with the snow deposited by the storm, she knew they wouldn't be driving anywhere any time soon.

After pinning up her hair, Angel whispered a prayer for the day and then opened the door. Ava called out, "Papa! She's awake!"

Angel paused, wondering what was going on. She looked at Ava for a moment and then stepped from the room. Vincent and Benjamin came in from the dining room.

"You look like Christmas," Vincent said with a smile. "A beautiful angel."

"Well, thank you." She didn't know why, but his compliment embarrassed her a bit. She glanced toward the rug. "I'm sorry for sleeping so long. What time is it?"

"It's almost noon. You needed the rest. Benjamin and I have been heating up lunch, so it's just about ready."

106

"And I set the table," Ava declared.

"That was very kind of you all. I appreciate my Christmas gift."

"We have another for you," Benjamin said. He came to Angel and took hold of her hand.

Angel was surprised by his touch. He'd had nothing to do with allowing her to get too close, and for him to take her hand was a big step. She looked up to see where he was leading her, and that's when she saw it.

The rocking chair. His mother's rocking chair.

Benjamin brought her to the chair and stopped. "We talked about it. You're our ma now, and we want you to have this chair."

Angel couldn't keep the tears from falling. She knew what it meant . . . what they were saying to her. She had finally been accepted into the family . . . in full.

Ava hurried over. "Sit down, Angel. Sit down."

She looked to Vincent, who was smiling. He nodded as if to reassure her. Angel sank onto the wooden seat and eased against the back.

"Don't cry, Angel." Ava came to her side.

"These are tears of happiness," she assured them.

Benjamin touched her arm, patting it as if to comfort her. Angel's heart was full to overflowing.

"I love you all so much. Thank you for this . . . and for letting me be a part of this family."

Vincent came and knelt in front of her. "We love you, and we're grateful to God for bringing us an angel."

She gave a little laugh. "And I got my shepherd and a family. Merry Christmas."

Vincent touched her cheek, his expression overflowing with love. "Merry Christmas, Angel."

No Room
at the
Inn

MISTY M. BELLER

CHAPTER 1

Hope Palmer slid her knife through the last of the dried apple pieces, letting them drop into the bowl on the table in front of her. These should be enough for their Christmas tradition of dried apple pie. That special day was still four days away, but she wanted to make an early version and test a different ratio of spices.

As she set the blade aside and reached for the towel to wipe her hands, the front door opened with a gust of frigid air.

Her brother, Martin, stepped inside and closed the door quickly before he stomped his boots on the rug. "That's quite a storm."

She nodded, her gaze drifting to the small window, where the snow swirled in a curtain of white. The wind howled, its gusts whining through the rafters of the cabin. "Sam's stage is probably holed up at the last stop. I guess we'll have a quiet Christmas." A storm like this usually kept the roads blocked for a few days, especially with them being so far away from any town or even another house.

Martin turned to face her, his expression softening. "I know how much you love having guests this time of year. But we'll make do. It'll be nice, just the two of us."

She bit back a sigh and even managed a small smile. "It'll be wonderful."

He moved to the fire to warm his hands. "This time next year, we'll have the bunkhouse rebuilt and the new trading post open. People will come from miles around, and you'll be ready to run them off."

She chuckled, though she couldn't imagine turning anyone away. She loved their stage stop and inn being a place of refuge for weary stage travelers. Many people who came through here had been traveling for weeks from the east and relished the warm food and comfortable beds she and Martin provided.

But the bunkhouse had burned down two weeks ago, and with only one small extra bedchamber in the house, they had little right now to offer any guests. The few travelers who had come through recently had to make do with a mattress tick and heater in the barn.

Hope carried the bowl of apples over to the large wooden worktable and began measuring out the spices—cinnamon, nutmeg, allspice. The familiar scents filled the air, mingling with the aroma of the roasting venison Martin had brought in that morning. For a moment, she could almost forget her troubles.

Almost, but not quite. As she worked the spices into the apples, her thoughts kept circling back to the burned-out bunkhouse and what it meant for their future. They needed that extra space and the income it brought in to keep afloat—and to expand, like Martin dreamed of doing with the new trading post. Now those plans seemed so terribly far away.

Her brother was right that they would rebuild and come

back stronger. But the prospect of facing the long winter months without the steady stream of guests felt like a heavy weight on her shoulders. The inn was more than just a business to her. It was a calling, a way to show God's love and hospitality to those who passed through their remote corner of the world.

As if sensing her melancholy thoughts, Martin crossed the room and wrapped an arm around her shoulders. "We'll get through this, Hope. We always do."

She nodded, leaning into her brother's hold. "I know. It's just hard. Christmas is meant to be shared with others."

"And it will be." He gave her a squeeze. "We'll make it special. We'll sing the old carols, read the story of the first Christmas, and thank God for all the blessings He's given us."

She lifted her head and smiled up at her baby brother. "How did you ever get to be so wise?"

A particularly strong gust rattled the windowpanes, making her start. She glanced through the window again at the worsening blizzard.

Somehow, it felt like this storm was only the beginning.

<hr/>

The wind howled like a wounded beast, rattling the stagecoach as it lurched through the blinding snow. Noah Bentwood pulled his wool coat tighter around him as he strained to see anything beyond the frosted window. Across from him, Miss Whitmore sat huddled in her own layers, her face pale in the faint light through the glass.

"Hold tight, folks!" Sam, their driver, called over the roaring storm. "Split Rock Inn is just ahead."

Noah eased out an exhale. They were almost to safety.

"Good." Miss Whitmore breathed the word into a cloud of

white. He'd promised her father, his mentor, that he would see her safely home to San Francisco. He wouldn't fail Charles now when it mattered the most.

His mission hadn't gone as smoothly as he'd intended so far. Had there been so many delays the other times he'd ridden the stage? And here in the wilds of the Nebraska Territory, keeping Miss Whitmore safe was proving a more daunting task than he'd expected. Between rough men and fierce weather, he had to stay alert.

The coach slowed as the driver shouted to the horses. Then the rocking ceased with a jerk more sudden than usual. Had they arrived at the inn? Or had a wagon wheel caught on a rock—or worse yet, broken off the axle completely? The rig wasn't listing, so probably not the latter.

The handle of the coach door twisted, and he tensed, bracing himself for whatever the news would be.

Yet when the door swung open, ushering in a thick flurry of white, a woman's face appeared. At least, it looked like a woman's, though a muff covered her chin and neck, and a hood framed the rest of her features. What little he could see appeared too delicate and feminine to belong to a man.

"Come in. Quickly now." She waved them out even as she scanned the interior. When her gaze landed on Miss Whitmore, a frown gathered between her brows. "You must be frozen."

Indeed, a sophisticated young woman like Miss Whitmore didn't belong in a rattletrap stage during a blizzard like this.

Noah climbed out first so he could help her down. The moment he left the shelter of the rig, the bitter wind rushed around him, biting at his exposed skin. He turned and offered his hand to his charge. She took it, and he helped her navigate the slick step in her long skirts the best he could.

He breathed a prayer of thanks when Miss Whitmore got her footing. The woman who had opened the door motioned them toward the roughhewn house, snow swirling around them.

At last, they stepped inside, and blessed warmth enveloped him, pressing like a thick blanket over his chest. He released Miss Whitmore's elbow and stomped snow from his boots. The main room was small but tidy, with a fire crackling in the hearth on the left. A long table with benches on either side filled the center. They were probably accustomed to feeding much larger crowds than the three of them—including the driver.

Their hostess unwound her scarf to reveal a young, pretty face framed by wisps of dark hair. Not at all like the other innkeepers they'd met along the way. Most of the stops during the first week had been run by families—solid men, harried women, and children scurrying around.

As they'd traveled farther west, they'd stayed with a middle-aged couple, then the inns had all been operated by men. Sometimes brothers, once a father and son, and most recently, three grizzled friends who'd spent several years trapping in the Idaho Territory until the game dried up. They'd shared a great many tales—many of which could have only possessed a single thread of truth wrapped in many layers of exaggeration, but it was still entertaining. He'd stayed up far too late into the night listening to their escapades.

But a stop like this, even farther west . . . The young woman must run the place with her husband. She looked far too innocent to have lived in this demanding land for long, though her manner appeared confident and easy.

"I'm Hope Palmer." She smiled, mostly speaking to Miss Whitmore. "Please, warm yourselves by the fire." She motioned to the flames leaping in the stone hearth. "I'll fetch blankets and warm tea."

He cleared his throat. "I'm Noah Bentwood. And this is Miss Ellen Whitmore."

Miss Whitmore had already started toward the fire, but paused and dipped her chin. "Please, call me Ellen." Her teeth chattered slightly as she spoke.

Mrs. Palmer's eyes softened. "You poor dear, you're chilled to the bone. We'll get you warmed posthaste."

As the innkeeper scurried toward the cookstove, Noah wrapped his coat tighter around himself. His charge appeared to be in good hands, so he'd best help Sam. "Excuse me, I need to help the driver with the horses." He pulled the latchstring and braced himself for the cold, then cracked the door enough to slip out.

The frigid air struck him like a fist, but he pushed forward through the vicious wind and swirling snow. Sam had been out in this mess all afternoon, and though Noah had offered to switch places with him, the older man had refused, determined to get them to the next stop.

Even through injury. Sam had received a nasty gash on his arm not long after they left Kansas, while hitching an unruly team to the coach. He'd not complained, but he'd favored the limb ever since, especially these last few days.

When they'd stopped to rest the horses at noon, Sam's eyes held a glassy sheen, and he'd been sweating, despite the cold. Noah should have asked if something was wrong then, but Sam had mentioned the coming storm, which then consumed all their focus.

Maybe Mr. Palmer could look at the injury to see if it had festered. Would he have medical skills? Even a basic knowledge would be more than Noah possessed. He'd never been exposed to illness or injury. Gram had always taken care of such, and he and his brothers had rarely been sick.

Noah hated this helpless feeling when he was so used to taking charge and being in control. Though they'd reached shelter from the storm, he had a feeling their troubles were far from over.

CHAPTER 2

Thank the Lord the stagecoach had arrived unscathed by the blustery storm raging beyond these walls. Hope stirred the bubbling stew, scraping the bottom of the pot to make sure the potatoes and carrots didn't stick. The venison she'd been cooking for dinner wasn't ready yet, so she'd added the leftover stew from their noon meal so their new guests could eat something warm right away.

She glanced up at Miss Whitmore, who'd perched on the edge of a ladder-back chair close to the fire. The young woman was a beauty, no doubt about it. Judging by the elegant fur-lined coat she'd finally unbuttoned, she was clearly accustomed to far more amenities than could be found on this wilderness plain. Her husband must not have much experience with the harsh winters in the west to allow her to travel during these months.

But . . . Her mind snagged on an important detail she'd forgotten in the hurry to make the woman comfortable and then ready enough food for the five of them. Mr. Bentwood had called her Miss Whitmore—*Miss*, not Missus. They couldn't be husband and wife. Not with different surnames too. Nor brother and sister.

Perhaps they weren't traveling together.

The door opened and the wind howled, tossing in a flurry of snowflakes and three weary men. Martin entered first, shifting over to the rag rug to stomp his boots. Behind him, Mr. Bentwood and the stage driver, Sam Thompson, straggled in, both men hunching their shoulders against the chill.

"It's even worse out there than before." Martin shook the snow from his arms, then removed his gloves and worked loose the buttons on his coat. "We'll be lucky if we don't get snowed in for a week."

Mr. Bentwood's head jerked up at the comment. "A week? Do you think so?"

Martin shrugged. "This weather has a mind of its own, but I'm sure it'll still be snowing by morning. That storm looks locked in."

Hope motioned to the blaze in the hearth, as she had before. "The fire's warm, the stew's almost ready, and there's hot tea on the table."

Within minutes, the men and Miss Whitmore settled around the table, each nursing a cup of steaming tea. Hope stayed by the cookstove, stirring the stew so it didn't scald.

Mr. Bentwood turned to her brother. "Mr. Palmer, by chance do you have any medical training? Sam here suffered a gash on his arm, and we've not had it properly tended."

Before Martin could answer, Mr. Thompson waved off his concern. "It's just a scratch. Nothing to worry about."

Martin frowned. "I'm not good with that sort of thing, but my sister is." He glanced her way. "Hope, would you mind?"

She sent the driver a smile to put him at ease. "Of course." The man had always been kind. He came through here with stages often enough that she considered him a friend. He took proper care of his horses, too, and treated his passengers with respect. That pairing was harder to find than one might think.

Mr. Thompson looked ready to object again, so she added, "Maybe after you eat and thaw all the way through."

His gaze dropped to the table. "I reckon." He was still shivering, so it might be a while before he recovered from all those hours in the storm. Yet . . . was that sweat on his forehead? She'd assumed the red splotches on his cheeks were from the weather, but they could be from fever instead.

She scooped out stew into the bowls for them all, careful to make sure none of the servings included potatoes not yet softened. Once their guests were eating, she settled onto the bench beside her brother. This might be a good time to discuss sleeping arrangements for the night.

She glanced at Miss Whitmore, who had remained quiet since their initial introductions. She ate hungrily, though not without the poise that was surely ingrained as deeply as the need to be hospitable had been embedded in Hope. Her parents had built this stage stop before she was born, though it served as a trading post and refuge for travelers back then. Growing up here had always been exciting—meeting new people nearly every day, learning where they came from and hearing stories from their lives. This was the perfect life for her, no matter how challenging the winters were or how hard it might be to say farewell to new friends when they boarded the stage and disappeared forever.

She'd learned to guard her heart, though. She'd always become too attached to the guests they had, too devastated when they would leave. Though many promised to write, few ever had.

Miss Whitmore glanced up at Hope, as though she felt her gaze. The woman smiled, but her delicate features were drawn with fatigue. She had to be younger than Hope, judging by her smooth skin. Younger than Martin, too, who was three years Hope's junior. Maybe twenty? Or perhaps a little less.

She shifted her focus to Mr. Bentwood. He and Miss Whitmore barely spoke to each other, but it didn't appear to be tense silence. More . . . indifference. He seemed to respect her, yet there was no sign of special regard or tenderness between them.

Well, whatever her situation, this young lady was clearly far from home and in need of rest.

Hope infused welcome into her voice. "Miss Whitmore, we have a spare room you're welcome to use. It's a bit crowded with supplies, but there's a comfortable bed."

The woman's expression brightened. "Thank you. That sounds wonderful."

She might change her tune when she saw the tiny chamber and cot. Probably like sleeping in the barn compared to the home she came from. But it was the best they could manage.

Martin piped up. "Sorry to say our bunkhouse burned a couple weeks ago. We have a few mattress ticks laid out in the barn and a little heating stove. It'll have its work cut out for it during this storm, but we'll send extra blankets out there. I think it won't be so bad."

Hope fought a wince at her brother's description of the only other lodging they could provide. The barn had worked fine for the other drivers and passengers who'd used it these last weeks, but this storm would test the abilities of that little heater. At least they'd stay dry.

Yet she hated the thought of giving unsuitable accommodations to anyone who had come to take shelter at their inn. She leaned around her brother to see Mr. Thompson and Mr. Bentwood at the same time. "If either of you is uncomfortable at all, please come in, and we'll do our best to remedy the problem. No matter how late. I'll leave a pot of water on the stove so you can have something warm to drink if you need it."

Mr. Thompson nodded his thanks, but the movement seemed

to pain him. He shifted his injured arm, his good hand moving up to cup the elbow. The sooner she could examine the wound, the better.

After the meal, she quickly showed Miss Whitmore her room while Martin and Mr. Bentwood went out to unload the passengers' belongings from the coach. Then she retrieved her box of medical supplies from the shelf and placed it on the table next to Mr. Thompson. "Let's have a look at that arm now."

The man hesitated but then worked the arm out of his coat with effort, revealing a bloodstained shirtsleeve. She rolled it up, and her stomach clenched at the sight of the angry red flesh surrounding the jagged gash. Yellow pus oozed from the wound, and heat radiated from his skin even before she touched him.

"Oh, Sam, this is bad." She kept her voice low. "Why didn't you have it seen to earlier?"

He grunted. "Didn't have time. Had to keep the stage moving."

She shook her head, but there was no use scolding him now. The man was as stubborn as the mule Martin had raised when he was a boy.

She cleaned the wound as quickly and gently as she could, spreading a salve on the festering gash before wrapping it with a cloth bandage. That would help pull out the pus. Then she retrieved one of Martin's clean shirts to replace Mr. Thompson's soiled one. She would have her work cut out for her in washing the stench of infection out of that sleeve.

After Mr. Thompson had changed, he resumed his seat at the table, his eyes unfocused and shoulders slumped. He looked like he might fall asleep right there. If she tried to move him to a more comfortable chair by the fire, he might attempt to go out and help the other men.

She stood and moved to the cabinet where she kept her dried

herbals. She pulled out a jar of garlic cloves and dropped several into the kettle of tea, then added a spoonful of willow bark powder. The liquid would need to simmer a few minutes, so this would be a good chance to check on Miss Whitmore.

She strode past Mr. Thompson to the door of the little storage room and tapped a light knock. "Just checking to see if there's anything you need."

A pleasant voice sounded from within, though she couldn't make out the words. Then came a rustle, and the door opened. Miss Whitmore offered a tired smile. "Thank you so much for your kindness, Miss Palmer. I have everything I need for the night."

Hope returned the expression. "Please, call me Hope. And don't hesitate to let me know if there's anything at all I can do to make you more comfortable. Travel can be exhausting, even in the best of circumstances. I imagine coming west by stage in the dead of winter is especially taxing."

The young woman's expression turned wry. "Indeed. My father wanted me to wait until spring, but now that my classes are finished, I only want to go home."

Curiosity flickered in her chest. "Classes? You were attending school in the east?"

Miss Whitmore nodded. "Yes, but my home is Sacramento. That's where I was born, and I only left because Father was so set on a Boston finishing school." Her eyes brightened. "I can't wait to get home. I'm grateful Mr. Bentwood also needed to return to Sacramento and was willing to escort me."

Hope's heart picked up speed. An escort. So there was no affection between the two. Nothing scandalous, anyway. Surely there was a *little* attraction. A man as handsome as he was and a lovely young woman like her . . .

She kept her tone as innocent as she could. "Mr. Bentwood

is a friend of your family?" Perhaps the two had long been intended for marriage. Since childhood, maybe.

Yet, why did it matter? These two lovely people could marry if they pleased.

Miss Whitmore nodded. "He works for my father. Handles negotiations in the east, while my father takes care of dealings in the west."

Hope murmured, "Ah, I see," then stepped back. "Well. I hope your sleep is pleasant. Do let me know if you need anything."

"Thank you." The young woman glanced past her to the main room. "Is Mr. Thompson all right? He looked quite unwell at supper."

Hope turned to study the man now slumped over the table. Asleep, maybe. Though his pain and fever might not allow it. Likely he was too exhausted to hold his head up. "The wound on his arm has festered badly. I've cleaned and dressed it, and I'm making a medicinal tea for him now. But he's feverish and needs close watching through the night."

Miss Whitmore's hand fluttered to her throat. "I'm sorry to hear that. Please let me know if there is any way I can assist you in caring for him."

"That's kind of you." Even with the privileged background the woman must have enjoyed, she appeared to have a caring heart. "I plan to have him sleep out here where I can tend him. Speaking of . . ." She looked at the kettle on the stove. "I should get that tea to him. Sleep well, Miss Whitmore."

"Ellen, please. And thank you again. For everything." With a final smile, Ellen retreated into the chamber and shut the door with a soft click.

While Hope returned to the main room and poured a cup of the pungent garlic tea, her mind worked through all the new details. An escort. Ellen's father's business associate. Yet that didn't mean Mr. Bentwood was unattached.

And once more, why did this matter to her?

It shouldn't. She loved life here, running the stage stop. A man like Noah Bentwood could never be happy in such a remote, toilsome life. She'd seen too many people pass through here, acting like they might want to stay, but they never returned. She had to guard her heart from anything more than distant admiration.

She forced those thoughts away and set the cup in front of Mr. Thompson. She touched his shoulder. "Mr. Thompson. Can you sit up and drink this tea? It'll help with the pain and cleanse your blood."

With a groan, he lifted his head and straightened, then took the cup with his good hand. He sniffed the contents and wrinkled his nose. "Smells awful."

She couldn't help a chuckle. "I know, but it'll do you good. The garlic will fight the infection, and the willow bark will help with the fever and pain. Drink up now."

The man grimaced but took a tentative sip. He shuddered, then tipped the cup back and gulped down several swallows. When he lowered it, only a third of the liquid remained. "Tastes as bad as it smells."

She strode to the trunk against one wall and pulled out an armful of blankets. "You'll need to drink a cup of it every few hours." She deposited two of the blankets on the floor where there was enough room to fit a mattress tick. "I'm going to make up a bed for you here so I can tend you through the night."

"I can't put you out, Miss Hope." He shook his head and tried to stand but fell back onto the chair with a wince. "As soon as I rest a bit, I'll bunk down in the barn with Bentwood."

She fixed him with a stern look. "You'll do no such thing,

Sam Thompson. You're ill and you need care. I won't take no for an answer."

The grizzled man sighed but surrendered with a nod. "I hate to be a burden on you and your brother."

Hope stepped to the door, the rest of the blankets in her arms. "You could never be a burden. You need rest and prayer, and I'll provide both. Wait there while I bring a mattress tick from the barn."

He waved her off as he pushed to his feet once more. This time he made it. "I only need a blanket. A warm room and a dry floor are luxury enough." He shuffled toward the quilts she'd placed on the floor and eased down to sit beside them.

She pinched her lips together. This point wasn't worth arguing, but she'd bring the mattress tick inside anyway. The next time he woke, she could have him climb onto it.

Now it was time to see to the comfort of their other guest— one Noah Bentwood. Even the thought of him made her middle tighten. He had to be the most handsome man who'd come through their inn, at least that she could recall.

Those warm eyes and smile made her heart beat faster. And his manners! He comported himself as a gentleman. Yet he'd gone out in the snowstorm to help put the horses away. He'd even gone back out with Martin after dinner to unload the coach. In her experience, most gentlemen didn't willingly roll up their sleeves any time there was menial work to be done.

She took in a breath and exhaled. She needed to keep her silly mind focused on the task at hand. They had two guests to make comfortable despite the snowstorm outside. And one very injured stage driver who would need her care through the night and the next few days.

CHAPTER 3

The wind howled around the barn, making more noise than a pack of wolves.

Noah shifted on his bedroll and pulled the blanket tighter around him. The nearby woodstove put out plenty of heat, but his mind wouldn't settle enough to allow him to sleep.

Maybe he should go inside for that cup of tea Miss Palmer had offered. The family would be asleep by now, but she'd reminded him before he went out to the barn that she would keep a pot of tea on the cookstove all night, and he was welcome to it any time.

With that thought to fuel him, he rolled to his feet and found his boots. His fingers fumbled with the laces until they were tied tight enough to withstand the snowdrifts between here and the house.

When he stepped into the biting cold, the wind nearly stole his breath. He pulled his coat tighter around him and trudged through the snow, his boots sinking deep with each step.

At last he reached the house and pulled the latchstring they'd left out. The door opened, and he slipped into the warmth, closing the door quickly to keep out the wind. He breathed out an exhale and straightened his shoulders as he turned to check on Sam in the dim light from the hearth fire.

A figure sat beside the bed pallet. Miss Palmer.

She'd turned to face him, and weariness lined her eyes. "Mr. Bentwood." She kept her voice soft. "I didn't expect to see you until morning."

Noah stretched out his cold-numbed fingers. "I couldn't sleep. Thought I might take you up on that offer of tea, if it's not too much trouble."

Hope's lips curved into a tired smile. "Of course. I'll fetch you a cup."

She started to get up, but he motioned for her to stay seated. Then he gestured to the still form beside her. "How is he?"

She glanced back at Sam, her brow furrowed. "His fever's worse. I've been cooling his face, trying to bring his temperature down."

Noah stepped closer, studying the driver's flushed face in the flickering firelight. The man's breathing was labored, each breath rattling in his chest.

A knot of worry formed in Noah's middle. "What can I do to help?"

She glanced around, then picked up a large wooden bowl and held it out. "Would you get more snow for me?"

He took the container and made quick work of the task. When he returned to their patient, she had moved down to Sam's feet. She motioned toward the man's head. "Will you wrap snow in that cloth and place it on his forehead? I'm going to rub his feet to bring some of that warmth down to his limbs."

Noah eyed the old driver's bony appendages. Maybe he should offer to do that part and let her bathe his face. But Miss Palmer had already settled into the task and didn't seem bothered by touching a stranger's feet. A natural nurse, this woman.

He sat down next to the man to do as she'd directed. When he placed the snow-filled cloth over Sam's brow, the heat rising from the man's skin nearly burned him.

Lord, heal this man.

He glanced over at Miss Palmer, who was looking down, focused on her work. Her dark hair had begun to escape its practical bun, and a few tendrils curled around her face. The flickering firelight cast a warm glow on her skin, highlighting the compassion in her eyes. Despite the weariness that lined her features, there was a strength about her that he couldn't help but admire.

She glanced up, catching him watching her.

He worked for a casual expression. "What else can be done?"

Her gaze roamed Sam's body, halting on his injured arm. Her lips rolled in, her expression turning uncertain. "I've done everything else I can. Everything I know to do."

Noah studied the fresh bandage on Sam's arm, the clean shirt covering his good arm and most of his abdomen. "You've done more than I would have been able to." He looked up to meet her gaze. "I'm thankful you were here to help. I suppose we wait now?"

She gave a small nod.

He pushed to his feet. "Would you like a cup of tea?"

"Thank you." Her quiet voice trailed behind him as he moved to the cookstove. The kettle sat where she'd promised, and he grabbed two mugs from the shelf.

As he carried the steaming cups, warmth seeped into his chilled fingers.

She accepted the cup from him with another "Thank you." When she took a sip, her eyes closed briefly as the hot liquid worked its magic.

He almost smiled. Observing her was a unique pleasure.

He eased down in his previous spot and sipped his own drink.

The warmth spread to his insides, and after swallowing, he released a long, slow breath.

Miss Palmer was watching him, her green eyes catching the firelight. "Thank you for your help, Mr. Bentwood. I know you must be tired after your long journey."

He shook his head. "I actually came in because I couldn't sleep. I'm glad to help at least a little."

She nodded, understanding. "You're traveling to California?"

Noah shifted his gaze to the fire, watching the flames dance. "To Sacramento. My mentor and employer, Mr. Whitmore, is Miss Whitmore's father. I needed to return to California to meet with him, and he asked if I would escort his daughter home at the same time."

Miss Palmer studied him over the rim of her mug. "It sounds like he has a lot of faith in you."

"I suppose so." He allowed a small smile. "I first met him when I was barely more than a boy. He was traveling through our town and bought fruit from our little stand. He told me later I reminded him of himself as a youngster. He offered me an apprenticeship, taught me everything I know about business. Eventually, he sent me east to handle the business dealings on that side of the country." It might sound like bragging to mention Mr. Whitmore's offer to make him a partner in the business. Best to focus on his mentor, not himself. "He's a man of integrity. I owe him a great deal."

They lapsed into silence for a moment, the only sounds the crackling of the fire and Sam's labored breathing.

Her gaze returned to the ailing driver, her brow furrowed with concern. "I wish there was more I could do for him."

"You're doing everything you can. The rest is up to God."

She glanced at him, her eyes widening a little. "You're a man of faith?"

He nodded. "I am. My faith has seen me through many difficult times."

"Mine as well." She hesitated, then added softly, "Would you pray with me? For Sam?"

Warmth spread through his chest that had nothing to do with the tea. "Of course."

They bowed their heads together, and Noah searched his heart for the right words. He asked for God's healing touch on Sam, for strength and wisdom for him and Hope as they cared for the driver, and for safety and protection for all of them during the storm.

When he finished, Miss Palmer whispered a soft "Amen."

They settled into a quiet more peaceful than before as they drank their tea. Even Sam's breathing seemed to have settled. Miss Palmer's eyelids began to droop, and a yawn slipped out that she quickly covered.

"Why don't you get some rest?" he asked. "I can sit with him for a while."

She looked like she might protest, but then she yawned again. "All right. But wake me if anything changes?"

He nodded. "I will."

With a grateful smile, she rose and slipped from the room.

He added more snow to the cloth over Sam's brow. The skin didn't feel quite as hot this time. *Thank you, Father.*

There didn't appear to be anything else he could do, so he refilled his mug and settled on the floor against the wall.

It might be a long night, but he was ready for whatever might come.

———◆Y◆———

Hope placed the steaming platter of ham on the table next to the porridge, the savory smells of the morning meal filling the cozy room. She glanced over at Mr. Thompson, still asleep on his bed pallet against the wall. His face gleamed with sweat, but his breathing seemed steadier now, more even. Thank the Lord his fever had lessened as the night progressed.

She turned back to the others gathered around the table—Martin and their two stranded guests. Mr. Bentwood still wore his coat, his eyes flicking to the frost-covered window. Miss Whitmore kept her hands folded in her lap, her posture poised.

"Thanks." Martin gave Hope an appreciative nod. "This looks fine on a cold morning."

Hope smiled at her brother's compliment as she took her seat. "We'll need our strength for all the Christmas preparations ahead of us. The holiday is only three days away now." She passed the platter of ham to Mr. Bentwood.

He accepted it as he sent a glance toward one of the frost-covered windows. "The storm seems calmer this morning. Any idea when the snow'll stop?"

Martin cleared his throat. "From the looks of it, the worst of the storm has passed. But with the snow piled so high and Sam laid up . . ." He shook his head, his expression grim. "I reckon travel won't be possible until after Christmas, at the soonest."

Mr. Bentwood's face tightened, but he nodded and returned to his meal.

As the others finished eating and she began to clear the table, she glanced at Ellen. "Perhaps you'd like to help me string popcorn garlands for the tree? It's one of our traditions."

Her face brightened. "I'd be delighted. I confess, I've never had the opportunity."

"You're in for a treat." Martin grinned at their guest. "Hope's garlands are the prettiest in the valley. She's got a real knack for it."

Ellen's lovely smile slipped out with a hint of shyness. "Well then, I shall have to watch closely and learn her technique."

Hope fought to keep in a grin as she gathered her sewing kit and the sack of popcorn she'd popped yesterday. Ellen had a sweet disposition, just like her brother did. Those two would be so sweet together. "Here we are. Everything we need." She settled in her usual rocker and tugged a comfortable armchair closer. "Come, sit with me, Ellen. I'll show you how it's done."

Ellen joined her with a graceful rustle of skirts, her rosewater scent drifting in the air.

Martin was pulling out the pails to make cider, and he'd already drawn Mr. Bentwood into helping with the task. Beating the apples and tightening down the corkscrew took a great deal of strength. A task best left to the men.

She focused on showing Ellen how to thread the needle, tie off the end of the string, and pierce the center of each fluffy kernel or dried cranberry. Ellen proved a quick study, her slim fingers moving with an easy grace as she slid the decoration down the string.

"You're a natural." Hope smiled at her progress. "I daresay your garlands will rival mine."

Ellen laughed, the sound like silver bells. "You're too kind. I'm afraid I'll need far more practice before I can claim such an accomplishment."

As they worked, Hope couldn't help but watch the men. Her brother kept them moving efficiently. She spoke quietly enough that only Ellen would hear. "Martin's always been such a help with Christmas preparations. He's the best at making cider."

Ellen glanced up at him. "Is that so? I imagine that must take a good deal of strength to beat the juice from those apples." Was that a hint of admiration in her eyes? Perhaps.

"Indeed. My brother's never been one to shy away from hard work. It's one of the things I appreciate most about him. Of course, he's a quick thinker too. Educated in Philadelphia." She added that last bit so Ellen didn't think him a boorish frontiersman who could hardly sign his name.

Ellen hummed thoughtfully. "I have a cousin who attended a secondary school in Philadelphia. At Haverford."

Hope raised her brows. "Interesting. Martin attended the Hill School. I'm not sure if the two are near . . ." Mama had paid every last cent she'd saved for Martin to have that opportunity—and to hire a boy to help at the inn while Martin was away—so surely the Hill School wasn't a slum, though it may not be on the level of Haverford.

But Ellen's smile brightened. "I know of it. I believe my cousin had outings with boys from the Hill School." She slid a look toward the men, probably at Martin. A gaze that held far more interest than before.

As they worked, Hope kept the conversation on light topics—favorite Christmas treats, memorable presents, silly mishaps from holidays past. More than once, she caught Ellen sneaking glances at Martin, a rosy blush coloring her fair cheeks. Martin, too, threw looks Ellen's way when her eyes were focused on her task, admiration plain on his face.

Hope bit back a grin. Probably nothing would come of it, but at least Martin could enjoy the company of a pleasant lady for the holiday.

A floorboard creaked, and she glanced up as Mr. Bentwood approached. He gave a slight bow in front of them. "Martin has moved to the cider press, leaving nothing more for me to help with. Can you put me to work here?"

His voice sounded more formal than usual, and Hope paused her thoughts of budding romance between Martin and Ellen.

Had he noticed the surreptitious glances as well? Perhaps he really did have tender feelings for his charge.

Something tightened in her chest. Not jealousy. Just unease. After all, Ellen's father likely didn't want her escort carrying on with her when he should be looking out for her protection.

But even as the thought took hold, something inside her rejected the idea. She knew little of Mr. Bentwood. But he seemed too serious and restrained to allow himself to entertain such notions. He also seemed like a rule-follower. Though now that she thought about it, she couldn't say what gave her that impression.

Ellen motioned Mr. Bentwood toward a chair across from them, and he pulled it closer before sitting. Hope handed him the needle and thread she'd just prepared for herself. "We'd welcome your help, Mr. Bentwood. Just tie a knot at the end of your string and then slide a piece of popcorn or cranberry to the end before making a stitch through the center to secure it in place. You can string them in any order you like, making designs or whatever pleases you."

He looked over at the garland she'd just finished, then the cord Ellen worked on. After a moment, he set to the task, his large hands surprisingly deft with the delicate materials. His brow creased as he focused, as if creating Christmas decorations was a mission of vital importance.

They worked in silence for a few minutes, the only sounds the crackle of the fire and the rhythmic thumps of Martin working the cider press in the kitchen. Mr. Bentwood seemed to have brought a pall to their earlier conversation.

She lifted an inconspicuous gaze to study him. He'd finally shed his wool coat in the warmth of both fires, and the lines of his shirt accentuated the breadth of his shoulders. Were men of business always so muscled and . . . well, handsome? His dark hair hadn't been pomaded flat but brushed across his brow with a wave that looked perfectly contained at first glance. Yet the way the strands curled up at the ends gave it a roguish touch. Much like the man himself?

Why was she allowing her mind to entertain such ponderings? The man's hair had nothing to do with his personality. And why did it matter to her anyway? As long as he paid his bill and was pleasant company, she should be satisfied.

CHAPTER 4

Noah stretched a little higher to secure the end of the garland on the nail at the top of the cabin wall.

"There." Miss Palmer's tone rang with satisfaction. "Perfect."

He stepped back to study their work. All the garland had been hung on the cabin walls, draped in a pretty swag that made the place feel more festive than most homes decorated by a staff of servants. Especially with the aroma of cooked apples filling the room.

He sent the ladies a nod. "Well done."

Miss Palmer turned to gather the empty bowls that had held the popcorn and cranberries. "Thank you both for your help."

"What's next on your list?" Miss Whitmore looked to Miss Palmer.

Miss Palmer crossed the cabin in long, efficient strides and placed the bowls on the work counter. "You can take a break. I need to run to the barn now that the snow has nearly stopped. I've some herbs there that might help Mr. Thompson."

Noah's gaze shifted to their driver, still lying almost motionless on his pallet. Only the steady rise and fall of his chest showed he lived. Miss Palmer had changed his bandage once during the morning and woken him several other times to have him drink a tea concoction.

He turned to Miss Palmer, who was already pulling on her coat. "I need to retrieve something from my bag too. Do you mind if I accompany you?"

Miss Palmer looked up at him, brows lifting. "Of course not. I would welcome the company." She finished buttoning her coat and wound a scarf around her neck.

Noah grabbed his own coat and hat, then followed her out the door into the icy air. The snow had indeed slowed to a light dusting, the flakes dancing on the breeze that seemed to constantly blow through this open country. They trudged through the knee-deep snow, their boots crunching with each step.

As quiet stretched between them, he was too aware of the woman's presence beside him. Her skirts must be hard to manage through the snow they had to push through.

He motioned behind him. "Do you want to follow in my steps? That might be easier."

She shook her head, her mouth curving in a soft smile. "I'm fine."

And stubborn.

But they'd nearly reached the barn. He lifted the bar to push the large door in, then motioned for her to step inside first.

As he followed, the earthy scent of hay and horses enveloped them. Miss Palmer moved purposefully to the back, where bundles of dried herbs hung from the rafters.

He focused on his own task, retrieving his carpetbag from beside his mattress tick. As he rummaged through the contents, his fingers brushed against the worn leather of his Bible.

He pulled it out, the weight familiar and comforting in his hands.

When he turned back, Miss Palmer was carefully selecting sprigs of dried herbs and placing them in a cloth sack.

When she finished, she turned to face him, her expression unreadable in the dim light of the barn. "Did you find what you needed?"

He nodded, holding up the worn leather-bound book Charles had given him. "I did, thank you." He hesitated a moment. Now was probably the best time to broach the subject weighing on his mind. "Miss Palmer, I wonder if I might have a word with you before we return to the cabin?"

She paused in her stride toward the door. "Of course. What is it?"

He took a deep breath, choosing his words carefully. "As you know, I've been tasked with ensuring Miss Whitmore reaches her father safely. In order to fulfill that duty, I think it unwise to encourage any . . . attachments during our journey." Would she understand he meant with her brother, or would he have to be more specific?

Her brows rose. "Attachments?"

She would make him state his exact meaning, then, though he could tell by her expression she knew what he meant.

He pinched his mouth. "I've seen how you've been subtly pushing them together. And while I'm sure your brother is a fine man, Miss Whitmore and I will be leaving as soon as we're able. It wouldn't be fair to either of them to nurture affections that can't last."

Miss Palmer's brows rose. "I wasn't intending to nurture affections. I was only being friendly, as was my brother."

Was she telling the truth? Her cheeks held extra color, though that might be from the cold. He dipped his chin. "I'm glad to hear it. I'm sure it's best for them both to guard their hearts, especially during this delay." As he spoke, his wayward mind nearly distracted him by admiring the way the soft light filtering through the barn walls illuminated the hints of gold in her brown hair. Her eyes, a vivid green even in the dim interior, held his for a long moment.

He knew well the power of a locked gaze. In a business transaction, he could spot a lie when a man couldn't hold his gaze without twitching. But he'd not suspected the effects of staring into Miss Palmer's eyes, the way his chest would clench and his middle flip. How had he not noticed what a beauty she was? He'd not allowed himself to look at her long enough to see it, and he shouldn't do so now.

Her posture relaxed as she smiled, finally breaking her gaze, allowing him the freedom to glance aside. "Of course, Mr. Bentwood. I apologize if I said something amiss. To make amends, I'd like to bake your favorite sweet for our Christmas dinner, if I've the ingredients for it. What would you like?"

He blinked and slid a quick glance to her face to catch up with the shift in conversation. He'd not expected her to apologize so quickly. Her expression seemed earnest, but better they end this conversation now. "That's not necessary."

"I insist." Her smile turned hopeful. "What's your favorite? Sugar cookies? Mincemeat pie?"

"Chess pie." The words slipped out before he could think better of it.

Her eyes sparkled with pleasure. "Chess pie it is."

Had he just played into her hands? Hope Palmer was a shrewd negotiator, and he couldn't quite shake the feeling that he'd just been outmaneuvered.

As they made their way back to the cabin through the snow, he couldn't help but be both impressed and slightly unnerved by the woman beside him. She was unlike anyone he'd ever met, and he had to wonder what other surprises she had in store.

Hope set down her charcoal pencil and surveyed the list before her. Christmas plans were coming together nicely. The spiced cider, the garlands . . . even a chess pie, Lord willing. She glanced over to where Mr. Bentwood and Miss Whitmore sat across from each other, both reading quietly by the fire.

Mr. Bentwood's position outlined his chiseled features in the warm firelight. The strong lines of his jaw, the straight nose, the furrow of his brow as he concentrated on the pages before him. He'd surprised her with his forthright request that she not play matchmaker between Ellen and Martin.

Maybe she should have expected it, though. He seemed the kind of man who possessed the courage to speak up when he had to, even when the conversation would be uncomfortable. A man of integrity and honor.

No wonder Miss Whitmore's father had entrusted his daughter into this man's care.

Shaking her head, she turned her attention back to the list. Maybe she shouldn't have agreed so readily to make a chess pie. Was it even possible to get it to set without eggs? If she used cornstarch and saleratus, perhaps. She should test it beforehand. If she had to, she could ask his second-favorite sweet.

With that unwelcome possibility leaving a bitter taste in her mouth, she turned the paper over to focus on the matter of gifts. She and Martin would exchange gifts, of course. But she always tried to have something for guests to open on Christmas too. Just as Mama had done. She sometimes worked on such gifts during the long winter evenings so she'd have scarves or mittens or handkerchiefs ready when the holiday came.

For Ellen, she'd almost finished embroidering a handker-chief, stitched with three of the wildflowers that would grow in the meadow come spring. For Mr. Thompson and Mr. Bentwood, she had scarves already finished. These would be very practical for the remainder of their journey.

Her gaze lifted to Mr. Bentwood once more. Giving both men the same gift would be most proper. She couldn't let herself add anything special to Mr. Bentwood's, no matter how much she craved doing so. His initials? No. She would need to do it for poor Mr. Thompson too.

No matter how much Mr. Bentwood drew her . . . No matter how handsome he was . . . and good . . . and completely desirable in every way she'd let herself consider . . .

He was *leaving*. Traveling on in just a few days. She knew not to allow herself to fancy any of their guests. She had to guard her heart.

She dropped her pencil to the table and pushed to her feet. She might as well gather the men's gifts and wrap them. Then she wouldn't be tempted to add anything extra to one of the scarves.

As she made her way to her tiny bedroom, the floorboards creaked beneath her feet. She knelt beside the trunk at the foot of her bed and lifted the lid. The rich scent of cedar rose up to greet her, and she breathed it in. Nestled among the folded quilts and spare linens inside was the small wooden box that held her most cherished possessions.

She extracted the box from its resting place and set it on her lap. Her fingers traced the intricate carving of roses that adorned the lid, the swirling patterns worn smooth by time and countless loving touches. This box had belonged to her mother, and her grandmother before her. It held the treasures of generations, each one full of memories and meaning.

Her heart quickened as she lifted the lid. Martin would love the gift she had for him. She'd almost given it to him last year, but it hadn't felt like the right time yet. The knife had been passed down from father to son for three generations, the deer antler handle bearing their surname, *Palmer*. This treasure was more than just a tool—it was a symbol of their family's strength and resilience. Of the way they treasured their history and the foundations laid by the members of their family who had gone before.

But as she focused on the contents of the box, a cold dread settled over her. The knife was gone. She pushed aside the lace gloves her mother had embroidered. The tobacco pipe that had been her father's favorite. The buttons from her grandfather's cavalry uniform.

Where was the knife?

She stared at the vacant space, her mind reeling. The blade had been there. She'd taken it out to clean yesterday, but she'd put it back. Hadn't she? Yes, her mind could bring back the image of placing it atop the lace gloves.

Had one of their guests taken it? The idea made a knot in her stomach, but what other explanation could there be? The knife had been secure in this chest yesterday morning, before the stagecoach arrived.

Her hands trembled as she lowered the lid, her vision blurring. She couldn't bear the thought that one of them had betrayed her trust, had violated the sacred space of both her room and her family's history. Not Ellen, with her gentle grace and her kindness. Certainly not Mr. Bentwood, who radiated such honor and integrity.

Yet . . . would he have the most motive? She knew nothing about his background. Not whether he came from a large family or was the only child of the richest couple in all of California.

She did know he'd never strung garland before, but that told her nothing of consequence.

What of Mr. Thompson? He'd not moved off that pallet except once to relieve himself. Was it possible he could have slipped into her room when no one was looking?

Tears burned her eyes as she closed the chest's lid. She'd have to ask them all. As much as it pained her, she had no choice.

She had to know what had happened to her father's knife.

Taking a deep breath, she stacked the two scarves on the top blanket in the chest and closed the lid, then made her way back to the main room. She would wrap them in paper later. For now, she had to solve the mystery of the knife.

She paused in the doorway, her gaze drifting once more to the two sitting in front of the fire. From this angle, she could see Mr. Bentwood's face well. The light from the flames danced across his features as he turned a page in his book, oblivious to her turmoil.

How could she ask him if he'd stolen from her? How could she ask any of them? The question lodged in her throat, sharp and painful.

She eased out a breath and moved to the work counter beside the cookstove. Best put beans on to simmer for the evening meal, then she could begin her search.

CHAPTER 5

Noah copied the numbers from his ledger onto the clean paper, keeping his script as neat as possible. He only had a few more pages to finish this report for Charles, then he'd head back inside. Though the barn was large and drafty, having the heater so near his mattress kept his sleeping area warm. But the house felt so much more . . . cozy. And festive. A place that beckoned him.

The barn door creaked open, and he looked up to see who would enter. Probably Martin, tending the animals.

But Miss Palmer peered around the door. When she saw him, she slipped inside. Something in her manner made his chest tighten. Her expression looked drawn. Worried or upset, maybe.

She approached him almost on tiptoe. "Mr. Bentwood."

He put his work aside and stood. "Miss Palmer."

She stood with hunched shoulders, her hands clasped at her middle. She looked distraught.

His insides twisted. "What's wrong? Has Sam taken a turn for the worst?"

She shook her head. "I was wondering . . . I mean . . . have you seen . . ? I'm missing a knife. A hunting knife. About this long"—she moved her pointer fingers about two handsbreadth apart—"with a handle formed from an elk antler. Our surname

147

is carved into it." She ended with a pleading gaze, as though he could produce the knife from his pocket.

He frowned. "Where did you see it last?"

"In my trunk. In my chamber. I don't know where it could have gone. I'm sorry to ask, but I don't know what to do. Have you seen it anywhere?" Her voice broke, and she paused to take in a breath that made her shoulders rise and fall. "The knife has been handed down through our family as far back as I know. My mother entrusted it to me before she died, to give to Martin when I felt he was ready. I'd planned to present it to him this Christmas."

She'd been robbed of a cherished family heirloom, a final gift from a departed mother. He knew all too well the weight of such a loss.

"I know you must be worried. But it must be somewhere," he assured her. "Have you asked the others?"

She shook her head. "Not yet. I searched the trunk and my entire room. It didn't fall out anywhere."

He nodded as determination settled inside him. "Maybe someone saw it and put it in a safe place. I'll help you look, and I'm sure we'll find it. It can't have disappeared like a mist."

As she looked up at him, a glimmer of hope lit her eyes, though she looked hesitant to let it bloom.

The first step would be checking with the others. Maybe individually, just in case someone had a confession to share. "Perhaps it would be best if we approached the others separately. I can ask Miss Whitmore. She might have seen it if the knife somehow ended up in her room."

Hope rolled her lips inward. "I'll speak with Mr. Thompson and Martin. My brother went hunting, and might be gone the rest of the afternoon, but I'll catch him tonight."

She sniffed, and though she didn't look as devastated as she had a moment ago, his chest ached with the need to bring a smile back to her face. To see her eyes alight with merriment.

He dipped his chin to be on eye level with her. "We'll find it, Miss Palmer. Have faith." If the knife was anywhere on this property, he would locate it. Even if he had to dig through the knee-high snow.

A ghost of a smile touched her lips. "Call me Hope. And I pray you're right."

Hope. What a wonderful name. Especially at Christmastide.

His fingers itched with the sudden urge to reach up and stroke her cheek, maybe brush those tendrils of hair back from her temple. He couldn't do that, but he offered a smile. "Call me Noah, then. Shall we set to work?"

———— ⋎ ————

Noah raised his fist to knock on Miss Whitmore's door, pausing as doubt crept in. Was he overstepping bounds, intruding on a lady's private quarters, especially at this late hour? He'd volunteered to speak with Miss Whitmore so he could make sure it was done in as polite and respectful a way as possible. Not that Hope would have been rude, but . . . this was Charles's daughter, and Noah had promised to protect her.

He'd planned to speak with her about the missing knife much earlier, but when he and Hope had returned to the house that afternoon, Sam had needed help with several things. Hope had taken care of most of them—changing the bandage on his arm and helping him eat the stew she had ready—and Miss Whitmore had assisted her. Then Noah had taken his turn when Sam had needed support to hobble to the outhouse, then back inside to change into fresh clothing. He was still so frail.

He couldn't possibly be fit to drive by the day after Christmas. It would be at least a week later, surely. That thought should tighten the pressure in Noah's chest, but for some reason, he couldn't summon much worry. They wouldn't leave until they had a driver and a trail passable for the stage, so fretting about the delay was a waste of energy.

Instead, he could simply enjoy this unexpected adventure. A bit of pleasant company while being hidden away in a place so remote that no worries of business or family could reach him.

He squared his shoulders and tapped his knuckles against the wood. Muffled footsteps approached, and the door opened to reveal Miss Whitmore, her auburn hair slightly mussed and a shawl draped over her shoulders. Thankfully, she still wore her green dress. He'd not waited so late that she'd readied for bed.

At that thought, heat crept up to his ears.

In any other place, approaching a woman's bedchamber after dark would mean ruin for her reputation, but this was different. He simply had to make sure he kept his search completely proper.

"Mr. Bentwood." Surprise flickered in her eyes. "Is everything all right?"

The heat in his neck intensified. "I apologize for disturbing you. I know it's late. I just . . . I needed to ask you something."

Her eyes widened a little more. "Yes?"

He cleared his throat. No one would accuse him of improper intentions. Hope knew why he was speaking with Miss Whitmore, and her brother still tended chores in the barn. Sam had fallen asleep again, his snores drifting through the main room.

He refocused on Miss Whitmore. Best get this done quickly. "I meant to ask you earlier, but the day got away from me. I was wondering if you might have seen a knife? A hunting knife." He held his fingers apart like Hope had done to show the size.

Her brow furrowed as she studied his hands. "A knife? I don't

. . . I don't think I've seen anything." Her gaze rose to his face. "Could one of the kitchen knives work?"

He shook his head. He was making a bumble of this. "I mean, it's a particular knife. Hope—or Miss Palmer—she's missing it. The handle is made of antler, and it's for Martin. An heirloom, passed down through their family."

Miss Whitmore's frown deepened. "I see. Well, I'm certain I haven't come across anything like that. But . . ." She hesitated, glancing back into her room. "I'll look through my trunk and bags, if you'd like. Perhaps it got mixed up with my things by accident."

He hesitated. "Would you mind if I searched the supply crates stored in here? I'm helping Miss Palmer in the hunt." As much as he loved her given name, he should do his best to use Hope's surname when speaking of her to others. He couldn't lose all his manners just because they were snowed in so far from polite society.

Once more, her eyes widened. "Of course." She stepped back and motioned toward the boxes stacked in the corner. "Please. Help yourself."

As he entered, the soft scent of rosewater enveloped him, making him feel even more out of place. He paused just inside the door, not wanting to venture too far into her private space.

Miss Whitmore moved to the corner and lit an additional lamp on the shelf, brightening the room a little. Her trunk sat at the foot of the narrow bed, and her two carpetbags against the far wall. He'd carried those two himself when they'd arrived here amidst the fierce wind and swirling snow.

He turned to the crates at his right, opposite the bed, and lifted the lid of one on top. Fabric stared up at him, and when he removed the yellow flannel on top, he found a red plaid. A variety of folded materials filled the container, and he unpacked them carefully. He didn't have to unfold each cloth, thank the Lord. He only had to bend them to be certain nothing long and stiff had been tucked inside. Though who would have done the tucking, he still couldn't fathom. The next crate proved equally as fruitless, but he didn't allow himself to move so fast that he missed a clue.

After a few moments, Miss Whitmore's voice sounded. "I've emptied the trunk. Would you like to come check to see if you find something I haven't?"

He stood and turned. She'd laid all her clothing across the bed—dresses, bundles of frilly white lace, and other things he'd rather not know the names of. He'd only had brothers, and only one faint memory of his mother. Nana hadn't possessed anything with this much lace, at least not that she'd hung on the line on washing day.

He turned his focus to the trunk first. She'd emptied it well, and he made quick work of inspecting the upper tray and tapping the bottom for hidden compartments. What must she think of him, treating her as though she would willingly steal from the family that had offered them such gracious hospitality. But he wouldn't be able to rest if he had any lingering questions about places he hadn't looked.

He straightened and attempted an apology. "I'm sorry for such a search. It's just . . ."

She waved his words away. "Think nothing of it. It's awful to be missing such a priceless treasure. If an evil fairy mixed it in with my belongings, I certainly want it discovered and returned. Poor Hope."

He eased out a breath. "Thank you for being so gracious."

She turned to her belongings spread across the coverlet. "Help me watch for anything I missed as I pack them away."

He did his best not to feel like a cad as he studied each item for something solid hiding within. She was careful to hold the garments with her fingertips and shake them out, and by the time she'd repacked the trunk, he had no shadow of a concern that she might have hidden away a knife in her belongings.

He finished searching the crates while she laid out the contents of her two carpetbags, then they repeated the process. He searched the bags, then watched as she carefully inspected each item and tucked it back in one of the satchels. He'd never wanted to know everything women carried with them, but he now possessed the knowledge, though he couldn't remember half the names she'd mentioned for the items he wasn't familiar with. Best he forget altogether.

At last, she turned to him. "Where next?"

Only the bed remained, and it didn't take long for the two of them to remove the blankets and search the mattress tick. The cornhusk filling likely made her sleep as uncomfortable as his, but he'd slept on worse—a stone floor was far more uncomfortable.

After what felt like an eternity, she pulled the coverlet up over the bottom blanket and turned to him with sad eyes. "I'm afraid it's not here. I'm so sorry."

She truly did look sorry. Charles should be proud of this excellent young woman he'd raised. Charles *was* proud. He said that often. And he was counting down the days until she returned from school.

That reminder dulled Noah's relief, and he stepped toward the open doorway. "Thank you for helping me be so thorough." He turned back and gave a half bow. "I'll leave you to your rest."

As he pulled the door closed behind him, the mixture of emotions in his chest felt like they might combust within him. He'd just done something that would be a scandal in proper circles. But he'd done it to help Hope, and he didn't regret the search. If only it had been successful. Not that he wanted Miss Whitmore to be a thief, but surely there would have been a logical explanation.

And at least he would have been able to return Hope's treasure to her. He could well imagine how her expressive eyes would light. That pert mouth would probably open in surprise. And maybe she would even hug him—something impulsive and strictly for celebration. He could practically feel her warmth beneath his hands.

He shouldn't be imagining such things.

As he strode through the main room, Hope sat beside Sam's still form. She looked up at him with a curious expression, but he didn't stop to answer her questions. He could share the details of the search in the morning.

Just now, he didn't trust himself to be so close to her. Not with the darkness and cold thick outside and the warm fire making the room feel intimate.

He turned away from her as he pulled on his coat and hat. "Good night, Miss Palmer."

As he opened the door, her voice drifted behind him. "Good night . . . Noah."

His name spoken in her lovely voice, her tone so hesitant, made him want to turn back into the warm, bright cabin. He stepped farther into the icy wind and closed the door behind him.

Watch yourself, Bentwood. You've no business tangling with a woman who lives here in the middle of nowhere. He had his life laid out for him. And falling for a woman who lived and planned to stay in the wilderness of the Nebraska Territory wasn't part of that plan.

CHAPTER 6

The cabin lay quiet in the morning stillness except for the crackling of the fire. Hope stepped softly to Mr. Thompson's side
to see if he might be awake. Should she rouse him to ask about
the knife?

She'd intended to talk with him yesterday right after she and
Noah planned their search, but the poor man had been in need
of a great deal of care. By the time he'd been cleaned up and
fed, he was too exhausted to keep his eyes open.

Then Martin had finally come in from the barn, too weary
and cold to be civil. She'd decided to ask him about the knife
when he came back from hunting today.

As she stood beside Mr. Thompson, his eyelids slowly lifted.

She eased out a breath. Good. She settled cross-legged beside
his bed, adjusting her skirts to cover herself properly, and sent
him a smile. "Good morning. Are you feeling better?"

His gaze drifted to her face, distant at first, then focusing.
"Might finally be on the mend." His voice rasped so much it
was hard to understand his words. At least his spirits were
returning.

She rested her fingers on his brow. "I'm glad to hear it. Your fever hasn't returned, so I do think you're recovering. The important thing now is to get your strength back."

He gave a small nod even as his eyes drifted shut. "I've imposed on your hospitality too long."

"Nonsense. You're always welcome here. The snow is still too deep for the stage to get through anyway." He looked like he was about to drift off again, so she spoke quickly. "I was hoping to ask a question."

His lashes fluttered, opening a crack.

She pressed on. "By chance, have you seen a knife? One with an antler handle and the name *Palmer* carved into the grip?"

Mr. Thompson's brow furrowed. "A knife? No. I . . . the last few days are hazy." He spoke slowly. "I wouldna taken somethin' of yours. Surely not in my right mind."

She did her best to hide her disappointment. Should she take him at his word? She hated to search his bag without his consent, though it would be easy enough once he slept.

His eyes cracked a little wider and looked toward his bag on the floor. "You can check my things, just in case. I'd look for ya, but you'll be faster at it."

She reached for the worn leather satchel and set it on her lap. The brass clasp was tarnished and the leather straps nearly worn through. She unfastened the latch and folded back the flap.

Inside were a few spare articles of clothing, all of them threadbare and so dirty they almost crackled when she unfolded the bundle. Aside from those, the bag held a tin cup, a wooden spoon, a comb, a small sewing kit, and a very worn knife with its blade scratched from so many sharpenings. A leather-wrapped bundle held several strips of dried meat—a snack for the road, most likely.

And that was all. No books. Nothing for pleasure. He likely couldn't read and probably found entertainment in visiting with friends at the stops along his route. And these probably weren't his only possessions, just the small supply he needed when he drove.

At first, she'd felt sorry for the man who had so few belongings to carry. But maybe he'd learned the wisdom in relishing the gifts that came his way every single day. Like when Jesus sent his disciples out two-by-two to preach about the Kingdom of God. He told them not to take even an extra set of clothes. They would be fed and cared for along the way. How hard it must have been to trust so fully.

"See it anywhere?" Mr. Thompson's quavering voice brought her back.

"No. The only knife in here is yours." She slipped everything back into the bag except the cloth bundle. "Do you mind if I wash these clothes while you're here?"

He blinked at her. "I'd be obliged, Miss Hope."

Rising, she settled him more comfortably on the pillow and drew the quilt up over his chest. "Rest now. I'll check on you again in a bit."

As she turned to leave, Mr. Thompson's voice stopped her. "Miss Hope?" His words were slurred with fatigue. "I truly hope ya find that knife. Seems like it means a good deal to ya."

Emotion welled in her throat. "It does. It's been passed down through the men in our family for several generations. I was planning to give it to Martin on Christmas." She swallowed hard against the burn in her eyes. "But don't fret about it. You focus on getting well."

His eyes had already drifted shut, but he managed a small nod.

She watched him a moment longer, his chest rising and falling in a steady rhythm. At least she could rule him out as a suspect. But that still left the mystery unsolved.

With a sigh, she turned to put the clothes with her other washing. Now would be a good time to share her findings with Noah.

⸺⸺⸺⟶Y•⸺⸺⸺

As Noah brushed the gelding's neck in the dim light of the stall, the barn door creaked open. He peered around the wall to see who had entered. Maybe Martin had returned from his hunt.

But Hope stood in the doorway, the light framing her in silhouette. Even as a solid shadow, she was beautiful. Her stray curls gave her a feminine look, but she carried herself with a confidence all those fainting flowers in the elegant ballrooms would do well to learn.

She must have seen him, for she stepped inside and let the door fall shut. The lantern's soft glow shone on her face, making her look like a dark-haired angel with that soft smile on her lips. Yet as she approached and he could see her expression better, the worry there tightened his chest.

As she approached, he moved back to brushing the gelding. He'd been careful to do everything he could think of to care for the stage horses since Sam couldn't.

Hope halted in front of the stall where he worked. "I hope I'm not disturbing you. I thought we could compare notes on our questionings." Disappointment weighed her voice.

"I take it you didn't have any luck?"

She shook her head, her shoulders slumping. "No. Mr. Thompson said he hasn't seen it. He had me go through his pack, and it's certainly not there."

Noah grimaced. "The same with Miss Whitmore. I searched

the crates in her room, and she looked through her trunk and bags." He tried not to let the heat rise to his face again at the memory.

She sighed, the worry lines deepening on her forehead. "It's like the knife just vanished into thin air." She stared down at her hands.

His fingers itched to wrap around hers. It would be a normal sign of comfort between friends, wouldn't it?

But just as he'd convinced himself to reach out, she looked up. That desperation from before glimmered in her eyes. "I don't know what else to do. I've looked everywhere."

He hesitated. "Is there any chance your brother has it?"

She stilled, then a flicker of pain flashed on her face. Maybe he shouldn't have asked it. But her expression turned thoughtful. After a moment, she shook her head. "Martin doesn't even know the meaning behind the knife. And he would have no reason to go through my trunk."

Noah nodded. "Well, then . . . I suppose it might be good for us to do one final search of the rest of the house and barn. Just in case there's a clue we might have missed." He tried for an encouraging grin. "Maybe a mousehole big enough a little rodent could have carried the knife through."

She scrunched her nose. "I'm not sure I want that to be the answer."

He chuckled, then reached for the rope across the stall doorway. "Is now a good time to start looking?"

She nodded. "Martin's still out hunting, so we can search his room and mine. Then the main room and the barn . . ."

He raised his brows. "Think he'll be upset if we go through his things while he's gone?"

She scrunched her nose. "I wouldn't do it with anyone else except him. He's my younger brother, and he's always been happy for me to put away his clean clothes or all the knick-knacks he leaves around the cabin." She glanced in the direction Martin had ridden earlier, as though she could see through the barn wall. "I'll ask him about the knife and let him know we searched his room as soon as he gets back."

Noah nodded, then motioned for her to lead the way from the barn.

CHAPTER 7

Martin's room was a small, tidy space—a bed, a chest of draw-ers, a trunk at the foot of the bed. Together, Noah and Hope methodically searched in the chest, under the mattress, and between folded shirts and trousers in the drawers. No sign of the missing knife.

Hope's shoulders slumped as they moved on to her room. "I've searched in here several times already."

As she stepped inside, Noah hung back. "Do you want me to look in the main room while you go through yours once more?" His mouth went dry at just the thought of being in there.

She shook her head, her eyes turning glassy. "You might notice something I haven't. This is the last place I saw it too." She glanced inside. "If you'd rather not be in here with me, I'll go through the kitchen again while you search here."

That sounded like an even worse idea. He couldn't go through her belongings—her unmentionables—without her there. He would have to think of this as simply a job to be done. A task to get through.

"I . . . it's probably best for us to work together." His voice cracked on the words, but at least he got them out.

She turned and stepped inside, and he followed. But he only

161

made it as far as the doorway, then stopped to let himself take in the space.

Hope's room was cozy and simple, yet filled with feminine touches. A patchwork quilt in cheerful colors covered the narrow bed. A vase of dried lavender sat on the wooden dresser, filling the air with a subtle, sweet scent. Noah swallowed hard, suddenly all too aware he was standing in the private space of the woman who'd begun to take up too much space in his thoughts.

She moved to the trunk at the foot of her bed and knelt beside it. "I've gone through this at least three times now," she said with a sigh as she opened the lid. "But maybe a fresh set of eyes will spot something I missed."

Noah stepped forward, honing his focus again. This was about finding the knife, nothing more. He knelt beside her, and they removed and inspected each item inside. Folded fabric, shawls, stockings, a few treasured books.

When she pulled out the wooden box where she'd kept the knife, his chest tightened. The expression on her face said its contents were special.

Hope lifted the lid of the box with trembling fingers. Inside lay a collection of trinkets and mementos—a pipe, ladies' gloves, and two gold buttons. Cavalry, if he wasn't mistaken.

She fingered the smooth cedar bottom of the box. "This is where I kept it." The reverence, the longing in her tone made him want to know about these other pieces. They were special to *her*, so they mattered.

He reached out a single finger to touch the bowl of the pipe. "What are these treasures?"

She picked up the pipe, cradling it in both hands. "This was my father's. He only smoked it in the winter, when we'd have long evenings inside. He'd sit in an armchair with a tall back and smoke the pipe."

Her gaze turned unfocused. "I don't remember him ever reading during those evenings. We all talked, and he watched what the rest of us did. Like he simply enjoyed being with us." Her voice caught at the end, and the tears shimmering in her eyes looked like they might spill over.

She sniffed, and her gaze focused again, landing on him. "He died when I was seven. A heart condition that kept him in bed those last weeks."

He nodded. There weren't words that could ease the loss, but at least he could show his own feelings. "I'm sorry you lost him so young."

Her mouth formed a shaky smile. "What of you? Are your parents still alive? Where did you grow up?"

That old familiar knot balled in his throat, but he summoned his usual casual tone when sharing these details. He didn't speak of them much, but he needed Hope to know this part of him. To understand how low his background had been. He was no prize. Not the kind most women sought.

"I never knew my father. My mother died when I was four, during the birth of my younger brother. My grandparents raised us. There was an orchard in the yard, and we sold oranges in town." Why had he added that last part? He didn't tell people that.

Sorrow filled her gaze, and she looked like she wanted to lay her hand on his. He would have welcomed the touch, but he didn't want pity.

"Were your grandparents kind?" she asked. "You had other siblings?"

He nodded. "They did their best. It's not easy for an older couple to raise three boys without much of a livelihood. My older brother is Tom and the younger Mose."

She studied him, and his neck itched at the way she seemed

to see so much with that gaze. After a moment, she spoke in a soft voice. "I'm sorry it was so hard, but I can see how that upbringing made you the man you are today."

He swallowed, still trying to work loose the knot in his throat. "Yes."

"Are your grandparents still alive?"

He shook his head. "They passed within a year of each other. Mose had already left to apprentice to a pharmacist, so they had a few months to themselves again before the end." He'd loved his grandparents, even though not all the memories were good. It couldn't be easy to raise another round of children unexpectedly.

A new round of tears glimmered in Hope's eyes. For him? He couldn't let her grieve a past he'd moved on from himself.

He turned back to the trunk—empty now and ready for a thorough inspection. He spoke as he rose up on his knees to feel the bottom. "I'm wondering if there's a crack or something the knife could have worked into."

But nothing was obvious, and after an incredibly thorough search, he had to give up that possibility. No cracks in the wood or joints. No hidden compartments. No glint of silver.

"It's just not here." Hope sighed. She scanned her room. "Maybe I should give up on it. It's just a knife. Losing it doesn't change our past. Maybe I can write out the memories as a Christmas gift for Martin instead." She offered a feeble attempt at a smile that made his belly twist.

He reached for the blankets that had been at the bottom of the trunk. "Let's put these back in and finish searching your room. If we don't find it anywhere in the house or barn, maybe we'll think about giving up."

But *he* wouldn't stop searching. Not if he had to dig up all the snow in the yard, he'd look until he found this treasure for her. Until he'd removed this sorrow lining her face and lit those beautiful eyes again.

Hope nodded, then reached to help him fold the blankets and place them back inside the trunk.

As they worked, his fingers brushed hers, and a tingle spread up his arm. He focused on the task, willing away the growing warmth in his chest at her nearness.

They finished with the trunk and turned their attention to the rest of the room. Noah checked under the bed while Hope opened the drawers of her dresser. He tried not to let his imagination wander to what feminine items might be tucked inside. Although it was hard to ignore the subtle scent of lavender that clung to her linens.

After a thorough inspection yielded no clues, they moved to the main room of the cabin. The knife had to be here somewhere. It couldn't have just vanished.

He lifted the braided rug near the hearth to check the floorboards while Hope rummaged through a basket of mending. Neither turned up any sign of the heirloom. With growing frustration, they opened chests and crates, looked in and behind the stove, even moved the logs around in the hearth to make sure it hadn't been tossed in there.

Nothing.

As he closed the last trunk, he turned to Hope, who stood by the window, her arms wrapped around herself as she stared out at the snow-covered landscape. The defeated slope of her back made his heart ache. He crossed the room to stand beside her, close enough that their shoulders almost brushed.

"I'm sorry we haven't found it yet." He did his best to keep his voice soft, since Sam still slept near the far wall. "But we're not giving up. There's still the barn to search."

She nodded but didn't look at him. "I know. It's just . . . that knife is one of the few things I have left of my parents. Losing it feels like losing a part of them all over again."

Noah reached out and took her hand in his, giving it a gentle squeeze. It was a bold move, but she seemed to need more than words. "I understand. But your memories of them live on in your heart, not an object. And we'll keep looking until we find it."

Finally, she turned to face him, unshed tears shimmering in her eyes. "Thank you, Noah. For helping me search. For understanding."

He smiled down at her, suddenly very aware of how close they were standing, of the softness of her hand in his. "You're welcome. That's what friends are for, right?"

Something flickered in her expression, there and gone too quick for him to decipher. Then she stepped back, pulling her hand from his grasp. "Yes." She cleared her throat. "Well, I suppose we should check the barn. Just in case."

He followed her outside, the cold air a sharp contrast to the warmth that had enveloped him moments before. They trudged through the snow on the worn path to the barn, shoulders hunched against the wind. Inside, they split up to cover more ground—Hope checking the stalls while Noah investigated the hayloft and equipment. He even searched under his bedding and in his satchel, just in case.

By the time Hope joined him near his belongings, his optimism had dwindled.

It simply wasn't here.

He turned to Hope, condolence on his lips, but the words died at the sight of the silent tears tracking down her cheeks, leaving glistening trails on her skin.

"Hope . . ." He reached out a tentative hand to her shoulder. She startled at his touch, quickly dashing away the tears with her sleeve. "I'm being foolish, I know. Crying over a knife." Her voice cracked. "It's just . . . it was the last thing Mama ever gave me. Her most prized possession. And now it's gone forever."

His chest squeezed tight. Before he could question himself, he stepped closer and folded her into his arms. She resisted only a moment before melting against him, hands fisting in the fabric of his coat as quiet sobs shook her frame.

Her tears soaked into his shirt, but he didn't mind. If he could absorb some of her sorrow, take away even an ounce of her pain, he'd gladly do it. Her grief was a palpable thing, radiating from her in waves that crashed against his own battered heart. He knew well the ache of losing loved ones, of clinging to the smallest reminders of them.

After a few moments, her sobs quieted, and she pulled back a little to look up at him. Tears still clung to her lashes, but a hint of her usual strength had returned. "I'm sorry. I don't usually fall apart like this."

He shook his head, reaching up to brush away a stray tear with his thumb. He kept his other hand around her waist. He wasn't ready to let her go yet. "You have nothing to apologize for. It's all right to grieve the things we've lost. The people we've lost."

Hope searched his face, those eyes so deep and full. "You've lost so much too."

He swallowed. "The loss . . . it leaves a scar. An empty place inside you."

Her features softened. "Yes. Exactly." She took a shuddering breath. "When I hold that knife, it's like I can feel them with me again. Mama's gentle hands. Papa's steady presence. Without it . . ."

"They're still with you, Hope. In here." He laid his palm

over his heart. "No one can ever take away what they meant to you, knife or no knife."

Her eyes filled again, but she blinked the tears away. "I know. I do. It's just . . . harder to remember that sometimes." Her hand came up to cover his where it rested on his chest. "Thank you, Noah. For being here. For not thinking I'm ridiculous."

"I could never think that." If only she knew how much he wanted to be here. Right here. Just like this. "You're one of the strongest people I've ever met, running this stage stop the way you do. But even the strong need comfort sometimes."

Her lips curved. Not quite a smile, but close. "Well, you're very good at it. The comforting."

He huffed a self-conscious laugh. "I've . . . never been the best with feelings."

"Could have fooled me." Her eyes held his, something warm and soft in their depths that made his breath catch.

They still stood so close, his arm around her waist. Her hand covering his over his heart. He looked into her upturned face, her eyes shimmering with unshed tears but also with a tender warmth that drew him in like a moth to flame. In that unguarded moment, the yearning he'd tried so hard to ignore surged to the surface, strong and undeniable.

Almost of their own volition, his fingers drifted from her waist to the small of her back, pressing her closer. She inhaled sharply but didn't pull away. If anything, she leaned forward, her body a whisper from his. Her gaze dropped to his mouth, then flicked back up to meet his, a silent question in their amber depths.

He shouldn't. This could change everything between them. But with her so near and everything in him craving her, he could find the will to resist no longer. Slowly, giving her time, he lowered his head until his lips hovered a hairsbreadth from hers.

"Hope." His voice came out rough. "Tell me to stop."

Her lips parted. Then she whispered, "I don't want you to stop."

Closing the last bit of distance between them, he captured her mouth with his own.

CHAPTER 8

Her lips were warm and soft, pliant beneath the gentle pressure of his kiss. She made a little sound in the back of her throat, her fingers curling into his shirtfront as she rose up on her toes to meet him. His hand splayed across her back to anchor her to him.

He lost himself in her taste, her warmth, the perfect fit of her slender body against his. It was both achingly familiar and exhilaratingly new, like coming home and setting out on uncharted waters all at once.

It took every ounce of willpower he possessed, but he gentled the kiss, easing back until their lips parted. He rested his forehead against hers as they both fought to settle their breathing.

He worked to form words. "Hope, I . . ."

Her eyes blinked open, hazy and unfocused before sharpening on his face. "Noah . . ." Something like wonder colored her tone.

He swallowed hard, struggling to say the right thing. "I'm sorry, I shouldn't have . . . that wasn't . . . I didn't mean to take advantage."

She gave a small shake of her head, her nose brushing his. "You didn't. I wanted . . . I've wanted that."

His heart stumbled in his chest. "You have?"

A rosy flush climbed up her neck to her cheeks. "I know I shouldn't. We're so different, from such separate worlds. But I can't seem to help how I feel when I'm with you. How much I don't want you to leave."

His breath caught at those last words. He didn't *want* to leave her. But he had to. He had a duty. A job. A life.

With that cold bucket of water dousing him back to reality, he eased his hold. He had to think. Had to pray.

Hope's gaze turned questioning. The last thing he wanted was to make her think she'd done something wrong. He reached up for her hand and wrapped it in his. Then he pressed a kiss to the backs of her fingers. He needed to be honest with her. "Hope, I don't know how this could work, something more between the two of us. But I've seen God sort things out in ways I could never have imagined. I think I need to do some praying." He held her gaze as he pressed another kiss to her fingers.

Let her see my heart, Lord. Don't let me hurt her.

Maybe God answered his prayer, for no sign of pain flashed in her eyes. She only nodded. "I need to do the same."

A bit of tension eased from his shoulders. "I suppose we should get back to the house." Away from the temptation to kiss her again. Would it hurt to brush his lips against hers one more time? He had a feeling one more would never be enough.

So he released her, and they both turned toward the barn door. Back to reality—one that looked far different from the way it had an hour before.

———— • ∀ • ————

Hope dusted the sugar from her hands as she mentally reviewed the recipe for chess pie. Without eggs, it would take some creative substitutions to achieve the right consistency. She glanced at the small bag of precious cornstarch. Hopefully, it would be enough.

If only they still had chickens, she could make Noah's favorite Christmas dessert properly. But the last group of hens Martin had ordered from Kansas had only survived two months. The varmints in this country were able to break through any number of wires and wood cages to snatch the fowl.

So, she'd learned to cook without eggs. Not too hard if one avoided baking cakes and custards. And chess pie.

Using cornstarch and saleratus might just do the trick, though. *Lord, let this work. Let Noah love the outcome.*

The scent of cinnamon and nutmeg from the simmering wassail on the stove mingled with the aroma of the bean soup she'd started cooking for their evening meal. Martin still hadn't returned from another long day of hunting, but when he did, he would be hungry. After they ate, she would ask him privately about the knife.

As she measured out the cornstarch, the thought of the knife led her, of course, to thoughts of that kiss.

Sweet mercy, what a kiss. The way Noah looked at her with such intensity and longing had made her heart race. And when he'd pulled her close, his strong arm encircling her waist, she'd felt a sense of rightness, of belonging. As if everything in her life had led her to that moment.

She sighed, pouring the filling into the pie crust. It was foolish to dwell on what could never be. Noah had his own life, his own responsibilities. And she had hers. Their paths had crossed for a brief moment in time, but soon enough, he would be gone. She'd learned this the hard way too many times, when she'd wallowed after guests left. Why had she let it come to this once more?

Because Noah is different.

Even as the thought slipped in, she shook her head to send it away. But clearing her mind of him felt impossible.

Lord, I really want this man. Not only is he one of the most handsome men I've ever met, but he's honorable and honest—and more than those wonderful qualities . . . he loves You.

When she finished the prayer, her spirit still churned. Noah had a life, responsibilities to his job and probably to his brothers. Could he really give all that up for a life here with her?

Could she give up Martin and the stage stop for Noah? The idea made her want to sink down on the bench and cry. *Lord, is that what You want me to do?*

She slid the pie into the oven, her heart heavy with unanswered questions. Best to keep busy and let the Lord sort it out.

The door to Ellen's bedchamber opened, and the woman stepped out with a cheery smile. "Hello. I didn't know you were out here working or I would have come sooner. I suppose I was too engrossed in my book."

Hope returned the grin, grateful for the distraction. "I'm just putting together a few things for our dinner tonight."

Ellen's eyes brightened as she took in the array of ingredients on the work counter. "It smells heavenly in here. Is there anything I can do to help?"

She glanced around the space. "If you're sure you don't mind, these vegetables need to be chopped for the soup." She motioned to the pile of carrots and potatoes on the counter.

Ellen stepped forward. "I'd be delighted. Just show me what to do."

As they worked together in the small space, peeling and slicing, Ellen's friendly chatter drew Hope in. She'd not expected a genteel lady to possess such a quick wit and a keen eye for detail. Her stories of city life and high society were downright funny.

Still, Hope found herself wondering what Ellen truly thought of their simple frontier existence. Did she find it quaint and charming, like something out of a dime novel? Or did she secretly long for the comforts and refinements of her former life?

Before she could ponder it further, the sound of footsteps on the porch announced Martin's return. Only her brother would stomp with those heavy thuds. The front door opened, and Martin paused on the threshold as he shook off the snow that clung to his coat.

"There you are." She moved the pot to a cooler part of the stove. The vegetables should be cooked by now. "Did you find anything?"

Martin shook his head as he pulled off his gloves and coat, though his scowl could have answered for him. "Snow's still too deep. Not many animals out yet."

She sighed as she ladled him a bowl of soup. If he couldn't bring in fresh meat, she'd have to parboil some they'd dried. It would fill their bellies, but what a sorry excuse for a Christmas dinner. That wasn't Martin's fault, though. "The soup is ready, so have a seat. I suppose everyone can eat at their leisure tonight."

He moved to the table. "Smells good."

Ellen filled a bowl with soup and sat across from Martin, then the door opened and Noah stepped inside. His eyes found hers right away, and her breathing hitched. His presence always filled the room. She gave a small smile so her tumultuous feelings weren't too obvious in case anyone else watched her. "Are you hungry? It's a simple bean stew, but it's ready."

A twinkle lit his eyes as he removed his coat. "It smells wonderful. A double helping, please, if there's plenty."

Warmth slid through every part of her as she filled his bowl to the top.

The men exchanged small talk about Martin's hunt and

what kind of animals were usually found in this area during the winter.

Then Martin pushed to his feet. "Miss Whitmore, I'd be happy to show you the sleigh you wanted to see, if now is a good time."

Ellen's head jerked up, but Hope couldn't see her expression. "I'd love to, Mr. Palmer." She stood, far more gracefully than Martin had.

Martin ran a look from Noah to Hope. "You two are welcome to come if you want."

Hope hesitated. The chess pie would need to come out in another five minutes or so. After so much work, the last thing she wanted was to let it burn. "I can't leave the food unattended right now. But you go ahead, and I'm sure Noah would be happy to accompany you."

Though she trusted her brother and Ellen, a chaperone would be wise. Another waft of heat rose up to her cheeks at the memory of her and Noah's private time in the barn.

Noah met her eyes, his gaze sharp. He might be remembering those moments too, and he clearly didn't want his ward to experience the same thing. Not under his watch.

Her brother would keep things respectable. Noah didn't have to turn into a brooding guardian. She raised her brows at him to add a little levity. Then pressed a hand to her chest and gave her head a slight shake. She'd had nothing to do with this invitation.

Noah's gaze softened, as though he might be chuckling inwardly. Then he pushed up from the table, leaving his half-full bowl of stew. "I'd like to see it too." He glanced at Hope. "I'll be back to finish this. Never fear."

The final look he sent before he donned his coat with the others made butterflies flit through her middle. He almost sounded like he'd be back to finish their silent banter. Or maybe even finish their kiss from earlier. Or the conversation after it. Maybe he'd made a decision and planned to take her aside and share it.

Settle down, Hope. The man only meant you shouldn't take away his bowl from the table.

But as Noah's handsome form stepped out of the cabin and he closed the door, the ache inside twisted harder than ever. *Lord, either show us how we can work things out together, or take away all of my yearning for him.*

Because if the Father's answer was no, how could she stand to watch Noah leave?

CHAPTER 9

I will lift up mine eyes unto the hills, from whence cometh my help . . .

The words blurred together as Noah sat in the barn the next morning. The warm glow of the lantern lit the area around his bed pallet, and the crackling fire in the cookstove took the chill from the air.

Help. In his case, God had sent help during the snowstorm. In the form of Hope.

She was a special woman—unlike anyone he'd ever known. Her vibrant smile, her fierce determination, the way her presence filled a room . . . filled his mind. Even when he was trying to focus on something else, like these quiet moments with the Lord.

He squeezed his eyes shut to clear his thoughts. But that only made him remember their kiss. He huffed out a breath. A lot of good he was at making himself focus.

He rested his head back against the cold barn wall and stared up at the rafters. "I'm sorry, Lord. Help me focus on You. Clear out these distractions."

His mind snagged on that last request. Maybe instead of

pushing Hope out of his thoughts, he should deal with his questions, here and now.

With a sigh, he searched for the words. "Show me Your will in this. Show me what I'm to do with all these thoughts she stirs up. We're so different. Our lives are in two very separate places. She's happy here at this stage stop, following the legacy her parents left for her. And I'm . . ."

What was he? Two days ago, he would have said he was a successful businessman, with a prosperous life ahead of him. But was that really what mattered to him?

He was good at his job negotiating shipping deals and lining up all the details. Many days, he wished he didn't have to be indoors so much. But he loved working with Charles. That part he did truly love. The man was so much more than an employer. Even more than a friend or mentor.

In truth, Charles felt like a father, a feeling Noah couldn't remember, since he'd never known his own father. Charles had become the family Noah always wanted.

So that left him with what? A friendship he valued and a job he appreciated. And where did Hope fit? Should she belong anywhere in his future? Or were all these thoughts and attractions merely the effects of being hidden away in this remote place for a few wonderful days? Getting to live a simple life without the complications of society or business deals or the expectations of others?

He focused on the rafters again. "Please, God. If you mean for me to leave Hope behind, take away these feelings. Help me to see clearly."

He stayed in that prayer for a long moment, letting his spirit commune with the Almighty, the Maker of heaven and earth, the One who knew everything about him, even the number of hairs on his head.

A sense of peace sank through him, so rich his entire body relaxed. "Is that a yes, Lord? Would you have me pursue courting Hope?"

That sense of peace lingered, settling his insides.

"If this is your will, I trust you to create a way for me to see her again. Make our way plain."

He closed his eyes and drew in a breath of the sweet fragrance around him. *Thank you, Father.*

At last he opened his eyes and finally stood. He should go to the house and see what he could help with. Martin had gone hunting again early this morning before breakfast, searching for meat for tomorrow's Christmas dinner.

As he left the barn, his boots crunched in the softening snow as he sank through the layers. The sound echoed in the stillness around him, shattering the tranquil silence of the morning.

As he closed the door behind him, the sun's rays warmed his back, glinting off the snow to send shafts of light in every direction.

A movement to the right caught his focus.

Martin strode from the trees, two plump wild turkeys dangling by their legs from one gloved hand. "Finally!" He grinned.

Noah couldn't help smiling back as he strode forward. Hope would be pleased. "Looks like they're beauties."

Martin's green eyes sparkled. "Reckon the warmer weather drew 'em out. Just in time."

Noah nodded his approval, eying the distinct red-and-blue heads and iridescent feathers of the large birds. His grandfather had taught him how to dress game. The unpleasant task had always turned his stomach, so he'd avoided helping Grandfather once he was old enough to do other chores instead.

But out here, skills like those weren't an option. And if he ever wanted to entertain the thought of joining Hope here—though he still had no idea how that would work out—he needed to see if he was man enough for everything it required.

He swallowed hard against the queasiness that rose in his gut at the thought of what would come next. "You want me to help clean those?"

Martin shot him a surprised look. "Sure, if you're up to it."

He nodded. "I think so." In truth, he wasn't sure himself, but he'd volunteered now. And maybe it wouldn't be as bad as he remembered.

He followed Martin to the woodpile behind the house where they could work without making a mess. Once they had everything spread out on the ground, Martin handed over one of the birds. "You know where to start?"

The cool weight of the turkey settled into his hands, the familiar shape bringing back memories of hunting trips with Grandfather. Those days held some good memories. He eyed Martin's knife, already poised over his bird. "I remember some, but you might need to talk me through it." He remembered enough to know there were tricks to accomplishing each step without making things harder and destroying precious meat.

Martin proved an easy teacher, voicing each step as he worked.

Once Noah remembered the process, they worked in silence, each focused on his bird. The knife Martin handed him cut through the skin more easily than he remembered, and the smell wasn't quite as bad as it had been when he'd helped Grandfather all those years ago. Maybe that was just because everything smelled different outside in the fresh air rather than the squalor of a row of shanties.

As he pulled feathers from the flesh, his thoughts drifted back to Hope. She was deeply rooted in this place, her love for the inn and the frontier life woven into every fiber of her being. Could he really ask her to leave all that behind for the bustle and noise of the city? And what of his own dreams and ambitions? The thought of disappointing Charles left a hollow feeling in his chest.

Noah let out a long sigh, his breath clouding in the chill air. If only there were some way to bridge the gap between their lives.

He glanced over at Martin, who'd begun to dig through his pack. Could this younger man be the key? If he were willing to take over running the inn, maybe Hope would be more open to the idea of life in the east.

Noah cleared his throat and did his best to sound casual. "So, do you and Hope plan to always run the inn together? Or has one of you ever talked about taking over completely?"

Martin looked up, surprise flickering across his face. "Well. I can't say I haven't thought about going back east, getting into bigger business ventures. But I couldn't leave Hope. She loves it here. She's poured her heart and soul into this place. And she can't run it by herself."

Of course not. And Hope would never be content as a businessman's wife, attending an endless stream of social gatherings and navigating the politics of high society.

She came alive in her role as the Split Rock's innkeeper. This business had been in her family for generations. And he wouldn't *want* her to change for him. He loved her just as she was.

No, if he wanted a future with Hope, he would have to be the one to come to her. Was he ready to do that? To turn away from everything he'd worked so hard to attain in order to pursue a relationship with this woman?

He was good at business, but it wasn't something he felt passionate about. If he were honest with himself, he didn't care about making money. He cared about meeting the expectations of the man who'd given him a chance when no one else would.

Martin glanced up again, eyeing him. "Why do you ask?"

Noah's chest tightened. Martin had been gone hunting so much these past few days, he might not realize how much attraction crackled between Noah and Hope. Maybe it was time to be up front with the man.

He took in a deep breath. "These past few days, getting to know your sister, have been some of the happiest of my life. I'd like to get to know her better, to court her, if she'll have me."

Martin's eyebrows shot up. "Really?"

Noah nodded. "It wouldn't be easy, with me living back east and her heart so tied to this place. I don't want to take her away from the life she loves or ask her to be someone she's not. And I have obligations of my own I can't ignore."

He gazed down at his knife. Laying it out like that made their situation sound hopeless. But if God was in this, he would make a way.

He lifted his focus back to Martin. "Your sister is special. Worth the challenge."

Martin studied Noah for a long moment, his expression unreadable. Then he nodded. "I appreciate your honesty. You seem like a good man, and I look forward to knowing you better." Then a corner of his mouth tipped as a twinkle touched his eyes. "The rest I'll leave to Hope. She's got a mind of her own, that one."

Noah huffed out a laugh. "Don't I know it."

Martin returned his focus to his work, and Noah did the same.

The glint of sunlight on metal caught Noah's eye, and he glanced over at the knife Martin was using. Its ornate antler handle bore a single word, carved with care into the smooth surface.

MISTY M. BELLER

He straightened. "That knife . . ." Realization settled in a rush.

Martin glanced up, then at the knife in his hand. One corner of his mouth tipped up as he raised the blade. "Nice, huh?"

It had to be. He reached out. "Can I hold it?"

The blade was half-covered with turkey innards, but the word carved into the antler handle was easy to make out. *Palmer.*

"Where did you get this?" He shifted his focus to Martin.

The man shrugged. "My other knife broke a few days back, and I remembered seeing this one in Hope's trunk a while ago. Figured I'd borrow it until I had time to forge a new blade."

A chuckle forced its way through Noah's chest. All this time . . .

He wiped both sides of the blade in the snow, then held the knife up to inspect it again. The blade was old, no doubt, but looked sharp and carefully cared for.

Martin was watching him, more patiently than Noah would have.

He shook his head and turned to him. "I'm pretty sure this is the knife Hope's been looking high and low for. We've searched every corner of the house and barn."

Martin winced. "I meant to ask her about it, but she was never around when I'd think to."

"Can I tell her?" Even if Martin said no, he wasn't sure he could keep the news from Hope more than a minute.

He shrugged. "Sure."

Noah pushed to his feet, holding the heirloom with care as he strode around to the front of the house. What would she say? Would she be angry with her brother? Probably just relieved.

Before he opened the cabin door, he tucked the blade into his coat pocket. When he stepped into the room, all three occupants turned to him. Sam sat up on his bed pallet, leaning

185

against the wall. He seemed to be finally feeling better. Miss Whitmore and Hope both worked in the cooking area.

He met Hope's gaze and tried to tone down his grin as he sauntered toward her. He was doing a poor job of looking casual, though, for her eyes narrowed at him.

"What is it?" She wiped her hands on a cloth and stepped toward him, and when he reached her, he slipped the blade from his pocket.

As she stared down at the knife, her beautiful eyes widened. "Is that . . ?" Her gaze lifted to his.

She must know it was the right knife, but he nodded anyway. "The blade on your brother's knife broke and he remembered seeing this one in your trunk. He forgot to tell you about borrowing it."

Martin had come in behind him. "I'm sorry, Hope. Didn't mean to make you fret."

She didn't respond to her brother, just refocused on the knife and reached for it. She took the tool in both hands and examined it, turning it around with her fingers like a roasting spit.

Then she finally looked up, and her gaze met Noah's. "He was in the barn until so late last night, I didn't get a chance to ask him about this. Thank you." Her words came quiet, for him alone.

She moved around him, placing the knife in her palm as she stood before her brother. "This knife first belonged to our great-grandfather on Papa's side. He carved our family name in it, then gave it to Grandad when he went west to fight the Indian wars. Grandad gave it to Papa. You were too young when Papa passed, so Mama asked me to keep it safe until you were old enough to truly appreciate it."

She extended the knife on both sets of fingers, like the gift of the Magi. "Now I give it to you, Martin Palmer. Keep it safe, and every time you use it, remember you come from a line of strong Palmer men. Men who've fought and suffered and worked for what mattered to them. Men who've loved fiercely and laughed loudly and lived life to the fullest."

Martin took the knife, and Hope stepped closer to wrap her arms around her brother. "I love you." Her words were muffled in her brother's coat, but Noah could still hear the way they broke.

Emotion clogged his own throat. He and his brothers didn't have an heirloom knife to remind them of their ancestors. But they did have each other, something he'd lost sight of these past years since he left his grandparents' home. But as soon as he had a spare week or two, he would visit his brothers. Then maybe he could talk his older brother into coming with him to see their youngest. The three of them hadn't been together since their grandparents passed.

For a man who mourned the loss of the family he'd never had, he'd certainly not been grateful for those he did have. He still needed to sort through how he could court Hope—what their life could be like and whether he could continue working for Charles.

CHAPTER 10

Christmas Day had been even better than she'd hoped. Mr. Thompson was able to join them at the table for the feast— though he barely touched his food plate. He'd seemed lost in thought, and not just because of the pain from his wound. Was he worried about driving the stage again?

Once the snow melted enough for the next stage to get through, Noah and Ellen could continue their trip. But Mr. Thompson might not like the idea of sitting here instead of accomplishing what he considered to be his job.

When they exchanged gifts, the thoughtfulness of each present made her eyes burn. Martin had carved her a beautiful wooden haircomb, and Ellen gave her a set of silver hairpins engraved with a floral design. When Hope offered an exuberant thank-you, Ellen's smile turned shy. "I hope they will help you remember me. I've so enjoyed coming to know you. Maybe we can write to keep up our friendship?"

Those tears pressed harder as Hope pulled her into a hug. "I would love that a great deal, Ellen."

She'd even heard Martin asking if he could write to Ellen. The woman had blushed as she quietly accepted.

And now that the dishes were washed and put away, Noah

and Martin enjoyed a game of chess by the fire while she finished tidying up. The cabin smelled of pine and cinnamon, the air warm and cozy despite the frigid temperatures outside. A perfect ending to a wonderful day.

As she bent to sweep some crumbs off the floor, a shadow fell across her work. She straightened and turned to find Noah standing there, his coat in his arms.

"I'm about to take a turn around the yard to stretch my legs." His voice was low, meant only for her ears. "Would you care to join me?"

Her heart fluttered at the invitation. They hadn't spent much time alone since that night in the barn, and she'd missed his company. Missed the way his presence settled something inside her, making her feel seen and understood in a way few people ever did.

Of course, maybe this outing had nothing to do with wanting her company and everything to do with needing fresh air after being cooped up inside all day. Either way, she welcomed the chance to be near him again.

She nodded. "Just let me grab my coat."

The late afternoon sun shone bright again today, though the air felt colder than yesterday. More snow had melted, which meant they were one day closer to the next stage coming through. One day closer to Noah leaving her.

She did her best to push away that thought as they walked side by side through the snow-covered yard. She wanted to enjoy this moment with Noah, to savor every second together.

He glanced at her, a small smile tugging at the corners of his mouth. "That chess pie you made was the best I've ever tasted. You have a real talent in the kitchen."

She scrunched her nose. "Thank you. It was a challenge making it without eggs."

He raised his brows. "Without eggs? Is that possible?"

"Turns out it is."

He stopped to stare at the barn, then looked around the yard. "I suppose you don't have chickens. I didn't think through my request very well." He met her gaze, his eyes earnest. "I'm sorry. I didn't mean to make the meal harder for you."

She rested a gloved hand on his arm. "I enjoyed the challenge, truly. I'm usually able to order eggs to come on the supply wagons, but winter makes it harder for them to get through."

Noah nodded. He knew that fact well now. He didn't start walking again, but reached for the end of his scarf, holding up the embroidered part. "Thank you for this too." He locked those remarkable eyes with hers again. "It's perfect. By far the most handsome scarf I own."

She couldn't stop the heat flaming her cheeks. "That's not true."

He shook his head. "I can tell you beyond a doubt that it is."

"I'm glad you like it."

His eyes turned serious. "I have something for you as well." He reached into his coat pocket and pulled out a small velvet pouch, then emptied the contents into his gloved palm. A delicate gold locket gleamed in the sunlight, its surface engraved with swirling designs.

"It was my mother's." He spoke softly, running a thumb over the pendant. "My father gave it to her on their wedding day. When she passed, my grandparents saved it for me." He shook off one of his gloves to open the locket. Inside, two tiny sketches stared up at them—one of a young boy, and the other of a man who bore a striking resemblance to Noah. "That's me and my older brother, Tom."

Hope stared at the necklace, her mind reeling. Surely he didn't mean for her to keep something so precious, so personal.

"It's beautiful," she managed. "I don't know what to say. Are you certain you want me to have this? I couldn't possibly—"

He closed his free hand over hers, drawing her focus to his face. "I want you to keep it safe for me." His gaze held a soft smile. "When the trail is passable, I'll have to continue my journey to escort Miss Whitmore home. But I've decided that I'm going to put a hold on that partnership discussion. Instead, I'm going to ask for a leave of absence. Our superintendent who's running things in the east while I'm gone can continue a few more months." His gaze held steady on hers. "I'd like to come back. To this stage stop. If that's all right with you."

Come back? It felt like the air had been stolen from her lungs. Tears blurred her vision as bright and overwhelming joy spread through her. This couldn't be real.

She managed to ask, "You want to come back? To stay here, with us?"

He nodded, a tentative smile tipping the corners of his mouth. "If you'll have me."

"But . . . are you certain? You had plans."

He squeezed her hand, his gaze unwavering. "I've never been more certain. These past days with you, getting to know you and your brother, have shown me what truly matters. My plans, my job—they all pale in comparison to the connection I feel with you. The future we could have."

The tears she'd been holding back spilled down her cheeks as a watery laugh escaped her. "I would like that very much. Having you here, with us . . . with me. It's more than I dared to dream."

His smile widened, eyes crinkling at the corners. "May I?" He held up the locket, a silent question.

She nodded, not trusting her voice. As she turned, he shucked his remaining glove. His cold fingers brushed the nape of her neck, sending a shiver down her spine. The weight of the pendant settled just above her heart, a tangible reminder of his promise.

When he finished, he turned her back to face him, his hands coming to rest on her shoulders, his gaze on hers. "I don't want you to forget me while I'm gone." His warm breath caressed her cheek. "This way, you'll always have a piece of me with you."

She removed her own gloves, dropping them to the snow beside Noah's, and reached up to touch the locket. "As if I could ever forget you, Noah Bentwood."

His eyes darkened, the intensity in them stealing her breath. "There's one other way I want to make sure you remember me."

A thrill slipped through her as her body recalled that kiss.

And then his mouth was on hers, gentle and searching at first, then insistent as she melted into his arms. The world around them disappeared, leaving only the two of them, hearts pounding in unison, a promise of all the beautiful moments yet to come.

When they finally parted, breathless and flushed, only one thought stayed rooted in her mind: She would wait as long as it took for this man to return to her.

Epilogue

The wind howled like a wounded beast, rattling the stagecoach as it lurched through the blinding snow. Noah pulled his wool coat tighter around himself as he strained to see anything beyond the frosted window. Across from him, the only other passenger slept through the noise.

"Hold tight, folks!" their driver called over the roaring storm. "Stage stop just ahead!"

Noah eased out a breath. He was nearly there. Nearly to Hope.

His heart quickened at the thought, a mix of anticipation and trepidation making his palms sweat inside his gloves. What would she say when she saw him? Would her eyes light up with joy, or would her feelings have ebbed?

They'd exchanged letters, but because of the distance between them and his traveling, it had been weeks since she'd written the last one. Maybe she'd changed her mind since then. Perhaps she'd decided theirs was only a temporary attraction. The result of too much proximity and the romance of the Christmas holiday.

Lord, if this is the direction you would have me go, let her affections have grown, not lessened.

A sudden jolt jarred him from his thoughts as the coach lurched forward, then slowed to a creaking halt. The driver's voice carried through the wind. "Split Rock Pony Express and Stage Stop! We'll be here for the night, so gather your things and head inside."

The slumbering man across from him jolted awake with a snort, then blinked as he sat upright. Noah straightened, too, gripping the handle of his leather satchel as he peered out the frost-rimmed window at the familiar wooden building nestled in the snowy valley. A plume of smoke rose from the stone chimney, and the golden glow spilling from the windows promised warmth and shelter from the biting cold.

He pushed open the stage door and stepped down onto the snow-covered ground, wincing at the icy chill that seeped through his boots. He made his way through the swirling snow, his heart pounding with each crunching step. The front door swung open, and a familiar figure emerged from the warm glow within.

When the man caught sight of him, he paused. "Noah?" A grin spread across Martin's face as he hurried forward, his hand outstretched. "By golly, it is you! We weren't expecting you for another month at least."

Noah clasped Martin's hand, a smile tugging at his own lips despite the nerves in his belly. "I made better time than I thought. The weather held out longer than expected." He glanced past Martin to the closed door. "Is Hope . . . ?"

"She's inside, making food for the passengers." Martin's grin widened, and he clapped Noah on the shoulder. "Go in while I see to the horses."

Noah nodded his thanks, then turned and climbed the wooden steps to the front door. The moment he stepped inside, a rush of warmth enveloped him.

The familiar scents of woodsmoke and simmering stew filled

his senses as his gaze swept the room—taking in the crackling fire in the hearth and the long table set for a meal.

Then his eyes found Hope, and all else faded away.

She stood at the stove, her back to him as she stirred a large pot. Her dark hair was pinned up in its usual bun, a few loose tendrils curling at the nape of her neck. A blue apron covered her simple brown dress, the fabric hugging her curves in a way that made his throat go dry.

She focused so intently on her task, she'd not heard him.

He cleared his throat, and she glanced over her shoulder. When her eyes met his, they widened in surprise . . . then lit with a joy that stole his breath.

"Noah!" In an instant, she abandoned the spoon and rushed toward him, skirts swishing around her ankles. "I can't believe you're here."

Before he could respond, she launched into his arms, wrapping her own tight around his waist. He stumbled a step back but regained his footing and pulled her close against his chest.

Her body molded to his, warm and solid and real. He closed his eyes and breathed her in—the scent of lavender and woodsmoke and something uniquely Hope. Something he'd missed even more than he'd realized.

His hands moved of their own accord, sliding up to cradle her head as his fingers threaded through her silky hair. He felt her shudder, heard her sigh his name against his shirtfront. And just like that, every worry and fear melted away, replaced by a sense of rightness that settled deep in his bones.

This was where he belonged. Here, with Hope in his arms.

———⋎———

The sudden relief at seeing Noah again, of feeling his strong arms around her, made it hard to breathe, much less speak.

When Hope finally found her words, they came out choked and broken. "You're here. I can't . . . I can't believe you're here."

He stroked her back, not letting her go. Just holding her. She'd already lost control of her tears. *He came back, Lord. He came back. Thank You. Thank You for bringing him back.*

She needed to see his face now. Every handsome part of him. She pulled away, just enough to look up at him, then wiped her eyes to clear the blurriness. "I didn't expect you so soon. I figured with the weather you would be another month at least."

Those beautiful brown eyes sparkled, pleasure curving his mouth. "Do you think I could wait that long? Two months already felt like two years."

Her chest squeezed. To know he'd missed her too, that these months apart had been as hard for him . . . it meant more than she could say. More than she could show.

Noah kept one hand around her back, then used the other to brush away the remnants of her tears. His hand settled on her cheek. "I missed you." His voice rumbled with emotion. "Every day, every hour, every minute. I thought of you constantly, wondered what you were doing, if you were thinking of me too."

Hope leaned into his touch, savoring the warmth of his skin against hers. "I was. I prayed for your safe return, for God to watch over you and bring you back to me."

"He answered your prayers."

"He did." She reached up to trace the line of his jaw. He was really here, standing in front of her. "Did Miss Whitmore reach her father safely? And was he upset about your leave of absence?"

A mischievous sparkle lit Noah's eyes, and a smile played at the corners of his mouth. "Yes, Miss Whitmore arrived without incident. And as for Charles, he didn't begrudge my leave at all. In fact, I have some good news on that front, but I'll tell you about it later."

Curiosity burned through her. News? What could he possibly have? She gripped his wrist. "Tell me now. Please, Noah. I don't think I can bear the suspense."

He chuckled and shook his head. "I should have known better." He took her hand in his. "This might sound a bit presumptuous, but . . . Mr. Whitmore has suggested that I consider a different partnership in the business. He thinks we could start a transport branch across the territories, with me stationed somewhere near the middle of the route to have access to both ends. We would hire another man to assist with the work in the east."

Hope's heart leaped. "That's wonderful. Do you like the idea?"

He removed his other hand from her back, cradling both her hands in his. His gaze locked on her, intense and unwavering. "I like it a great deal, since it means I'll have the freedom to court you. Officially. If you'll have me, that is."

Joy exploded within her, so fierce that it stole her breath. She blinked back a fresh wave of tears, her smile trembling. "Oh, Noah. That's wonderful."

He grinned, relief and happiness etched into every line of his face. "I was hoping you'd say that."

As he lifted her hands to press a kiss to her fingertips, her mind spun through the days ahead. "Where will you stay? We're the only shelter for miles around. We haven't made much progress rebuilding the bunkhouse with so much snow." And she was fairly certain Martin wouldn't allow Noah to live under the same roof while he courted her.

His eyes held that twinkle. "I was hoping you and Martin

wouldn't mind me staying in the barn. At least until I can build other accommodations."

Yes. Still proper, yet wonderfully close. She couldn't stop her endless grin. "I think that will be perfect."

As he lowered his mouth to hers, she sank into the rightness of his touch. His presence here. His arms around her.

This moment was everything she'd hoped for, everything she'd prayed for.

Noah was home, and he was hers. Truly hers.

A Star in the West

KAREN WITEMEYER

Now when Jesus was born in Bethlehem of Judea in the days of Herod the king, behold, there came wise men from the east to Jerusalem . . . and, lo, the star, which they saw in the east, went before them, till it came and stood over where the young child was. When they saw the star, they rejoiced with exceeding great joy.

Matthew 2:1, 9-10

CHAPTER 1

THREE WISE MEN FROM THE EAST TO ARRIVE TOMORROW

The headline caught Stella Barrington's eye as she cleaned up her father's breakfast dishes. Grinning, she set aside the bowls she'd just stacked and picked up the folded newspaper.

Always one to appreciate a clever bit of writing, she unfolded the paper to view the column in its entirety. Stella already knew the basic details the article would cover since her father headed up the symposium committee at Baylor that was responsible for bringing the guest lecturers to town, but any columnist possessed of enough wit to draw in the nonacademic populace by teasing them with a nativity reference at this time of year deserved a read.

> Professor Albert Boggess, Chairman of Baylor University's Department of Mathematics, has put his background in astronomy to good use in guiding a trio of wise men from the east to our humble town for the upcoming Christmas season. Three professors from the hallowed halls of Harvard University will arrive on Tuesday to bestow their gifts of knowledge, prestige, and academic prowess upon a mathematics program still in its infancy.

203

Professor Ignatius Barrington called the visit "quite a coup" and expects the impact on students to be substantial. "These men represent some of the finest scientific minds our country has to offer," Barrington said. "Their combined research in the fields of mathematics, astronomy, and physics is groundbreaking. Exposing our students and faculty to such talented minds is a gift beyond price. A continued partnership with these learned men will propel our program into the next century as one of the top programs in the West."

Oh, Papa. You do have a flair for the dramatic. Stella grinned as she shook her head. Baylor might be the oldest university in Texas, but it couldn't yet compete with the top national programs in mathematics. Agriculture, yes. Mathematics . . . well, she loved her father's optimism, but she doubted his theoretical numbers lined up with those rooted in reality.

The article went on to highlight some of the visiting gentlemen's accolades. Professor Goldstein's recent article in the *American Journal of Mathematics*. Professor Muir's pioneering research on electromagnetic waves. The third professor was a protégé of James Mills Peirce, son of the late Benjamin Peirce, who many considered to be the father of American mathematics. One of her father's heroes.

Stella's stomach flipped as she read that last line. Surely it was mere coincidence. Mr. Peirce was bound to have more than one protégé. Her eyes flew over the rest of the article, searching for an unfamiliar name, one that would offer reassurance that disaster did not loom around the corner.

Considered one of the brightest young American minds in the field of mathematics, Professor Stentz recently received a prestigious Parker Fellowship to study in Germany under renowned mathematician Felix Klein at the University of Göttingen.

Stella's fingers lost all feeling. The newspaper plummeted to the floor.

No. It couldn't be. Professor Stentz coming here? Her stomach lurched. Why had her father not warned her? With all his excitement over the symposium, never once had he mentioned the names of the Harvard professors who would be visiting. Had he kept them from her intentionally?

She pressed a hand to her midsection, ordering it to settle. Of course Papa hadn't willfully kept things from her. He didn't have a deceitful bone in his body. Truth be told, he might have mentioned it in one of his evening rambles, and she'd not noticed. She'd been known to nod and offer the occasional *mmm* of encouragement without really listening when he started meandering down theoretical roads.

She'd inherited his love of academia, but literature interested her far more than mathematics. Yes, she was proficient in algebra, trigonometry, and the basics of Euclidean geometry, but when he started going on about various aspects of number theory, her level of comprehension, and therefore interest, dropped exponentially.

Even so, the probability of Frank Stentz's name being mentioned without her noticing was infinitesimal. Not with her heightened awareness of that particular personage. Every day she searched the mail in hopes of spotting his return address. And when she allowed herself foolish romantic daydreams, his was the name attached to her imaginary suitor. Yet in less than a day's time, he would no longer be imaginary. He'd be in her town, eventually in her home, very much in the flesh.

Good heavens. This was a disaster. Gripping the table's edge, Stella lowered herself onto the nearest chair.

She never should have started corresponding with the man. A part of her had known it to be folly. But she'd been in the middle of reading through all of Jane Austen's novels in the autumn of last year when Papa returned from a meeting of the newly formed New York Mathematical Society. The influx of happy endings for the Bennett sisters, Emma, and even the timid and plain Fanny Price must have temporarily altered Stella's brain chemistry with some sort of romantical infection, deafening her to the pragmatic voice that usually guided her actions.

Papa had been filled with stories when he came home, most of which centered around a young man he'd met with ties to the great Benjamin Peirce. Yet it wasn't just a love for pure mathematics that had bonded the two, but a shared faith as well. One of their discussions on the concept of infinity as developed from Cantor's set theory had taken a religious turn, and Mr. Stentz had invited Papa to Sunday services at the very church Papa had already planned to attend. Papa declared it a sign from above that God had a hand in bringing the two of them together.

"You'd like him, Stella. Polite. Devout. Absolutely brilliant, yet humble. Not one to toot his own horn, though he's not afraid to argue you into the ground during a theoretical debate. Respectfully, of course." He'd chuckled at that. *"He's near your age, too. Thirty, I think he said. Not the ancient scholars one generally meets at these types of functions."*

When a letter arrived the following week from Mr. Stentz, her father had read it to her, emphasizing the line where the gentleman had asked after his daughter.

"Why don't you scribble a few lines to the fellow?" Papa had urged. *"I'll include it with my letter. Might do the man good to have someone speak to him about matters not involving numbers."*

What a fool she'd been to agree. To think such a flirtation harmless. Writing a man who lived a thousand miles away had seemed safe enough. The two of them would never meet. He worked at Harvard, for pity's sake. She had nothing to fear in striking up a friendship. And when the letters had become more personal? Well, it was like living in her very own novel. A place where she could pretend to be beautiful and clever, the type of woman to engage the interest of a scholarly gentleman. A gentleman she'd come to respect and esteem. Perhaps even love.

Well, that book had just slammed closed, and reality had slapped her across the face. Frank—her Frank—was coming to Texas, and she'd no longer be able to pretend that anything romantic could exist between them. Because the moment he saw her, he'd see what every other eligible man in McLennan County saw—a plain spinster of eight and twenty years with no feminine attributes to attract a man's attention. Unfashionably tall, flat of chest and large of nose, with feet so long she had to have shoes specially made.

She'd accepted the truth about her destiny years ago. She'd not been built for marriage. God had selected another path for her. One that led her to take over the running of her father's household after her mother passed away ten years ago. One that gave her the freedom to serve as a volunteer sponsor for the Rufus Columbus Burleson Literary Society on campus, mentoring the female students who attended. One that allowed her to chair the nativity production committee at church.

Her life was fulfilling. Meaningful. She didn't need a man to validate her.

So why was the prospect of losing the regard of Mr. Frank Stentz slicing through her heart like an overzealous letter opener?

"Ready to begin collecting data, my boy?" Isaac Goldstein chuckled as he slapped Frank's shoulder, causing the bow tie he'd been straightening to go askew.

Frank frowned at his reflection in the small mirror hanging in the boardinghouse parlor and set the tie back on its proper axis, precisely perpendicular to the placket of buttons running down his shirt front. Perhaps revealing his experimental intentions to his colleagues had been an error in judgment. Yet any data collected needed to be analyzed impartially, and for once, Frank doubted his ability to be objective.

Besides, both Goldstein and Muir had wives, meaning they possessed a rudimentary knowledge of how to decipher feminine signals, an ability Frank found as impossible as dividing an integer by zero. Yes, they'd claimed their wives two and three decades ago, respectively, but they'd still accomplished the feat. And if he'd learned anything in the field of mathematical research, it was that one must build upon theorems already proven in order to advance one's understanding. Hence, his enlistment of the professors. Though, the amiable Goldstein was a more eager participant than the dour Mr. Muir.

"I still say this experiment is a waste of resources." Randolph Muir tugged on his shirt cuff until a small strip of white extended beyond the black of his coat sleeve. "You've been offered a chance to study under Felix Klein. At Göttingen! The most renowned institute for mathematical research in the world. You'd be a fool to give up the chance for a doctorate just to court a woman. Parker Fellowships don't grow on trees, you know."

Frank turned away from the mirror. "I'm aware."

He bit back the retort that sprang to his tongue. He couldn't blame Muir for speaking the truth. He'd had the same argument with himself for the last three months. Studying in Germany with some of the finest minds in the field was an amazing opportunity. It would undoubtedly launch his academic career and all but guarantee his tenure at Harvard. Yet he'd be alone. Oh, he'd have students and colleagues, and of course his numbers, but lately he'd developed an ache in his chest that flared at the lack of company at his breakfast table or when he crawled into bed alone at night.

If he turned down the fellowship, it wouldn't come again. But then, the chance to join his life to that of a woman who didn't find him peculiar and dull was proving equally rare. So which path should he pursue? Which offered the highest probability for long-term happiness? A complicated equation with hundreds of variables.

Achieving an advanced degree would put him on elite footing among his peers and deepen his understanding of a subject he'd loved since he'd first learned to count. Numbers were trustworthy and constant, though they could be mysterious and elusive as well. Untangling them and restoring order brought him rich satisfaction, like opening the drawers in a cabinet and finding everything precisely where it belonged. And discovering something new? Progressing the collective knowledge of mankind? Such an accomplishment could fulfill a man for a lifetime.

Academically.

But what about personally?

Accomplishments brought little happiness if one had no one with whom to share them. God had gifted him with a talent for mathematics, and he wanted to be a good steward of that gift, but there were many ways such a gift could be utilized.

The learned men who mentored him at Harvard had left an indelible mark on his life. They'd shaped his understanding of mathematical truth. Yet they hadn't shaped his character or his personality, his faith or his values. That impact had been made by people like his mother, his first-grade teacher, and the minister who shepherded the small flock in his hometown. People who loved and cared for him. People who invested in him as a person, not just an intellectual.

"Frank? Are you listening?"

Judging by the exasperated huff that accompanied the question, his colleague had been talking for some time.

"Sorry, Muir." Frank hung an imaginary sheet over the blackboard in his mind to hide the complex equations and probability analyses for predicting lifelong happiness. He'd have to ponder them later. "I drifted for a moment there. Calculating, you know."

Muir scowled. "You're worse than my first-year students, daydreaming about girls when there are serious scientific endeavors more worthy of your attention."

The shorter, plumper Goldstein inserted himself between Frank and Muir, a twinkle in his eye. "Now, Randy, I doubt your wife would appreciate being categorized as unworthy when compared to science."

Muir's face reddened. "That's not what I—"

"Of course it wasn't." Goldstein chuckled. "Now, let's quit arguing about Frank's future and start helping him collect data so he can see which hypothesis has the most promise." He leaned toward Frank and gave a wink. "I'm rooting for love."

"You can't root for anything while collecting data, you old windbag." Muir shook his head. "The experiment has to be impartial."

"That's why I'm rooting for love. To balance you pulling for Germany." Goldstein slapped Muir on the back and headed for the boardinghouse door. "No use pretending to be unbiased. You've already revealed your compromised state. Now, let's go. I don't want to be late for dinner."

Only then did Frank think to check the clock ticking on the mantel. Good heavens! How long had he been lost in thought? Grabbing his hat off the chair where he'd left it, he hurried out of the parlor. One couldn't impress a woman with punctuality if he failed to appear at the appointed time. And when a man possessed as few impressive qualities as Frank did where women were concerned, he couldn't afford to squander even one.

Most ladies found him odd and socially inept. Not that he could argue with their assessment. Facts were facts, after all. And since he possessed neither the wealth nor looks required to encourage women to ignore these well-documented oddities, he was already starting at a deficit.

Frank collected his overcoat from the stand and held the front door wide for his companions, silently urging them to hurry. Once outside, he quickly calculated the maximum stride length he could engage while still allowing his companions to match pace. Pressing them to greater speed produced the added benefit of limiting conversation, though he did feel a twinge of guilt when Muir began huffing slightly. Thankfully, Professor Barrington's home was nearby, though a creek forced them to walk an extra couple of blocks out of the way to find a bridge.

Each step that brought Frank closer to the Barrington home should have relieved his anxiety, but the opposite proved true.

What would Stella think of him? Her letters indicated a positive opinion had been formed over the last months of their correspondence, but he'd been able to show himself to best advantage in his letters. One had time to think of just the right phrase when writing a letter. To order his words in a pleasing fashion. To recall an amusing anecdote. He'd revised each missive at least three times before trusting it to the postmaster. Meeting in person didn't provide that luxury. Spoken words couldn't be edited or erased.

Don't let me bungle this, Lord.

Though if he did, he supposed he'd know the Lord intended him for Germany.

A cowardly part of him wanted to ignore the number on

the side of the small home on South Fourth Street and circle back to the boardinghouse. But he needed answers, and one couldn't solve a complex equation without directly engaging the problem.

So with a stiffening of his spine and a prayer in his heart, Frank mounted the steps of Number 1405 and rang the bell.

CHAPTER 2

The buzz of the doorbell pierced Stella's calm like the sudden sting of a bumblebee. She startled so severely, she nearly dropped the pot roast she was taking out of the oven.

Pull yourself together. Tonight is about Papa, not you.

Stella tightened her grip on the roasting pan and set it on top of the stove. Tossing the pot holders aside, she took a breath and steadied her nerves.

She could do this. Tonight was a work dinner, like any of the dozens of others they had hosted in their home. She would smile and serve during the meal, then disappear into the kitchen to clean up. Mr. Stentz need not be under any obligation to converse with her personally. Discussions would center on the symposium. She'd make sure of it. There'd be no need for awkwardness between them. No promises had been made, no expectations expressed. Frank—no, *Mr. Stentz*—was simply a friend. A colleague of her father's. She'd not embarrass either of them by fawning over him or behaving in any way flirtatious. Such actions would only paint her a fool. Besides, she admired him too much to force him into an uncomfortable position. He'd escape the evening unscathed, and their paths need never cross again.

Papa's voice boomed through the small house, his excitement adding to his volume as he welcomed the Harvard professors. Stella ordered her mind to focus on moving the roast and vegetables to the serving platter, but her ears rebelled, straining to pick out the unfamiliar voices so that she might identify which belonged to the man who penned her letters. She resorted to humming to drown out the foreign sounds and finally managed to get the roast sliced and the potatoes, carrots, and onions arranged in an orderly fashion. Scientific minds appreciated precision, and she aimed to please. For her father's sake. Not because she sought to make a good impression on any particular person.

The same rationale had inspired her choice of attire. She'd selected the pale green dress to reflect well on her father. The fact that the ladies of the literary society had once mentioned that the color complemented her complexion had little to do with it.

"As little as yeast has to do with dough rising," she muttered as she took the bread bowl from the warmer.

But there was no harm in wanting to look one's best. Even an unattractive woman could take pride in her appearance. Tidiness and cleanliness were worthy virtues. Besides, God had arranged her features the way he'd seen fit, and she'd not argue with the Creator over his artistic inclinations. He hadn't given her beauty, but he'd given her other blessings—ones she wouldn't trade even if offered the choice. A loving home, a supportive faith community, a passion for learning, and an empathy for others struggling to find their way. Things that carried lasting value.

Still, she dreaded seeing disappointment flash in Mr. Stentz's eyes. She'd had thirty-six hours to prepare herself for the inevitability of such an occurrence, but knowing what was coming wouldn't dull the sting.

Squaring her shoulders, Stella picked up the platter and backed through the swinging door that led to the dining room. Might as well get it over with. At least dispose of the dread hanging over her like a cloud.

The drone of male voices dropped away as she entered. She pasted a smile on her face as she turned to face the room.

"Ah, here's my daughter now."

She heard her father speaking, but her eyes had yet to find him. They'd snagged on a thin man standing near the hutch that displayed her mother's china.

He had red hair. She hadn't expected that. Red and a bit unruly. Her smile widened at that observation, then froze in place when his gaze met hers from across the table. Blue eyes. Lovely, intelligent blue eyes—that immediately shuttered as his gaze moved to somewhere in the vicinity of the nearest place setting.

A burning sensation flared in her stomach. At least he'd masked his disappointment by hiding his gaze. She supposed she should be thankful for that small kindness. Yet his rejection still hurt. Thankfully, she had years of practice hiding hurt behind false cheerfulness.

"Good evening, gentlemen." She held up the platter. "I hope you like pot roast."

"It smells divine." The shortest of the visitors smiled at her, his fluffy sideburns making up for the thinning hair on top of his head.

"Stella is a marvelous cook," Papa bragged as she set the platter in the center of the table. "You're in for a treat." He held his arm out to her. "Come, my dear. Let me introduce you to our guests."

She moved to her father's side, careful to keep her gaze from straying to the redheaded man with the loose-fitting suit and clean-shaven chin. Gracious. Had she really cataloged that many details about him in the fraction of time she'd allowed herself to look at him?

"This is Professor Goldstein."

Stella focused on the jovial man in front of her and offered a smile. "Welcome to our home, Professor."

"It's an honor, Miss Barrington."

"And this fellow is Professor Muir, our physics expert." Papa directed her attention to a man with a long face hemmed by a well-trimmed, dark gray beard. He didn't exactly frown at her, but his smile resembled more of a straight line than an arc.

"Miss Barrington." He spoke with the cultured tones of one long acquainted with the stature of elite academia.

"Professor Muir." She dipped her chin in deference, sensing that would curry more favor than a pleasant grin.

"And this young rapscallion is Professor Stentz."

Courage, Stella.

Locking her hostess smile in place, she turned her gaze to Mr. Stentz, who seemed to be looking everywhere *except* at her. A touch of sympathy rose within her. She understood all too well how it felt to have one's dreams dashed. And if he had harbored any romantic notions toward her at all, he was likely at a loss over how to pick up the scattered pieces without *looking* like he was picking up pieces. Perhaps she could relieve him of some of that burden.

"Welcome, Professor Stentz. My father has spoken of you often over the last year. The two of you have planned a remarkable symposium. I have no doubt that Baylor students will talk of it for years to come. I only wish I had time to sit in on some of the lectures, but I'm afraid that other responsibilities demand my attention during the Christmas season. I'll have to settle for hearing Papa recount the details to me."

Her father gave her an odd look, but she barely noticed,

for Mr. Stentz chose that moment to finally meet her gaze. And heavens, what an impact. Reverberations quaked in her chest. She'd expected relief, possibly even gratitude, to reflect in those keen blue eyes, not a soulful penetration that searched her depths for an answer to a complicated equation.

"I'm . . . ah . . . sorry to hear that, Miss Barrington." His gaze dropped to somewhere around her extra-large shoes, and his fingers subtly churned at the air. "I had hoped to d-deepen our acquaintance while in town."

Goodness. Had he just . . . ? No, surely she'd misheard. Even a true suitor wouldn't just blurt out his intentions while in the presence of others at a dinner party.

"Stella manages my correspondence," her father inserted into the charged silence, "and has exchanged a few letters with Stentz on my behalf regarding symposium business."

"Of course," Mr. Goldstein interjected with a wink. "Only natural for two people who have corresponded to wish to meet. Scientific minds are ripe with curiosity, and Frank is nothing if not scientific."

Mr. Goldstein chuckled, and Papa joined in at a heartier level than the comment warranted. Stella smiled, thankful to have a distraction to cover her retreat to the kitchen. She needed to collect the rolls—and her wits.

Because if Frank Stentz had meant what he said, she might have to recalibrate her expectations.

———•▼•———

Frank wasn't precisely sure where he'd stepped wrong, but if Muir's eye roll was any indication, he'd managed to plant his foot in a knee-deep manure pile. He bit back a groan.

Why must social interaction be so nuanced? Why couldn't a man just state what he was thinking without worrying about how it might be construed? This was why he preferred numbers to people. Numbers were exactly as they appeared to be. One didn't have to guess at their meaning. They spoke plainly and acted in a predictable manner. One needn't fret over inadvertently causing them offense or making them uncomfortable.

His shoulders sagged as he took his place at the table. He'd made Stella uncomfortable. Probably even embarrassed her. Two outcomes that would complicate his courtship calculations. Of course, there might not even *be* a courtship at this rate. Not if she didn't want to see him. Her statement, if taken at face value, seemed to indicate as much.

But her letters had revealed a different woman—one willing to share things with him. When she wrote of books she'd read or concerts she'd attended or of something she'd seen while walking along the river, she mentioned a wish that he'd been there to experience whatever had brought her delight. *That* woman had been eager for his company.

So which version more accurately portrayed the woman before him? The Stella who'd captured his heart with her letters? Or the Miss Barrington who couldn't rid herself of him fast enough?

Neither version said much during the meal. After her father said grace, Stella asked about the symposium, and as one would expect with a quartet of academics at the table, the conversation never veered back to her. A shame, that. Frank hungered for knowledge about the lady sitting across from him with the thick brown hair and big brown eyes. So far, all this evening had taught him was that she was a good cook and didn't mind being ignored by the men at her table.

Well, most of the men. Frank had not ignored her in the slightest. A fact she'd have to be obtuse not to comprehend, and from what he knew of her from her letters, she was anything but obtuse. However, each time she caught him staring, her mouth had flattened instead of lifting at the corners. He'd checked. After taking a heartbeat to gather his courage and lift his gaze out of his supper, where it inevitably dropped each time her eyes found his. Wouldn't a woman who welcomed a man's attention smile if that man showed interest?

Frank contributed few comments to the dinner conversation. Even Muir's obvious baiting by misquoting Peano's axioms failed to draw him from his distraction for more than the moment it took to point out that not all the axioms utilized first-order logic. Peano's principles of arithmetic clearly stated that the ninth axiom employed second-order logic.

Hmm. Second-order logic. Frank sat a little straighter as his gaze slid back to the woman pouring after-dinner coffee for the men. What if he considered Stella a *set* instead of an *individual*? A grouping of numerous variables, even those that seemed incongruous, that all related and informed the identity of the whole. If Stella was *both* the woman who wanted to share her sunset walks by the river with him *and* the woman who sought to avoid him when he was sitting in her dining room, a logical explanation must exist to correctly define her behavior. He just had to puzzle it out.

Frank grinned as anticipation eradicated his discouragement. Nothing like a good puzzle to raise a mathematician's spirits.

Yet one couldn't puzzle out variables if they were beyond his range of observation. Frank frowned at the door Stella had disappeared through. It no longer quivered on its hinges. How long ago had she departed? One minute? Two? He glanced back at the table and counted coffee cups. Four. In front of the men only. No cup sat at her place. She didn't plan to return.

That would never do. If he didn't speak to her tonight, he might not get another chance. Not if she chose to avoid him the entire time he was in town.

Excusing himself from the table, Frank exited the dining room in the direction of the entry hall and the small lavatory Ignatius had pointed out when they'd first arrived. He diverted at the last moment, however, and searched out another point of entry for the kitchen. Spying a doorway a few paces down on the left side of the hall, he tiptoed toward it and peeked inside. She sat at a small table, book in one hand, coffee cup in the other. A peaceful scene. One he oughtn't disturb.

Nevertheless, he squared his shoulders and crossed the threshold.

"Miss Barrington," he whispered.

She gasped, dropping her book onto the table with a rather loud *thump* as she spun in her chair to face him. "Mr. Stentz?" Thankfully she matched his hushed tone and didn't scream out her surprise. "What on earth are you doing here?"

"May I . . . speak with you?"

Her gaze flew to the swinging door that led to the dining room. "I don't think—"

"Please?" His mother had always insisted that word carried magical properties, and for the first time, he believed it might be possible. What else could explain Stella swallowing her protest and offering a reluctant nod?

She motioned for him to take the chair opposite hers.

Hope swelled within him. "Thank you." He hurried to seat himself and then leaned forward, keeping his voice pitched low. "Miss Barrington . . . Stella . . ." Was it permissible to use her given name? They did in their letters, but perhaps things were different in person. "Miss Barrington. It's my hope that you would permit me to call upon you while I'm in town."

She shook her head, and Frank's heart deflated. "You are under no obligation to call on me, Mr. Stentz." A smile curved her lips this time, but her eyes failed to illuminate. "And I will completely understand if you wish to cease our correspondence. I know I'm not the type of woman men wish to call upon."

What? All Frank could manage was a trio of blinks as he tried to assimilate a piece of information that made no logical sense whatsoever. "I assure you, my intentions are quite genuine."

"That's very kind of you to say, but I'm well aware that my appearance is, shall we say, lacking."

She smiled again, and the sad acceptance that accompanied it made him unaccountably angry. And confused. She thought herself lacking? Lacking what? All the appropriate parts were present and arranged in the typical manner.

"I see nothing lacking."

Pink colored her cheeks. "No need to be polite, sir. I saw you divert your eyes when you first beheld me." He began to protest, but she held up a hand. "It's all right. There's a reason I've reached the ripe old age of twenty-eight without having a suitor."

Her insinuation made his jaw clench. He looked her straight in the eye and refused to let his nervousness divert his gaze again. "You're right. There *is* a reason you haven't yet had a suitor. Because until today, I was in Massachusetts. I apologize for my tardiness."

Now it was her turn to blink. Once. Twice. Three times. "You're in earnest?"

He nodded. Then, just to ensure there was no misunderstanding, he added words. "I am."

Slowly, her lips curved into another smile, a small one that didn't even show her teeth. Yet it caused his pulse to pound in a terribly chaotic fashion. For this one, small as it was, reached her eyes and warmed her entire countenance.

CHAPTER 3

"Perhaps this wasn't a good idea."

Stella cringed inwardly as the young ladies of the R.C.B. Literary Society flocked around Frank on the lawn in front of Burleson Hall. They peppered him with questions and assaulted him with a mixture of batting eyelashes and antagonistic glares. Like an ill-prepared soldier thrust into battle, Frank flinched and dodged, tripping over both his words and his feet.

"Is it true they don't allow women to study at Harvard?" Rose Atwater accused, her eyebrows slanting behind her wire-rimmed spectacles.

Frank stumbled sideways a step. "Ah . . . technically, yes, but there's an Annex where, ah, females receive instruction directly from Harvard professors. I taught a course there last term, as a matter of fa—"

"So you condone the subjugation of women in institutions of higher learning?"

Frank's eyes rounded like a hunted animal cornered by a predator. "That's not what I—"

Annabelle Raymond sidled up so close to Frank that her black-checked skirt brushed his trouser leg. "Pay her no mind, Mr. Stentz. Rose is still sore from losin' our suffrage debate last week." Annabelle's accent thickened as she laid on the southern charm. The sound grated on Stella's nerves. Normally she adored Annabelle, but at the moment, Stella found her display of feminine wiles vastly annoying. "I'm sooooo lookin' forward to attendin' your lecture tomorrow on the transformational nature of pi, Professor."

"Transcendental," Frank corrected as he scooted a few inches away. "Lindemann proved pi to be transcendental *not* transformational." He cast an anxious glance at Annabelle's skirt, as if it were made of nettles that would sting him if they got too close.

A third young lady, Margaret Olson, jostled Annabelle out of the way and inserted herself into the vacated space. Stella bit back a groan. Could they not see how unsettled they were making him?

"The only pi you understand, Annabelle, is the kind you can eat." Margaret turned to Frank. "I, on the other hand, am in Professor Barrington's geometry class this term and am quite efficient in calculating circular areas."

"Speaking of calculating circular areas," Stella inserted into the quickly deteriorating conversation, "why don't we apply some of our mathematical knowledge, ladies." Before they henpecked Frank to pieces. "If Professor Stentz is the center of a circle with a radius of three feet and wishes to conduct conversation only with those standing at or beyond the circumference of said circle, where should each of us position ourselves?"

"Oh, oh, oh, I know this!" Annabelle bounced on her toes. "If the radius is three feet, then the diameter would be six—"

Margaret rolled her eyes as she took hold of Annabelle's arm and tugged her backward. "For pity's sake, Annabelle. It's not a real math problem. Miss Barrington is just trying to get us to stop crowding the professor."

"Oh." Annabelle's face flamed as she retreated.

"Your calculations were quite sound, though," Frank said, daring a quick glance at the young woman before diverting his gaze to a tree some distance away.

Stella's heart warmed. It spoke well of a man to look past his own discomfort to soothe the discomfort of another.

Annabelle brightened at the professor's approval, but she made sure to respect Stella's arbitrary boundary. "I'll see you at the lecture tomorrow, Professor."

Frank offered a tight smile. "I'll be there."

And he would probably be ready to run in the opposite direction should Annabelle approach him again. Stella bit back a grin. Poor man. She should probably warn her father about the ladies' reactions so he could take precautionary measures to keep Frank from being bombarded. Apparently Baylor's female population found Harvard men quite intriguing. At least the ones under forty. She doubted Professors Goldstein and Muir were experiencing the same flood of attention.

"Come on, girls," Rose Atwater announced with the authority that came from being the oldest student of the group. "Let's leave Miss Barrington to her beau. We don't want to risk receiving a demerit for failing to arrive at the library on time for study hall."

Annabelle's gaze flew to Stella. "Your *beau*? Mercy, Miss Barrington. Why didn't you say so?"

Now *Stella's* face was the one flaming.

The other girls tittered as they followed Rose away from the dormitory where their literary society met toward the main academic building. Annabelle, however, hurried to Stella's side and took her hand.

Leaning close, she murmured an apology in a quiet voice. "I never would have flirted with the professor had I known he was your fella, Miss Barrington."

Annabelle had struggled to fit in with the other girls when she first arrived at Baylor last fall. Her lack of academic focus and the inconsequential standing of her family had made it difficult to connect with other students. She'd been sent to school on scholarship since her father was a preacher, and while Annabelle had never admitted to anything scandalous in her past, Stella had pieced together enough of her story to infer that the Raymonds had sent their daughter to school to extricate her from a relationship they deemed unsuitable. As a Christian institution, Baylor had a reputation for strict propriety when it came to educating their female students. Policy prohibited young ladies from accepting the attentions of men while enrolled. Annabelle struggled to embrace the restrictive confines, and Stella did her best to provide gentle guidance as well as a sympathetic ear whenever Annabelle grew discouraged.

Stella patted Annabelle's hand. "Professor Stentz is not my beau. He's simply a friend and a colleague of my father's. Nothing more." At least not yet.

Not yet? As if a change was guaranteed. Nothing in life was guaranteed, especially her ability to win the affections of a man like Frank Stentz. Goodness! He was bound for Germany in a few months. Germany! An entire ocean away. Even if something did bloom between them, nothing could come of it for several years because she'd never abandon Papa to travel overseas.

But wouldn't she also be abandoning him if she moved to Massachusetts?

Her stomach churned. She couldn't leave Papa. He needed her. Who would make his breakfast and press his shirts? What had she been thinking? This was a mistake.

"Miss Barrington?" Annabelle squeezed her hand. "Are you all right?"

"O-of course." Well, that wobbly assurance would fool no

one. Least of all herself. She forced a smile onto her face, but Annabelle's grip on her hand only tightened.

"Don't let fear steal your chance for happiness, Miss Barrington," Annabelle whispered. "If God can make a path through the Red Sea, he can clear a way through whatever obstacles stand in front of you, too. So don't go running back to Egypt just yet."

As if the words had unlocked the door to a storm cellar, Stella dove inside the shelter they provided and closed the door on the tornado threatening to spin her mind out of control. Blinking, she peered at the young girl before her with new eyes. "What wise counsel, Miss Raymond."

An impish grin lit Annabelle's face. "I stole that advice from my eldest sister. It's what she told me the night before I left home to come to school." Her expression sobered, and her shoulders bobbed in a shrug. "It reminded me that holding tight to something just because it's familiar isn't always as safe or good as one might think. Sometimes we have to try something new to discover blessings only God can see."

The howling storm abated a little more, and Stella managed to inhale a full breath. "Excellent advice." She took another breath for good measure and let the brittleness around her forced smile soften into something more genuine. "How perceptive of you to recognize my need to hear it."

Annabelle beamed, and she stood a little taller. "I'm glad it helped." She gave Stella's hand a final squeeze, then hurried off to catch up with the other girls. "See you later!"

Stella raised her hand in farewell, then turned to search for Frank. She found him intently studying a set of bricks in the dormitory wall a few steps away.

Clasping her hands behind her back to hide her residual nervousness, she moved toward him. "They've gone."

He twisted to face her, his gaze glancing off her face to fall to the ground before making a slow climb back to her eyes. As she waited for him to reply, it dawned on her that he'd never made eye contact with any of the other young ladies either. Ladies who were all quite attractive, intelligent, and vibrant. Could it be that it wasn't *her* that he found difficult to look at, but people in general? Or at least *new* people with whom he hadn't yet established a level of comfort?

His eyes finally connected with hers, and she suddenly felt glad that he didn't share them with others on a regular basis. They were quite extraordinary. Bright blue, like a summer sky. Yet it wasn't their color that captivated her so much as what she saw in their depths. Intelligence mixed with an endearing uncertainty. Probing mixed with patience. Admiration mixed with . . . attraction? Her pulse fluttered despite the logic that insisted she must have misinterpreted that last element.

"I hope you don't think me cowardly for evading your friends. I've never been adept at conversing about things outside the realm of mathematics."

"I don't find you cowardly in the least," Stella assured him. "Anyone would have been caught off guard by that swarm of young ladies. When you offered to walk me home after my literary society meeting, I thought only of the convenience of us both being on campus at the same time. I didn't consider the likelihood of my ladies ambushing you."

Frank stepped away from the building and came alongside her. "I'll be better prepared next time."

Next time. How strange that two simple words could spread such warmth through a person. Feeling as if she'd just been hugged, Stella steered their trajectory toward the creek that ran along the west side of campus.

"When the weather is nice, I like to follow the creek home.

It's not a very direct path, but it's peaceful and affords a rather scenic view."

"Sounds like an excellent route." He fell into step beside her, allowing her to lead the way.

Neither said anything as they wound through the students milling around the buildings, but as they left the school behind, the silence between them began to grow uncomfortable. Stella searched for something to say that didn't have to do with the weather and came up empty.

Thankfully, Frank filled the void. "Tell me something about yourself that I don't know from your letters."

"All right. Let's see . . ." Her mind remained stubbornly blank.

She'd already told him of her hobbies and activities. He knew of the passing of her mother and her literature studies. She'd shared her favorite books, confessed her lack of singing voice, and even mentioned her fondness for the color green. What else was there to tell?

"How about your middle name? Do you have one?" Frank offered, and Stella latched onto the simple topic with relief.

"Celeste."

"Stella Celeste." His gaze left the trail ahead long enough to caress her face before dipping back down. "It suits you. A star in the heavens."

She blushed at the poetic-sounding compliment even though she knew he was just reciting the literal meaning. "My father has always been fascinated by astronomy, and I happened to be born one month after the discovery of Sirius B, the companion star to Sirius. Papa read the paper by George Phillips Bond on the subject and decided at once that I was to have a name fitting of such a find."

Frank's head came up. "I remember studying that paper. Bond

ran the Harvard observatory at the time. A pair of telescope makers in Cambridgeport alerted him of the find, I believe."

"That's right. Alvan Clark and his father." She smiled. Not many people around here knew of the Clarks or cared much about their work from nearly three decades ago. It was nice to share the story with someone who could appreciate it the way she and Papa did.

"How about you?" she asked when silence threatened to intrude again. "Do *you* have a middle name?"

"I do. Nothing quite as stellar as yours, however."

She chuckled softly at his pun. "I'm sure it's delightful."

"The name itself is fine. It's the repercussions that carry unfortunate results. In fact, I tend not to share it with anyone unless legally required to do so."

Stella slowed her steps as they reached the creek. Instead of turning to walk along the bank, she halted and pivoted to face him. He was choosing to share something private with her. Something intimate. Her pulse quickened. "You have me quite intrigued, sir."

"Like yours, my father has long been fascinated by scientific matters. One of his favorite hobbies around the time of my birth was to research historical mathematicians. His favorite was John Napier, a sixteenth-century Scottish scholar and the Eighth Laird of Merchiston. He apparently came to be known as the Marvelous Merchiston."

Stella stifled a giggle. "Oh my."

"Quite the moniker, isn't it? Father said he was deserving of the title since he discovered logarithms, invented a calculating device known as Napier's bones, and popularized the use of the decimal point."

"Three quite impressive accomplishments. I suppose those could qualify him for 'marvelous' status."

"My father thought so. Of course, he also thought it marvelous to saddle his son with the name *Napier*."

"It could have been worse. You could have been named for Anaxagoras, *my* father's favorite."

Frank chuckled, a rich, delightful sound that instantly made her heart lighter. "Yes. That's certainly worse. Although it would have helped with my secondary problem."

"And what problem is that? To my ear, Frank Napier Stentz carries a very distinguished ring."

Frank shot her a self-conscious grin. "Try just the middle initial. See how that rings."

"Frank N. Stentz?" It took a moment, but when she repeated it to herself silently at a faster clip, it hit her.

Laughter exploded from her in a burst. She slapped a hand over her mouth to try to hold it in, but when she caught the twinkle in Frank's eyes, she gave up the fight.

A man with ties to the nativity after all. And one apparently possessed of enough humility and humor to poke fun at himself while inviting her to know him better. Could anything be more charming? Or dangerous?

Losing her heart to this man would be so easy. But would it lead to losing her father?

Stella fell silent as she resumed their walk along the creek. She'd promised Mama to take care of Papa, and she'd not go back on her vow. If the Lord didn't make a path for her to somehow keep them both, she'd have to let Frank go.

CHAPTER 4

Frank surreptitiously flipped open the lid of his pocket watch and checked the time. His jaw clenched.

Wrap it up, Muir. You've already gone four minutes over.

He wasn't usually one to clock-watch, but these were extraordinary circumstances. For the first time in ages, the real world captivated him more than the theoretical one. And in the real world, a certain delightful lady had invited him to join her in a carpentry project at the church following the afternoon symposium session. A session that should have concluded—he checked his watch again—six minutes ago.

Muir's voice droned on about the apparatus German physicist Heinrich Hertz built in 1887 to generate and detect electromagnetic waves and the experiments Muir himself had been conducting on those Hertzian waves. Such an innovative area of research should have held Frank's attention easily, but he found his mind wandering to Stella instead.

He'd enjoyed her company five times in the last ten days. Twice, he and the other visiting professors had supped in her home. Once, he'd walked her home from her literary society meeting, and last Sunday he'd attended church with her and her father. Sitting next to her on the pew had made concentrating

233

on the preacher's sermon quite a challenge, but sharing a hymnal as they sang had been a complete delight. Even her slightly off-key singing hadn't dimmed his pleasure.

However, his favorite outing transpired yesterday, when they'd strolled across the Waco Suspension Bridge. The weather had turned chilly, driving most people indoors. He'd offered to take her home if she'd rather not be out in the wind, but she'd opted to brave the cold, which afforded them a bit of privacy on their stroll. They'd stopped halfway across the bridge, leaned against the railing, and simply watched the Brazos River flow beneath them. Despite the winter nip in the air that numbed their ears and chapped their cheeks, it had been a glorious outing. He'd had her all to himself for nearly an hour.

They'd spoken of his family and hers. Of the differences between eastern society and life in Texas. Of how mathematics and art blended in various forms, like music and kaleidoscopes and architecture. The very bridge they stood upon served as a ready example of how one enhanced the other.

It had been a rather obvious ploy to convince her that the two of them might make a suitable pairing, but she hadn't debated his points. In fact, she'd even brought up DaVinci's Vitruvian Man in support of his argument. A fact that brought him significant encouragement. Yet with the symposium scheduled to conclude at the end of next week, he needed more than encouragement. The early data he'd collected seemed to support his theory that a courtship with Stella was possible, but he lacked evidentiary confirmation.

Applause broke out around him, tearing Frank from his thoughts and bringing him back into the realm of time. Time! He checked his watch again, horrified to see it was now twenty past the hour. He lurched to his feet so quickly, he cracked his knee on the chair desk. Giving his throbbing appendage a quick rub, he limped toward the exit, scattering *pardon*s around him like seed among chickens as he forced his way upstream through the crowd of students flocking to the front of the room to speak to Professor Muir.

Once in the hall, Frank stretched his stride as far as it would extend and ignored the odd looks aimed in his direction. He was aware of the ridiculous manner in which his hips wiggled as he maximized his walking velocity. Snickering echoed in his wake, but he paid it no mind. Getting to Stella in a timely manner took precedence, and as long as he wasn't running in the halls, he was breaking no rules.

He took the steps a little faster and would have broken into a jog when he hit the lawn if he hadn't spotted Mrs. Georgia Burleson, the wife of Baylor University's president, exiting the women's dormitory next door. She raised an eyebrow in his direction that reined in his would-be canter before it could begin.

"Ma'am." Frank smiled and tipped his hat to her, forcing his feet to the stodgy pace expected of a university professor.

She smiled and nodded her approval. "Mr. Stentz."

He kept to his torturously slow pace until he passed a pair of trees at an angle sufficiently positioned to conceal his undignified flight. Launching into a run, he raced along the path up to Fifth Street, turned left, and hurried toward town.

After dashing down three blocks, Frank grew winded and was forced to slow. Probably a good thing. A gentleman was less likely to impress a lady if he showed up sweaty and panting. Thankfully, the cool December air kept his perspiration to a minimum, and by the time he crossed the railroad tracks and entered the churchyard, his breathing had returned to normal.

Until he rounded the corner and spied Stella smiling up at a tall, muscular fellow carting lumber on his shoulder with the same ease one would carry toothpicks. One of those burly types who were naturally athletic, coordinated, and capable of fixing or building things without understanding one iota of the science behind what they did.

Frank's stomach churned, but he strode forward anyway. He might not compare favorably as a physical specimen in this man's shadow, but Stella had invited him, and he'd not let old insecurities deter him. He had his own strengths to recommend him, ones that Stella seemed to appreciate.

As fate would have it, Mr. Muscles noticed him first. Frank braced himself for disapproval or even condescension, but he was greeted with neither. The man welcomed him with a big grin, as if he'd been eagerly waiting Frank's arrival.

"Professor!" Boards clattered to the ground as the fellow dropped his load, wiped off his hand, and jogged forward to greet him. "It's an honor to have you helping us today, sir."

Frank shook the man's hand and grinned in return, his genuine enthusiasm contagious. "Call me Frank."

"Norman." The carpenter tilted his head toward the framed crèche that would serve as the backdrop for the nativity production scheduled for next weekend. "Stella's been telling us all about you. She even hinted that you and your cronies might be willing to step into the role of the three wise men this year. We're bound to draw twice the usual crowd with you fellas involved. I'd wager half of the Baylor student body would show up just to see a trio of esteemed Harvard professors dressed in costume. Folks from the community will surely want to take a gander, too."

Stella quickened her step to join them, her worried expression making something pinch in his chest. "I merely mentioned the possibility, Frank. No promises have been made. I intended to speak to you about it while we worked." She shot Norman a chiding look before turning back to Frank and placing a hand

on his arm. "You're under absolutely no obligation to participate. The only reason I even considered asking you was because
the paper ran an article the day before you arrived, announcing
that three wise men from the east were coming to visit. I thought
to build on that bit of notoriety to draw more community interest to the nativity production. Perhaps convince some to attend
who wouldn't usually come to a religious event."

Her lovely brown eyes gazed at him as if he had the power to
grant her dearest wish. And the touch of her hand on his arm
had his pulse rate increasing in exponential fashion. "We'll be
happy to do it."

The smile that broke across her face made his chest expand
like an aeronaut's balloon. He had no idea how he would convince Muir to go along, but he'd apply whatever force was
required to overcome the stuffy fellow's inertia. Frank had a
chance to be Stella's hero, and he'd not squander it.

"Great!" Norman slapped him on the back and nearly sent
him stumbling off his axis. "My wife and I get to play Mary and
Joseph this year. The honor goes to the couple with the youngest babe in the congregation. We missed the cut two years ago
when our first was born in June, but Millie had the good sense
to arrive in September." He chuckled as he moved back toward
the crèche and pulled a hammer from a nearby toolbox. "You
don't have to worry about memorizin' lines or anything. The
parson reads the script, and all you gotta do is follow what he
says. Easy as fallin' off a log."

"That's reassuring. I have no prior experience as a thespian."

Norman picked up a board, laid it flush against the frame,
and reached into his leather apron for a nail. "Just follow
Stella." He looked away from the board he held and sent Frank
a wink. "I can tell you got a knack for that."

"Norman!" Stella's cheeks flamed red as the carpenter

chuckled. She turned her back on him and took a few steps away to separate herself from the source of her embarrassment.

Frank followed, then smiled at the irony. "The man's not wrong."

"I'm sorry. Norman likes to tease. Pay him no mind." Her hands fluttered in front of her like a pair of doves that didn't know where to land. "I play the role of the star in the play, you see. That's all he meant. I dress in black, cover my face with a mourning veil, and carry a long rod with a painted tin star attached to the top. The magi follow me to find the baby Jesus."

Frank captured one of her fluttering hands and nestled it between his. "Why do you veil your face?"

She stilled. Whether it was his touch or his question that had evoked the reaction, he couldn't determine, but he liked the feel of her fingers lying within his palm too much to release them just to test a theory.

"I'm supposed to be invisible," she finally said, her voice low. "It is the star that is supposed to garner attention, not me. I prefer it that way, actually. That's why I volunteer for the role every year."

"Ah. I guess I can understand the veil, then. Your lovely face would certainly distract me."

She dropped her chin and tugged her hand free of his hold. "Don't lie to me, Frank. I know my face is far from beautiful."

"I speak the truth, Stella." He crooked a finger under her chin and gently tipped her face up for his inspection. "Your eyes shimmer with intelligence and kindness, your lips are evenly distributed across both cheeks when you smile, and your nose is perfectly centered in the oval of your face. You've been blessed with beautiful symmetry."

She blinked at him, her brow furrowing slightly. "You find my face . . . symmetrical?"

Drat. He knew he'd bungle things. He might find geometric balance beautiful, but Goldstein had warned him that women preferred poetry to science. Too late to change streams now.

"Aristotle said that the chief forms of beauty are order and symmetry, and Socrates stated that measure and symmetry are beauty and virtue the world over. It's why humans are drawn to flowers and butterflies in nature, and columns and archways in architecture." Maybe he should stop before he made this any worse. He removed his hand from beneath her chin and dropped his gaze. "I'm making a hash of this, aren't I?"

She didn't answer right away, and her silence gnawed at him. He darted a glance in her direction, bracing for the worst, but instead of her features puckering in offense or sharpening in anger, they rounded in what looked to be . . . wonder?

"Mr. Stentz, I think that is the finest compliment I've ever received."

Like a magnet zipping through space to attach itself to its polar opposite, Frank's gaze flew to hers. His heart pounded. "Stella, I . . ." He swallowed and gathered his courage. "I care for you a great deal. We haven't yet had a chance to discuss our—"

"Hey! You two gonna stand there chattin' all afternoon, or are you gonna help?"

Norman's call nearly startled Frank out of his shoes. He'd been so utterly absorbed in Stella, he'd completely forgotten the man's existence.

"Coming," Stella sang out. But before she moved, she leaned close and whispered in Frank's ear. "Meet me at the Old Corner Drug Store at Fourth and Austin tomorrow at two o'clock. We can talk then."

Frank nodded. He'd be there. Though it might not be a bad idea to drop by the Baylor library to brush up on some poetry beforehand.

CHAPTER 5

Stella lectured herself on the importance of pragmatism during the entire walk between the small house she shared with her father and the Old Corner Drug Store. Yet the moment she spied Frank standing in front of the shop, his suit freshly pressed and his bow tie slightly askew, her pulse hiccupped, and her mind flooded with the words he'd spoken yesterday.

"I care for you a great deal."

Heavens. How was a woman supposed to keep her feet on solid ground when a man as fine as Frank Stentz spouted such a sentiment?

Stella halted in front of the bank across the street from the drugstore and took a moment to breathe. As tempting as it was, she couldn't allow the giddy waves of romantic happiness surging through her spirit to mute her wits. One had only to look to the disastrous fate of Jane Austen's Lydia Bennet to be reminded of the dangers inherent in letting emotional whims dictate one's decisions. Real love wasn't a fairy tale where *happily ever after* magically dissolved all obstacles a couple might face. Real love tackled obstacles together, even those that left bruises and scars. Real love entailed sacrifice. Perhaps even the sacrifice of letting go.

That thought added enough lead to Stella's shoes to reestablish her equilibrium. Moving through a cluster of ladies discussing the latest bonnet fashions, Stella stepped off the boardwalk and into the street. About halfway across, Frank spotted her. A smile bloomed across his face, immediately transforming the lead in her shoes into a bright, hope-filled gold. It seemed he was an alchemist as well as a mathematician.

Stella's steps quickened of their own accord, making her slightly breathless as she accepted his hand to ascend onto the walkway. Or perhaps the breathlessness had been induced by his nearness, because it persisted even after her movements ceased.

"You're early," she said, her brain currently incapable of producing conversation with an ounce of wit.

Frank shrugged, his shy gaze darting from her face to the street to somewhere in the vicinity of her neck before finally climbing back to her eyes. "After being tardy to dinner at our first meeting and again yesterday, I wished to establish that I do, in fact, possess the ability to be punctual."

Stella smiled. He really was quite endearing when trying to impress. Of course, the simple fact that he *wanted* to impress her had already weakened her knees. "I'll be sure to add punctuality to your list of favorable traits."

His eyes widened slightly. "You keep a list?"

She laughed softly. "Only in my mind. Though it is growing rather lengthy now that I've had the chance to get to know you beyond an epistolary context. Perhaps I should consider a written enumeration of traits. I wouldn't want to forget any."

"As long as you only record my positive attributes. It would be quite disheartening to think a list of my flaws existed where some undiscerning soul might stumble across it." He gave a little shudder. "I happen to know there are numerous datapoints in that particular subset."

"Are there?" Stella moved toward the shop door, casting a demure glance over her shoulder. "I've not had cause to observe many at all."

The corners of his mouth twitched upward before he recalled that he should open the door for her. Lurching forward, he clasped the handle and swung the portal wide so that she could enter the shop ahead of him.

A half dozen patrons wandered through the deep, narrow shop, perusing the medicinal and sundry items on display in the glass cases and shelves on the merchandise side of the shop. Stella gravitated to the right, toward the soda fountain, where a pair of boys sat on stools at the counter, sipping the dark, carbonated beverage she planned to order for Frank.

The clerk drying glasses behind the bar set aside his towel and nodded to her. "Howdy, Miss Barrington. What can I get for ya?"

"Two Wacos, please."

"Yes, ma'am." The clerk pumped dark syrup into a glass, then added soda water on top before giving it a stir with a long-handled spoon.

Frank leaned close. "I don't see *Waco* on the menu board," he murmured.

Stella smiled and pointed to the sign on the wall behind the clerk. "It's the one at the top."

Frank's forehead scrunched. "I readily admit that I'm an atrocious speller, but I'm pretty sure Waco starts with a W. The top flavor on the board is named for some doctor named Pepper."

The clinking of the spoon inside the glass diminished as the clerk finished the first drink and began making the second.

"The shop owner, Mr. Morrison, is trying to train us to use the new name," Stella explained, "but most of the locals still call it a

Waco. You'll see why when you taste it. The flavor is completely unique, and it's only made here, hence the tendency for residents to claim it as their own. One of Morrison's pharmacists, Charles Alderton, created the recipe a few years ago. It contains a mix of twenty-three different flavors, but no one knows precisely which ones." She winked and leaned in close enough to smell a hint of Frank's shaving soap. "I think Morrison keeps the recipe locked in a safe somewhere. Trade secrets, you know."

"Ah, a mystery." Frank waggled his brows. "I can't wait to taste this secret concoction."

Stella chuckled. "Oh, I doubt it will be a secret for long. From what I hear, Morrison plans to bottle and distribute it across the state. Who knows, in a few years, you might be able to order a Dr. Pepper in Cambridge, Massachusetts."

"Something else to make me think of you."

Stella smiled, but her heart drooped at the thought of him being back at Harvard . . . without her.

"Here you go, Miss B." The clerk set two full glasses of dark soda on the counter in front of her and poked a paper straw into each one.

Grateful for the distraction, she nodded. "Thank you, Lionel."

Frank slid a couple of coins across the counter, then collected the glasses. "Where to now?"

Recalling the reason she'd asked him to meet her here, Stella nodded toward the rear of the store. "There are some tables in the back." Tables that would afford a semblance of privacy while still being properly in public.

She led the way to a small table for two positioned against the side wall. Frank set their drinks down, then helped her with her chair.

"Thank you."

His smile shot straight to her heart, his eagerness to please palpable. And please her he did. So much.

Once he was seated, she took a sip of her soda and waited for him to do the same. "What do you think?"

His eyebrows arched in surprise a moment before a look of contemplation overtook his features. "You're right. I've never tasted anything like this." He sipped, then tipped his head. Then sipped and raised his gaze to the ceiling as if running a complex analysis. After a moment, he accepted defeat and grinned. "I have no idea what it tastes like, but I like it."

"I'm glad." After scanning the store to ensure no one she knew stood nearby, Stella took another sip for courage, then scooted her glass aside. "Frank. I'd like to talk to you. About . . . well, about what you said yesterday."

He gulped suddenly, then sputtered as a cough caught him off guard.

"Are you all right?" She started to get up, thinking to pound him on the back to help with the choking. "I'm so sorry. I shouldn't have sprung that on you with no warning."

He waved at her to keep her seat and fished in his coat pocket for a handkerchief. "I'm fine."

He didn't sound fine. He sounded like a strangled toad.

He cleared his throat and tried again. "I'm fine. Truly."

This time he sounded more like himself, and Stella released a sigh and leaned back in her chair. The few patrons at the rear of the store who had turned to stare resumed their shopping once the choking subsided.

Frank wiped his mouth and chin with the handkerchief, then gave a discreet swipe of the tabletop that Stella pretended not to notice. She busied herself with unbuttoning her outer coat and slipping her arms from the sleeves. Embarrassment was apparently an excellent heat conductor.

Having regained control of his lungs, Frank leaned forward slightly and kept his voice low. "Am I correct to assume that you are not referring to our discussion of the nativity production?"

Stella nodded. "I didn't have the chance to respond to your . . . statement yesterday, but I wanted to confirm that my feelings on the matter align with yours."

She doubted she would ever forget the smile that stretched across Frank's face at that moment. Such absolute delight. Over *her*. She'd never thought to find someone who would care so much for her good opinion. For her affection.

"I am glad to hear it." He glanced up at a man who'd approached a display of cigar boxes a few feet away before turning back to Stella. "Will your father be at home this evening? I would like to discuss the matter with him as well."

Talk to her father? So he *was* considering a proposal. Stella felt as if her chest had been hooked up to the soda water tap. Effervescence expanded within her, nearly making her dizzy. Only the recollection of the obstacles before them kept her from floating to the drugstore ceiling.

"Before you do, I'd like to share a few concerns, if I may."

Frank's expression sobered, but his eyes never left hers. "Of course."

Stella looked away first. "As you might have surmised, my father and I are very close. It's been just the two of us for the last ten years, and I'm not sure I can abandon him to follow a path that takes me hundreds or even thousands of miles away."

Frank leaned back in his chair, and a canyon seemed to open between them. "I see. That is a variable I had not considered."

The man shopping for cigars made his selection and moved toward the front of the store. Seeing no one else within earshot,

KAREN WITEMEYER

Stella seized the privacy of the moment and pushed aside vague conversation in favor of plain speech.

Placing her hands on the table, she leaned forward. A touch of pleading laced her words. "Perhaps we might continue our correspondence while you are in Germany, and a way will present itself for us to be together when you return."

His gaze focused on hers again, and the intensity of it made her heart throb. As if he had no care for who might see, he reached across the small table and clasped her hand. "Stella, if I can have you, I have no need for Germany."

"No need for Germany?" What was he saying? "You cannot forfeit such an opportunity, Frank. Not for me." The very idea was ludicrous. "Papa has told me about your fellowship. How Göttingen is considered the epicenter of mathematical thought and advancement. It's your dream. You've written as much to me in your letters."

His thumb stroked the back of her hand. "Dreams change. As do people." He released a sigh. "I have a confession to make. I didn't come here for the symposium. I came here for you. To see if the woman I'd grown to . . . admire through letters might consider a courtship in person. Family is important to me, too. So important that I'd gladly forfeit a fellowship to build one of my own with the right woman." His thumb ceased drawing its soothing circles, and all of his fingers squeezed hers. "I'm convinced that *you* are the right woman, Stella."

"But . . . Germany. You can't . . ."

His mouth tightened. "You sound like Muir." He pulled his hand away from hers, and it hurt as much as if he'd taken a layer of her skin along with it. "I don't need to study in Germany to contribute to mathematical advancement. Benjamin Peirce never left the States, and his research is considered on par with all the giants in the field. There are other ways for me to steward the gift God has given. Yes, I love research and delving into theories that have yet to be proven. But I also love teaching. For of what good is knowledge if it is not shared?"

"And this teaching you love . . . it is to take place at Harvard, correct?"

He fell silent, and her heart panged. She understood the dilemma too well. His family or hers? They couldn't live close to both, and moving somewhere between the two would only leave them close to neither.

It was a problem with no solution. At least not one she could see. But she wouldn't give up hope just yet. Her heart belonged to a mathematician, and judging by his expression, he'd already started ciphering. If there was an answer to be found, Frank would find it.

And if there wasn't? Well, she served a God with the power to break the rules of science and nature, so anything could happen.

CHAPTER 6

Sitting at the desk in his boardinghouse room, Frank stared at his symposium notes without really seeing them. His mind still reeled from his conversation with Stella a few hours ago. She cared for him. Even implied that she would welcome a proposal. *If* marriage didn't entail leaving her father.

Frank rubbed at his forehead, trying to manually stimulate a creative solution, since cogitation alone had failed to produce anything of use.

He should have foreseen this complication. He'd fallen prey to his own masculine assumption that wives simply followed husbands. Wasn't it logical that his employment would dictate where they built a home? In his experience, a significantly large percentage of marriages operated in this fashion. But therein lay the crux of the matter. There must first be a marriage. He hadn't considered that Stella might balk at tying her life to his because she didn't want to follow him to Massachusetts.

Stella had been running Professor Barrington's household for years. They'd been a family of two for more than a decade, their shared loss of her mother bonding them in an unbreakable fashion. Of course she'd not want to leave him behind. And

Barrington wouldn't leave Baylor behind. Building the mathematics program here was his dream.

A knock on his open door brought Frank's head around. Goldstein stood on the threshold, a triumphant smile beaming across his face. "You won't believe it, but I finally convinced Muir to agree to play one of the magi in the nativity production your young lady is putting together."

Frank swiveled in his chair. "Astonishing! How did you manage it?"

Goldstein shrugged as he stepped into the room. "Extortion."

A strangled laugh tickled Frank's throat. "What?"

"I threatened to chatter at him for the entire train ride home if he refused." Goldstein shined his knuckles on his vest as if they were made of silver. Though it was his silver tongue that had won the day.

"Ingenious strategy, Isaac. Verbal torture. I wish I had thought of that."

Goldstein chuckled. "He wouldn't have taken the threat seriously if it had come from you. He knows you like to be left alone with your books and your thoughts as much as he does. But me? Well, I can converse with a tree stump, and Randy knows it." He sat on the edge of the narrow bed and studied Frank's disorganized desk with a far-too-perceptive eye. "Are you all right? It's not like you to be untidy. Especially with your presentation notes."

Frank waved off his friend's concern. "I'm fine."

"And I'm a scientist trained in observation. You're not fine." Goldstein raised a brow. "Did something happen between you and Miss Barrington?"

Maybe having more than one mind working on the problem would speed the production of a solution.

"She gave me reason to believe that she would be amenable to a proposal—"

"That's great!" Goldstein thumped Frank's arm. "Isn't it?"

"It is. Except that she also intimated that leaving her father behind in Texas to follow me back to Harvard would break her heart. It might even keep her from accepting my proposal altogether." He sighed and ran his palms down the length of his thighs. "I love her, Isaac. The last thing I want to do is cause her pain. Perhaps it would be better for me *not* to propose. That way she won't have to choose between us."

"Hmm." Goldstein stroked the white mustache that connected his matching sideburns. "All right. Let's analyze our findings so far." He ticked items off on his fingers as if they were abacus beads. "One. Miss Barrington is favorably disposed toward your suit in general. Two. Professor Barrington has given no indication that he would oppose a match between you and his daughter. Three. You are madly in love with the woman." He switched to the other hand. "On the negative side of the equation we have . . . One. Miss Barrington's dedication to her father makes her reluctant to leave Texas. Two. The love she shares with her father is of a longstanding nature, giving it the potential for greater weight when measured against new feelings that have not yet had the chance to mature. Three. Your current position requires you to reside in Massachusetts with an option for relocation to Germany, neither of which are in Texas."

Frank ran his hand through his already-mussed hair. "That's an accurate summary of the datapoints." And rather depressing to hear it rattled off in such blunt fashion.

"It seems to me that the variable causing the most disruption is geographical in nature. Have you considered taking a job here? Barrington's been dropping hints for almost a fortnight about how they wish to expand their department. I'm surprised he hasn't offered you a position outright yet. Maybe he's waiting for the symposium to finish."

Frank straightened. "What hints? All I recall is his pride in showing off the new classrooms and the telescope they use for astronomy."

Goldstein chuckled. "My boy, you've never been one for subtlety. Besides, you've been so distracted by the man's daughter, I'm surprised you've paid any attention to Ignatius at all."

Frank fell silent. Could Goldstein be correct? Would Baylor hire him?

The bigger question was if he would want them to. Harvard was the most prestigious university on American soil when it came to mathematics. Working there would allow him to partner with some of the greatest minds in the field. To collaborate on advanced theorems and visionary research. Here he would teach basic tenets without much to challenge him. He could conduct his own research and correspond with his colleagues, but it wouldn't be the same as meeting up in James Peirce's office to talk through ideas.

He'd already come to terms with giving up Germany. Must he give up Harvard as well?

"I see I've given you something to chew on." Goldstein stood and laid a hand on Frank's shoulder. "Take some time to pray about it, son. You don't have to decide today. Talk to Stella. Share your concerns and your hopes. She's only just met you in person. She's known her father her whole life. Perhaps with a little time, she'll get used to the idea of living elsewhere."

Goldstein let himself out of the room and quietly pulled the door shut behind him. Frank barely noticed. He'd already disappeared into his internal laboratory and started covering a mental blackboard with tabulations comparing the benefits of returning to Harvard versus taking a teaching position at Baylor, should one be offered.

The results were completely lopsided. He'd enumerated more than a dozen items in the Harvard column, and only one on the Baylor side. Yet Stella's name had been chalked in letters ten times larger than any of the other items, and he was fairly certain that should he place everything on a scale, his growing love for Stella would tip things in Baylor's favor. But was it wise to base such a life-altering decision on emotion?

He turned back toward his desk and braced his elbows on its surface as he bowed his head and pressed his fingers against his brow.

What is the right path, Lord? My heart urges me to choose Stella, yet my mind warns against trusting an organ that ignores empirical evidence. You have gifted me with mathematical understanding, and all my life I have felt the weight of your calling upon me to steward that gift in a responsible manner. Is it irresponsible of me to leave a higher seat of learning in order to please a wife? Didn't you instruct that wives are to be subject to their husbands?

Of course, if Stella refused to marry him, she wouldn't be his wife, would she?

A thought brightened his mind like a lamp being lit in a dark room. Data. He needed spiritual data. Grabbing the leather-bound book at the top edge of his desk, he began flipping through the holy pages, searching for examples he could draw from.

Abraham. Sarah left her home, her family to follow him to a new land. And Isaac. Rebekah left her father's family to join him in Canaan. And Ruth. She left her homeland and married a man in a land foreign to her. Although, to be fair, it was her mother-in-law she followed to the new land, not a husband.

And now that he thought about it, Ruth's first husband left *his* homeland and lived among *her* people. Which brought Jacob to mind. He stayed with his wife's family for fourteen years before returning to his own. And what of Moses? He lived among his wife's family for years. Even worked for his father-in-law until God called him to return to Egypt. Then again, Moses really had no home of his own after killing the Egyptian. Should that invalidate his inclusion in this inquiry?

Frank ran a hand through his hair and fisted a thick tuft until pain radiated over his scalp. Nothing was more frustrating than inconclusive data. All he had to do was look at David. Abigail left her home to marry him, but with his first wife, Michal, David left *his* family to join hers.

What was God trying to show him? That it didn't matter who followed who? That there was no right answer? But Frank *wanted* an answer. Something clear and quantifiable to reassure him that he wasn't making a mistake. Yet even the passages that spoke of wives being subject to their husbands also spoke of husbands loving their wives and making sacrifices for them. How was he to know what to do?

Later that evening, Stella sat in her favorite chair with a copy of her favorite book, but instead of finding comfort in the story, *Jane Eyre* only stirred up more uncertainty. For Jane had fallen completely in love with her Edward, and he with her. But marriage between them was a mistake. Doomed to fail before it began. Perhaps she should take heart that the two eventually found their happy ending, but it came at such a steep cost. Would the same be required of her? Of Frank? She didn't want Frank to suffer, to forfeit all he'd worked so hard to achieve. He deserved a wife who could come to him with no reservations, who wouldn't hesitate to support him in his work, and who would gladly follow him wherever that work took him. She couldn't do those things. Not yet, anyway.

"If you frown at that book any harder, it's going to combust."

Stella glanced up to find her father studying her from his chair across from her. He'd set his own book on the table near his elbow.

She offered a smile, hoping he'd not look too close or analyze too deeply. "Miss Brontë and her characters are made of stern stuff. They can handle a few contemplative stares."

"A few?" Her father raised a brow as he removed his feet from the ottoman and planted them on the floor. "You've been scowling at that same page for the past quarter hour." He leaned forward, his eyes brimming with concern. "Want to talk about it?"

Yes. But how much should she say?

"Does it have anything to do with a particular redheaded mathematics professor?" Papa's eyes began to dance. "Is the courtship not going well?"

"Papa!" Heat flushed her cheeks. "We're just friends." Mostly.

Her father chuckled. "Don't you be fibbing, girl. I've seen the way you light up whenever he's around. And Frank's making all kinds of departures from his usual character. Leaving symposium sessions early, agreeing to participate in public performances, and walking on eggshells around me. The man is my intellectual and professional superior. There's only one reasonable explanation for his sudden nervousness in my presence. He's completely besotted with my daughter."

Pleasure rushed over her at his words, yet it failed to make her dilemma any smaller.

"You care for him. Don't you?" Her father's gentle tone caused her eyes to mist.

Stella nodded. "I do. I fear my heart will belong to him forever."

Papa rose from his chair and moved to sit on the side of the sofa closest to her chair. He reached over the sofa arm and clasped her hand. "Why does loving him make you afraid?"

She couldn't meet his eyes. "Because I know how much it will hurt when he leaves."

"You don't think he will offer for you?"

She shook her head as the first tears began to fall. "Just the opposite. I'm pretty sure he will. But I don't see how I can accept. Not when marrying him will mean leaving my home. Leaving you." She sniffed as she raised her head and peered into her father's face. "You are all the family I have, Papa. I can't leave you."

His grip tightened around her fingers, and his voice choked slightly. "Oh, my sweet girl. How I love you. And if you move to the East Coast, I will miss you terribly. But you'll only be a train ride away. I can visit you during university holidays, and we can correspond between visits."

Stella twisted to face him, her chest feeling as if it might burst. "But who will take care of you? Fix your eggs the way you like them, press your suits, darn your socks? Who will make sure you don't forget your keys and keep your ledgers organized? You're a terrible bookkeeper, you know."

He smiled. "That I am." He reached up to wipe a tear from her cheek with his thumb. "No one will ever tend to me as well as you do. As well as your mother did. But I'll manage. I *am* a grown man, after all."

"I can't leave. I promised Mama I'd take care of you." The secret blurted out of her with no warning. She expected to see shock arrest his features, but his tender expression never changed.

"And I promised her to take care of *you*." He patted her arm. "Your mama wanted us to take care of each other so that neither of us would fall prey to grief. She wished for our family ties to grow stronger in her absence, not to weaken from neglect. But she never wished for us to hold so tightly to each other that we let no one else in. Why do you think I encouraged you to write to Professor Stentz all those months ago? I hoped the two of you would form a connection. He impressed me as an intelligent, godly man. One with a kind spirit and a humble manner. One who would appreciate a woman who shared his faith and his love of learning. One who could take care of my little girl when I am no longer around to do so."

Stella's breath stuck in her throat, and her head began to spin. "Papa. Never tell me that you've been playing matchmaker all this time."

His eyes twinkled. "It seems I have a knack for it. I might have to go into business if the professorship doesn't work out."

A laugh bubbled out of her. A joyous, freeing laugh that cleansed her heart and infused her spirit with hope. She still didn't want to leave her papa, but for the first time, considering the idea didn't feel like a betrayal.

Stella sat in the rear of the lecture hall, her attention fully captivated by the man at the front of the room. In the six days since
their discussion at the soda shop, he'd been just as attentive as
before. Walking her home from her literary society meeting.
Helping construct the nativity production props. Even taking
her to a musical performance at the Garland Opera House.
He still courted her, though there was a slight restraint to his
manner now that had been missing before. Caution curbed his
enthusiasm. A caution she'd forced upon him.

Yet nothing about his manner at this moment felt the least
bit curbed or cautious.

The Frank Stentz she'd met in letters was intelligent, witty,
and full of stories about his family. The man she'd gotten to
know in person over the last two-and-a-half weeks was shy, a
little awkward in social situations, but exceedingly kind and
considerate of others. Especially her.

And *this* Frank? The mathematical genius with a passion
for number theory and higher learning? She couldn't take her
eyes off him.

How easily he commanded the attention of a filled-to-
capacity auditorium during the final lecture in the symposium
series. Not a chair in the hall remained unfilled. Latecomers

stood along the edges of the room, and a few even sat on the floor at the front. Word had spread over the last fortnight of Professor Stentz's charisma in the classroom, and it seemed the entire student body had turned out to see him for themselves. Even President Burleson and his wife were in attendance.

Stella hadn't thought it possible to admire him more, but as she listened to Frank's oratory on the Frobenius method for finding series solutions to linear differential equations, she found herself utterly enthralled. A strange effect, when she couldn't understand ninety percent of what he was saying. He spoke of analytical power series, coefficients, and recurrence relations. Regular singular points, indicial polynomials, and radii of convergence. It might as well have been a foreign language.

Yet she savored each incomprehensible word. He radiated such fervor and joy. Gone was his shyness, his hesitancy. Before her stood a man brimming with confidence and a tantalizing level of enthusiasm that beguiled his listeners. No dry recitation of findings with Frank. No condescension or inflated ego. He loved his subject, and he loved sharing it with others. The sharing seemed to energize him, for he roved the stage with animation alive in his limbs as well as his voice.

He was utterly magnificent.

If only she understood more of his subject matter so she could fully appreciate his giftedness. Beside her, Papa took copious notes, occasionally shaking his head and murmuring, "Brilliant!" under his breath, reinforcing her impression of Frank's remarkable talent.

"Professor Stentz." Albert Boggess, chairman of Baylor's Department of Mathematics, rose from his chair in the second row. "What occurs if the difference between the roots is not an integer?"

Undaunted by the interruption, Frank pivoted to address his

host. "Excellent query, Professor Boggess. Allow me to demonstrate." He moved to an unused section of the blackboard and began drawing out a complicated series of equations containing more letters and punctuation than actual numbers. "If the difference between the roots is not an integer, we must calculate a second, linearly independent solution in the other root."

By the time the lecture concluded and the hall erupted in applause, Stella had been convinced of two truths. Frank Stentz had been born to teach, and she'd been born to love him.

His gaze found hers through the incredibly crowded room and lingered. He smiled, and her heart expanded to such a degree, her lungs couldn't manage a full breath.

Frank suddenly held up his hand and called out in a voice loud enough to carry over the fading applause and rising conversation. "Don't forget to attend the nativity production at the Baptist church later this afternoon. Academic knowledge is meaningless if one lacks knowledge of the Savior. Besides, when else will you have the chance to see three Harvard professors parading about in tunics?"

Laughter filled the hall, and warmth spread through Stella's chest. In his moment of triumph, with dozens of people clamoring for his attention, he'd thought of her. Better than that, he'd supported her. Publicly. Endorsing and promoting her project.

"Who you share your life with is more important than where you live it," her father said in a low voice, his mouth close to her ear. "Wouldn't you agree?"

"I can't believe I let you talk me into this. I look ridiculous!" Muir huffed a disgusted breath as he peered down at the three inches of trousers that showed beneath the hem of his tunic.

Goldstein adjusted his papier-mâché turban so it no longer

covered his right eye like a pirate patch. "Trust me. No one will be looking at your ankles, Randy." He bent down to pick up his small wooden chest filled with rocks covered in gold paint. The turban slid forward again, covering both eyes this time. "Fiddlesticks! How am I supposed to see where I'm going with this thing sliding around on my head like a runaway toboggan?"

"Here." Frank set aside his urn prop and straightened Goldstein's headgear. An intricately wrapped scarf had been attached to the papier-mâché base to give it a more realistic look, but Goldstein's head was obviously a size smaller than whoever had worn the costume in the past. Frank angled the turban toward the back of Goldstein's head, uncovering his eyes.

"Oh dear." Stella rushed over to help. "Did no one explain about the woolen cap?"

Goldstein shared a look with Frank, then shrugged. "We saw a knit cap in the costume box, but it didn't seem to match the rest of the gear. We assumed it had fallen in the box by mistake."

"Hold on. I'll be right back." She disappeared inside the church for a moment, then came out with the brown knit cap clasped triumphantly in her hand. "If you wear this under the turban, it will keep it from sliding around. I'm sorry I didn't think to tell you about it sooner."

Goldstein smiled as he accepted the cap. "No harm done, Miss Barrington. Randy will help me get it situated properly." He shot a glance at Muir. "Won't you, Randy?"

Muir grunted.

"See?" Goldstein chuckled. "As agreeable as ever." He strolled over to the frowning Muir, giving Frank a moment of privacy with Stella.

"Maybe I should help." She started to follow Goldstein, but Frank stopped her by taking hold of her hand.

She spun around to face him, her eyes round. Even dressed in head-to-toe black, she made his pulse thump a lively beat.

"They'll be fine." Frank tugged her closer, his chest constricting beneath a tourniquet of erupting nervousness. "Stella, I . . ."

Now was not the best time for this. A couple hundred people milled about the churchyard, waiting for the production to begin, and he was dressed in a Middle Eastern tunic and robe with a dish towel banded to his head. However, with the symposium concluded, he had little time left. He'd lacked the courage to broach the subject earlier in the week, and now his departure loomed. Muir had purchased tickets for the three of them to leave on tomorrow's train. This might be his only opportunity to speak his heart.

"Yes?"

Frank peered into the face he saw in his dreams each night. "I . . . I love you, Stella. And I want to marry you. I know we still have a lot to figure out about where we might live and what my professional life will entail, but I believe we can find a mutually beneficial solution."

He squeezed her fingers, then drew them upward and pressed a kiss to the back of her hand. Her skin felt even softer than he'd imagined, and if it weren't for being surrounded by such a great cloud of witnesses, he'd gladly experiment with her lips as well.

The catch in her breath and slight tremble in her hand encouraged him to continue.

"I've analyzed the data and proven the hypothesis I came here to test: that sharing my life with you means more to me than accruing academic acclaim. I'm willing to do whatever it takes to make things work between us. That is . . . if you . . . are similarly inclined."

Her beautiful brown eyes glimmered in the pre-dusk light as

liquid pooled along her lower lashes. She blinked and pressed her lips together, and for a torturous second, he thought he had made an irredeemable blunder. But then her head bobbed in silent affirmation, and a broken whisper found its way into the air between them.

"I'm very much inclined."

His elation multiplied at a staggering rate until he was certain it exceeded the bounds of quantification.

His arms ached to pull her tightly against him, and his gaze seemed incapable of looking anywhere other than her lips. How he longed to press his mouth to hers, to seal their understanding with something more tangible than words. As he watched, her lips parted, and without conscious thought, his body leaned closer to hers, hungry to hear whatever she wished to say.

Unfortunately, her would-be words were drowned out by the booming tones of the minister as he announced the start of the production.

Stella startled and twisted away from him, stealing her hand from him in the process. "We had better take our places."

She swiped at her eyes with the back of one hand, then lowered the netting of her black veil over her blushing cheeks. Frank collected his urn and lined up with Muir and Goldstein behind the church, where they would be hidden from view until their cue to enter the scene. Ignoring Muir's knowing look and Goldstein's waggling eyebrows, he positioned himself at the front of their line and locked his gaze on the woman standing in front of him.

Stella. His star. He had no idea where loving her would lead him, but just like the wise man he portrayed, he had faith that the journey would culminate in something glorious.

Stella tightened her grip on the black broom handle that served as the base of her celestial prop, her insides trembling so violently she feared she'd drop the Star of Bethlehem.

Frank loved her. He wished to marry her. His words replayed over and over in her mind, daring her to believe them. To believe that a woman no one else wanted had finally been chosen. Chosen and cherished. For that was how she'd felt when Frank touched his lips to her hand. Cherished. Desired. Loved.

"Hallelujah! Hallelujah! Hal-le-lu-jah!"

The singers representing the angels burst out with an abbreviated version of Handel's "Hallelujah Chorus," and for a heartbeat, Stella thought they rejoiced on her behalf. Until the preacher's rich voice proclaimed the birth of the Messiah to the shepherds.

Heavens. Had baby Jesus already been born? Her gaze zeroed in on the crèche where Norman stood beside his wife, a babe in her arms.

Get your mind where it belongs, Stella. You're here to honor the coming of the Savior and to share that good news with

*your community. Not to stare moon-eyed into the evening air
like a lovesick calf.*

Easier thought than done. She endeavored to put Frank from
her mind and focus on the nativity story playing out before her,
but each time he so much as shifted his weight or breathed a
little too heavily, her attention immediately diverted. By the
time the shepherds left the manger to go share the good news
with the townspeople, she'd become a bit frazzled from the
mental back and forth.

"'Now when Jesus was born in Bethlehem of Judaea in the
days of Herod the king,'" the minister intoned, "'behold, there
came wise men from the east to Jerusalem.'" He paused in his
reading of Matthew chapter two, and Stella realized with a
start that her cue had arrived.

Lifting her broom handle to chest-height to bring attention
to the large tin star at the top of the pole, she slowly walked
forward into the staging area, her three Harvard professors
dutifully following in her wake. One of the congregants wearing
a purple robe and a paper crown came out to meet her before
she neared the manger scene.

Frank obviously knew the story well, for he moved past her
to meet the man playing Herod.

"'The wise men asked, "Where is he that is born King of
the Jews? For we have seen his star in the east, and are come
to worship him."'"

Frank waved a hand in the direction of the star she carried,
but she would have sworn that his eyes somehow found hers
through the shielding of her veil.

The narration continued. "'After consulting with the chief
priests and scribes, Herod sent them to Bethlehem, and said,
"Go and search diligently for the young child; and when ye have
found him, bring me word again, that I may come and worship

him also." When they heard the king, they departed; and, lo, the star, which they saw in the east, went before them, till it came and stood over where the young child was.'"

Frank stepped back in line behind Stella, and she led them to the crèche where Mary, Joseph, and the Christ child waited. At the last moment, she shifted to walk behind the manger scene, climbing the small staircase Norman had built behind it until she reached the top platform behind the roof eaves. There, she held the star high and slid the end of the broom handle into the pocket Norman had installed to hold the pole in place.

"'When they saw the star, they rejoiced with exceeding great joy.'"

She crouched behind the top of the crèche as the preacher continued the story, wanting the star to be the focal point, not her. Moving quietly, she took a seat on the top step where she would be hidden from the audience, then peeked through a knothole to watch the rest of the production play out. Well, to watch Frank, at least. Her gaze seemed rather glued to that particular wise man.

"'And when they were come into the house, they saw the young child with Mary his mother, and fell down, and worshiped him.'"

Usually at this point, the men playing the role of the magi bowed their heads in a prayerful pose, but not Frank. He dropped to his knees and prostrated himself fully before the babe. Arms outstretched, face practically touching the ground, the urn extended deferentially before him.

Stella's heart squeezed, and her eyes misted. This was no overzealous acting. This was reverence. Pure and true. Frank's faith practically glowed, and she wasn't the only one who noticed. A decided hush fell over the crowd. Professor Goldstein slowly lowered himself to one knee, his older joints not as nimble as those of his younger colleague. Even the grumbly Muir bowed deeply at the waist as a spirit of worship filled the air.

The minister cleared his throat, as if he, too, had been overcome by the moment, then finally finished the reading. "'And when they had opened their treasures, they presented unto him gifts; gold, and frankincense and myrrh.'"

Norman stepped forward to accept the gifts, and as he did so, the choir resounded with "Joy to the World." The preacher urged the crowd to join in the singing, then set the example by doing so himself. All of the performers, including the wise men, stood and turned to face the audience as they joined in the caroling. Stella sang softly as she descended the stairs. She raised her veil and slid into place next to Frank, slipping her hand through his arm. His clear tenor voice lifted her spirit, and his beautiful smile urged her to greater volume as her need to praise her Savior overrode her self-consciousness about her lack of musical skill.

One carol blended into another as people linked arms and clasped hands in worship. Scores of voices lifted in song, drawing more and more people to the churchyard until the crowd spilled into the street. The choir director didn't stop after the usual three hymns; he started a fourth and a fifth, leading every Christmas hymn in the book.

Spiritual chills coursed over Stella's arms and through her chest as she sang. Never had she been so impacted by one of their humble little performances. Her heart overflowed with gratitude for the gift of Jesus, for the love and truth he bestowed during his life, for the grace and salvation he offered in his death, and the triumph and hope manifested at his resurrection. *This* was the good news of Christmas.

It took over an hour for the crowd to disperse after the final carol. Something special lingered in the atmosphere, and people seemed reluctant to leave. Church members struck up conversations with nonmembers. Children played around the manger, reenacting the story they'd just seen. Ladies shared recipes for favorite Christmas sweets, and men clumped together to jaw about the weather.

Baylor students and faculty chatted with the visiting professors, their discussions turning philosophical as they wrestled with the question of why a group of non-Jewish wise men from an eastern culture would follow a star to worship a newborn Jewish king. Angelic revelation proved a popular theory, since all the other major players in the nativity story—Mary, Joseph, and the shepherds—had experienced a direct call. A faculty member known for his Old Testament scholarship proposed a theory regarding Daniel's influence as a wise man in the courts of the kings of Babylon as well as the Medes and Persians—eastern peoples. Perhaps Daniel's prophesies had been studied by the wise men who came after him and led them to seek a messianic king at a calculated time. Hence why they would seek Herod for directions instead of having direct knowledge of where to go.

Stella found the discussion fascinating and incredibly stimulating. She could have listened for hours. Especially to Frank. His thoughts, his suppositions, the way he never disparaged an idea, even if it disagreed with his own. She could have stood there all night. However, the drop in temperature combined with the increasing darkness that encroached after the sun set finally convinced the group to abandon the mystery of the magi in favor of warm parlors and waiting suppers.

After leading Frank and the other Harvard men back to the church to remove their robes and tunics and collect their overcoats, Stella packed all the costumes away in the battered trunk that would hold them until next year.

"I say." Goldstein clapped Frank on the back. "What a grand evening. So glad you talked us into participating, my boy." He tipped his head toward Professor Muir. "Randy's glad, too. He just hides it better."

Muir drew himself up to his considerable height, his mouth edging downward in an impressive scowl. "I don't need you speaking for me, you old windbag."

Mr. Goldstein winked at Stella, his tone rich with laughter. "He offers no denial!"

Mr. Muir practically growled as he stormed from the church, which only made Goldstein chuckle harder. Though he did follow his comrade outside. Whether to apologize or further pester the man, Stella couldn't surmise.

She pushed away from the trunk and allowed Frank to help her with her coat.

"It really was a remarkable evening, Stella," Frank said as she turned to face him. "You should be very proud."

She shook her head as she did up the buttons on her coat. "No. I've helped put on this production for several years, and we've never had the kind of reception we had tonight. This was different. Special. I feel as if . . ."

Frank searched her face. "As if what?"

Stella dipped her chin. "You'll think me fanciful."

His hand touched her face, and she nearly forgot to breathe. Her gaze flew to his, where she found nothing but curiosity and gentle encouragement. "I deal in abstractions all the time, Stella. Fanciful is one of my favorite frames of mind."

His thumb rubbed the edge of her cheek, and she nearly lost

270

the thought she'd been holding back. Yet his touch, his regard, made her feel completely safe in exposing the inner workings of her heart.

"I felt as if . . . as if God were present." Her lashes lowered. "Which is quite obvious, I suppose. God is always present. Everywhere. It is his very nature." She raised her lashes and met his eyes. "But tonight, it felt as if his presence was purposeful. As if he were not only present but at work."

Frank nodded. "I felt it too. I think everyone did, at some level."

Was it her imagination, or was he drawing her closer? Stella's belly tightened as she stared into his eyes. Eyes filled with desire. And love.

"Frank?" Her mouth suddenly dry, she struggled to make herself heard over the pounding of her heart. "I don't want you to leave tomorrow."

"All right. I'll stay." He leaned close, his mouth mere inches from her own.

"Just like that?"

"Mm-hmm." His hand slid around her waist. A good thing, since her knees seemed to be weakening by the second.

"But what about your family? Won't they be expecting you?" Her gaze skipped down to his lips, and a delicious lightheadedness assailed her.

He tugged softly on her neck, bringing her so close to him, she could feel the warmth radiating from his skin. "I want *you* to be my family, Stella."

"I want that too." So much. Her entire being ached with it. "I love you, Frank."

His blue eyes darkened as he lowered his mouth to hers. Slowly . . . gently . . . with infinite sweetness, he kissed her, and she was reborn. The unattractive spinster she believed herself to be metamorphosed into a woman unafraid to take flight in the arms of the man she loved. Her palms spread across his chest as he deepened their kiss. She could feel his heartbeat through her fingertips, and the evidence of his desire filled her with wonder and exultation.

Along with a surge of unexpected shyness. She pushed against his chest ever so slightly, and he responded at once, separating his lips from hers and loosening his hold on her waist.

Her eyes opened and met his. Neither of them spoke, for what words could possibly do justice to what they'd experienced? Two hearts had melded into one. She belonged to him, and wherever he decided to live his life, she would follow. Without an ounce of regret.

"Frank! Stella! Come quick!"

Goldstein's shout tore through the church storage room like a cannonball. Stella and Frank jumped apart, then ran for the door.

Heart pumping for an entirely new reason, Stella raced outside, almost colliding with a visibly shaken Goldstein.

Eyes wide, he pointed in the direction of the crèche. "The manger. Hurry." He began to run, but since he was already winded, Frank and Stella easily outpaced him.

Mr. Muir stood at the manger, shoulders hunched and hands hovering above the trough as if unsure what to do.

"Randolph," Frank called as they approached. "What is it?"

But for once, the esteemed professor had no answer.

A few steps ahead of her, Frank skidded to a halt, his face taking on the same unbelieving expression as his colleague. A mewling cry penetrated Stella's senses a heartbeat before her feet brought her to the manger.

There in the straw, swaddled in a strip of blanket, lay a very unhappy newborn babe.

CHAPTER 9

"Oh, you poor dear." Stella brushed past Frank and scooped up the tiny human with the scrunched, red face.

Frank eagerly stepped back to make room for her. His competency relating to people in general was barely adequate, but relating to an infant? His skill level would be graphed in the quadrant of negative integers. The babe was so tiny, yet his plaintive cries tugged on Frank's heartstrings with powerful force.

Arranging the child in the crook of her arm, Stella turned her back to the wind and cooed at the baby. "What are you doing out here, little one? Where's your mama?"

An apt question. Frank looked to Muir, who couldn't seem to pull his gaze from the infant. "Did you see anyone by the crèche, Muir? Anyone leaving in a hurry?"

"What?" Muir blinked and finally managed to shift his attention to Frank. "No. No one. The churchyard was empty by the time Isaac and I came outside."

Goldstein joined the group, his breathing heavy and his cheeks red. "Who would abandon a child in such a manner? It's criminal!"

"Someone desperate, I would guess." Stella patted the baby's backside and curled him (or her, gender clues were in short supply at the moment) close to her chest. The baby's cries gradually subsided under Stella's comforting care.

Muir stepped close and raised a trembling hand to stroke the babe's bald head. "Someone who believed she had nowhere to turn." His voice quavered, nearly breaking at the end.

Frank eyed his friend more closely. The stoic, grouchy professor had tears shining in his eyes, an unheard-of happenstance. No statistics could have predicted the turn this night had taken.

"We need to visit the brothel."

Frank's lungs seized at Stella's flabbergasting declaration. A round of coughs exploded from his chest, prompting Goldstein to pound on his back. Isaac's face registered as much stunned disbelief as Frank felt, an outcome that would have been comforting had it not also confirmed that he had, in fact, *not* misheard his beloved announce her intent to visit a house of ill repute.

Regaining control of his lungs, Frank leaned close to Stella and murmured, "Did you say . . . *brothel?*"

She nodded. Rather enthusiastically, too. A stone dropped into his stomach.

"Do you see this embroidered *S* on the corner of the blanket?" She held up some extra fabric that hung past the baby's feet. "There's only one place in town that bears this insignia. Sherod's Sporting House in the Reservation."

Frank decided not to ask how she knew that particular tidbit. It really didn't matter. Her reputation was above reproach. Likely all local townsfolk were familiar with that emblem.

"The Reservation?" Goldstein asked. "As in Indians?"

"No. Some call it Two Street. It's Waco's red-light district. Down by the Brazos. Certain . . . entertainment is legal in that area. Entertainment that could lead to the conception of a child."

Prostitution. Good grief. How had a night that felt so holy deteriorated into something profane? Frank rubbed his temples, his head suddenly aching.

"The women who work there are forbidden to walk any street beyond the boundaries of that two-block area. In fact, if they wish to visit a shop in town, they must hire a horse-drawn cab to keep from being arrested for vagrancy." Stella finally looked up from the baby in her arms and caught Frank's eye, her expression equal parts determination and pleading. "Whoever left this child here took a great risk. If she wanted to rid herself of an unwanted child, she could have tossed him into the river. But she came here. To a church. Laid her babe in a manger just as God did with his own Son. She must have had faith that someone would find her child. Someone who could give him a better life. A life filled with love, unstained by scandal and godlessness. Don't you see, Frank? God led her here. He led Mr. Muir and Mr. Goldstein to find the child. God is still at work tonight, and my soul tells me that the Lord wants more than a safe haven for this babe. He wants to save the mother as well."

Stella's speech pierced Frank's spirit. He'd recoiled from the notions of brothels and prostitutes, repulsed by the salacity of what they represented. Such things were immoral and to be avoided at all cost. Not once had he thought of what the baby's mother might have suffered. Of what love might have prompted her to do. It seemed illogical that such a sinner could be directed by faith. Yet wasn't Rahab the harlot commended in Hebrews as a woman of great faith?

Shame washed over him. Who was he to stand in judgment of someone when he didn't know her story?

"We need to find the child's mother," Stella insisted. "Try to help her. If we can get her away from that life, offer her some kind of alternative . . ."

"I'll sponsor her."

Frank gaped at Randolph Muir, everything he'd thought he'd known about the man crumbling to dust.

Goldstein, however, didn't look surprised in the least. He looked . . . empathetic as he reached out to touch his colleague's shoulder. "Are you sure, Randy? It wouldn't be too much for Phyllis?"

Muir worked his jaw, his gaze unguarded as he turned to his friend. "It might be just what she needs to finally set her grief aside." He cleared his throat and straightened his posture, regaining some of his usual composure. "I'd need to meet the mother first, of course. But if she is not too hardened by her current situation and is willing to leave that lifestyle behind to start fresh, I'll bring her and her babe back to Cambridge and turn her over to Phyllis. If I know my wife, she'll have the young woman educated and trained in a marketable trade by the time the babe is weaned and will likely insist on being the child's honorary grandmother."

Frank had met Mrs. Muir a few times at faculty dinners, but she'd always been rather quiet and subdued. Not exactly the type to take on a charitable cause with enthusiasm. On the other hand, Frank had never suspected that stodgy Randolph Muir would volunteer to take a prostitute home with him either.

Stella shifted the babe to her shoulder and rubbed the small, rounded back. "You're sure your wife won't mind you bringing an unwed mother home with you?"

Randolph rubbed a hand over his beard. "I should have brought one home three years ago." He gazed above their heads and exhaled a shaky breath. "Our daughter, Geraldine, eloped with a young man we disapproved of. He promised to marry her but never did. What he *did* do was get her with child and abandon her to seek his fortune in the west. By the time we learned of her condition, it was too late. She believed we'd not welcome her home after she'd gone against our wishes and only wrote to us when her health declined to the point that she worried she'd not survive childbirth and wanted to secure a home for her babe. My granddaughter." Muir's voice cracked, and he had to swallow a few times before he was steady enough to continue. "By the time I found Geraldine, she was too weak to travel. She gave birth two days later. Neither she nor her daughter survived." He gave a sniff and straightened his shoulders. "If we find this babe's mother, I'll offer to take her home to her family. If she has none, I'll take her home to become part of mine. I failed Geraldine three years ago. Perhaps this is my chance to set things right for another man's daughter."

"I can't think of a better way to honor Geraldine." Stella leaned her cheek against the top of the baby's head, and something shifted in Frank's chest.

Would they someday cradle a child of their own like that? A longing, fierce and deep, surged to life inside him. He knew nothing of children. In fact, they rather terrified him. But to have a child with Stella—as dreadful as he'd likely be at dealing with tiny creatures who defied logic and order at every turn—he couldn't imagine any endeavor more fulfilling. Not even studying in Germany with the finest mathematical minds of his generation. As much as he wished to contribute to the advancement of scientific understanding for the whole of society, the chance to contribute to the advancement of an individual human would be even more remarkable. No calling could be more divine.

"Well, we've no time to waste, gentlemen." Stella, babe in arms, strode across the churchyard toward the street. "Let's be off."

An invisible hand clutched his heart with a ferocious grip as a single thought pulsed through his brain.

Stella is not to go to Sherod's. Send her home another way.

Frank could not explain the phenomenon, but his soul vibrated with undeniable urgency.

"Stop!" He jogged up to Stella and circled around in front of her. "You can't go to the brothel."

She bristled. "If you think I care one whit about my reputation when a child's life hangs in the balance, Frank Stentz, you don't know me as well as I thought you did."

Frank stood his ground. He had to. "I don't know if it is your reputation that needs protecting or if it is your life or the life of the child, but the moment you marched past me, a warning sprang to life inside my spirit. One that insisted I send you home another way. I won't ignore that, Stella. Not when every instinct I have tells me it came from above."

Her expression softened, then grew uncertain. She bit her lip as she glanced down and snuggled the child closer. "I hadn't considered it might be dangerous for the baby."

"Muir and I will go to Sherod's. I promise we will do everything in our power to find the babe's mother and get her away from there. We'll bring her to your father's house straightaway."

"No. Bring her to Norman's house."

Frank's brow scrunched. "The carpenter?"

"Yes. He lives two blocks down on Fifth. Small house. White picket fence. There's no telling how long your search might take. If the babe gets hungry or needs a change, I'd have no way to care for him at my home."

But Norman's wife would be well supplied. Having her own

278

infant, she could serve as a wet nurse and provide diapers and clean clothes should the need arise.

"Good thinking." Frank turned to Goldstein. "Will you escort her there, Isaac?"

He dipped his head. "It would be my privilege."

Reassured that Stella and the babe would be safe, Frank motioned to Muir and spoke five words he'd never imagined would pass through his lips.

"Let's go to the brothel."

CHAPTER 10

If it wasn't for the inconspicuous sign half hidden by the rocking chair on the front porch, Sherod's Sporting House would have looked like any other slightly rundown home in the area.

From the outside. The inside was another matter.

A hard-faced man with bulging muscles and an impressively curled mustache showed Frank and Randolph into a parlor decorated with thick red draperies, fringed lamps, and paintings of scantily clad and not-at-all clad women.

Heat engulfed Frank's face, and his gaze immediately dropped to the carpet. Not only to avoid looking at any of the inappropriate artwork but to avoid making eye contact with any of the other gentlemen in the room. What if someone recognized him and assumed he was here for . . . entertainment? The thought made him ill. Until he recalled Stella preparing to march over here to storm the castle herself.

Courage, man. You and the Good Lord both know why you're here. Just do what needs to be done and quit worrying about what others might think of you.

"Well, hello, gentlemen." A middle-aged woman with rouged cheeks and kohl-rimmed eyes sauntered over to greet them, her gaze carrying a calculating gleam. "Welcome to Sherod's." She coiled her fingers around Muir's arm, then leaned close and patted Frank's lapel. "First time, honey? No need to be nervous. My girls'll be gentle with you." She laughed softly, a husky sound that was likely meant to entice, but it accomplished the opposite effect.

"I'm not here for . . . that," Frank murmured in a low voice as he stepped backward and crinkled his nose against the cloying scent of the madam's perfume. "I'm looking for a woman who works here. One who gave birth recently. Could you arrange an introduction? I just want to talk to her."

Muir was working to disentangle himself from the bold female when Frank's words set off an unpleasant reaction.

The madam's smile tightened, and anger flashed in her gaze. "This ain't a talkin' house, boys. It's a sportin' house. And if you ain't gonna pay, I'm gonna have to ask you to leave." She motioned to the large fellow at the edge of the room.

"We'll pay," Frank blurted in a desperate attempt to stave off the advance of the muscled doorman currently cracking his knuckles and stretching his neck as if preparing for a physical altercation.

Frank fumbled for his billfold and pulled out a few dollars. He handed them to the madam, who raised an eyebrow at the sight of the money. She snatched the bills from his hand, folded them, and tucked them into the neckline of her dress.

"Fine. You can stay, but only for entertainment purposes. If I catch you askin' anyone else your insulting questions, Hastings will show you out. With extreme force. Do I make myself clear?"

"Yes, ma'am."

The sound of more knuckles cracking directly behind Frank sent a shudder through him, but he held his ground. Stella was counting on him. He'd not let her down.

The madam's eyes gleamed with malice. "None of my girls

would be foolish enough to get themselves with child, and I won't have you disturbing my guests with your unfounded accusations."

Because men facing the consequences of their actions would be bad for business. But if he couldn't ask around for the missing mother, how would they find her?

A blond woman in a blue dress that left most of her chest and all of her arms exposed pushed away from the bar she'd been leaning against and sashayed toward them. A leg wrapped in black stockings peeked through the slit of a skirt that stopped several inches above her ankles. Her attention seemed fixed on Frank, but he couldn't manage to hold her gaze. He trained his eyes on the floor until she pressed up against his side.

"Hey, sugar. Buy me a drink?" She leaned close and blew softly in his ear. He jerked involuntarily, which caused her to laugh, but she didn't pull away. In fact, she took hold of his arm and squeezed. "Leave this one to me, Opal. I'll make sure he has a *real* good time."

"And I'll take care of this one." A giggly redhead who looked younger than most of the female students at Baylor cozied up to Muir. "You know how I love older men."

At her age, *every* man was older.

Frank's companion tugged on his arm and drew him toward the bar. Deciding that going with her was less dangerous than engaging with Mr. Hastings, Frank followed. She ordered a pair of drinks, Frank paid, then she started doing the ear thing again. Only this time instead of blowing air, she whispered instructions.

"Relax, Professor."

Professor? She knew who he was? A mortified moan rumbled in his throat.

"I know who you're looking for, but you're gonna have to

play along, or Opal will get suspicious. You found the baby, didn't you?"

Frank reined in his surprise and dipped his chin in a subdued nod. It seemed his thespian skills weren't quite ready for retirement after all.

"Put your arm around my waist," his instructor whispered before reaching for the glass of whiskey he'd bought her. "What's your name, sugar?" She asked the question in a normal volume, cueing him that the performance had begun.

"F-Frank."

She beamed a smile at him, ignoring his stammer. "Strong name for a strong man," she purred, her flattery as empty as his wallet was sure to be at the end of this evening. She took a tiny sip of her drink, then walked her fingers up the front of his jacket. "I'm Pearl. You and me are gonna get along just fine, honey."

Frank swallowed hard. "You, ah . . . want to go upstairs?"

Her eyes lit with approval as her mouth curved into a well-practiced seductive smile. "I thought you'd never ask."

She slid her hand down his arm, laced her fingers through his, then led him past a distinctly uncomfortable-looking Muir, who was dancing by the piano with the giggly redhead.

Frank tugged Pearl to a halt. "What about my friend?"

She laughed as if he'd said something exceedingly witty. "Don't you worry, sugar. Miss Ruby will show him a great time."

Frank decided to focus on the *don't you worry* part of that statement, praying it meant Miss Ruby was in on the subterfuge. Offering no further resistance, he followed Pearl to the second floor and down a dim hallway. Instead of stopping in one of the rooms with an open door, however, Pearl led him to a narrow back staircase that led to the third-floor attic. A single long room with a ceiling that slanted on both sides stretched out before him. A series of cots lined each wall with a washstand on one side and an open wardrobe containing a handful of colorful dresses on the other.

"Wait here." Pearl released his hand and hurried down to the last cot on the left, where someone lay under a dingy-looking blanket. "Jade? It's Pearl. Wake up, honey. There's a man here to see you."

"I can't, Pearl. Not tonight."

Frank strained to hear her from across the room. Her voice was small and clogged with tears.

Pearl sat on the edge of the cot, her face aglow from the light of the candle next to Jade's bed. Pearl glanced back at Frank, her face suddenly looking years younger than it had downstairs. "He's not that kind of man. He's one of the wise men we saw in the nativity play this afternoon. He found your baby."

Jade gasped and sat straight up in bed, her wild gaze searching through the dark. "Curtis?" She grabbed Pearl's arm. "He can't be here. You *know* that. Opal will kill him."

Frank stepped into the room. "Your baby's safe, miss. He's with a friend of mine. On the other side of town." Thank the Lord. The idea of Stella or an innocent babe being anywhere near this place filled his chest with ice.

"It *is* the wise man." Jade's voice shook with awe as she pushed aside the blanket and swung her legs over the side of the cot. She wore a simple calico dress of modest design, likely one that had belonged to her before she'd come to work at Sherod's. "You found my baby? Is he all right? I hated leaving him out there in the cold, but I didn't know what else to do. Opal threatened to kick me out if I didn't get rid of him. I have no money and nowhere to go. No one to take me in. Without the protection of this house, I'd freeze to death on the streets."

Frank felt her desperation claw through him like a living thing, and his heart melted. "Your baby is fine. He's out of the cold and being tended to by a pair of ladies who'll see he has everything he needs." He walked deeper into the room. "But what Curtis really needs is his mother. That's why my friend and I have come. To offer you and Curtis a chance for a fresh start."

"I . . . I don't understand."

Footsteps on the stairs had all three of the room's occupants holding their breath. Frank turned to face whoever approached, ready to battle but praying it wouldn't be necessary. When he saw Muir's face emerge from the stairwell, he released his breath and smiled in relief.

He waved Muir forward, then turned back to the women. "This is my friend Randolph Muir. He's the one who found your son in the manger and the one who would like to help you be a mother to him."

When Muir came alongside him, Frank made the introductions. "This is Jade. The babe's mother."

"Gladys," she corrected. "My real name is Gladys. Jade's my working name."

Muir stepped forward and sketched a small bow. "Miss Gladys. I'd like to tell you a story, if I may. And ask you a few . . . personal questions."

She gave him an odd look but nodded. "All right."

Muir seated himself on the cot across from hers and began telling the tale of his daughter.

Pearl rose and gave the two a bit of privacy, moving to Frank's side. "You fellas really gonna get her out of here?"

"If she's willing." Frank considered the woman beside him. "We could get you out as well. Give you a fresh start in a new place. Ruby too." He frowned and looked around. "Where is Ruby?"

286

Pearl smiled. "Down in one of the sporting rooms, jumping on the bed." She chuckled softly when Frank's forehead wrinkled in confusion. "In case anyone should walk down the hall to check on us." Pearl winked. "She's making sure they hear what they need to hear. And probably having the time of her life." Her smile faded. "Genuine pleasure is rare in this line of work."

"You don't have to stay here. Either of you. We can get you out."

Pearl swiveled her head in the direction of the single window at the end of the room, a touch of wistfulness softening her features before she forced it away with a shake of her head.

"You're sweet to offer, Professor, but I'm stayin'. Ruby swears she has a cowboy savin' up his pay so he can come back and marry her. I tried telling her those kind of promises are empty, but she insists her cowboy is different. That he's comin' for her. She won't leave. And I can't go knowin' she's here. Someone's got to look out for the young'uns. Heaven knows Opal ain't gonna do it. All that woman cares about is linin' her pockets." She manufactured a smile and patted Frank's chest. "Don't you worry 'bout savin' me, Professor. I got a little nest egg set aside. When the time is right, I'll save myself."

"I'm sure you will." He prayed that day would come soon. The longer she stayed in this life, the harder it would be to leave.

Before he could say anything more, Muir rose to his feet and turned to face Frank. "Gladys has agreed to return to Cambridge with us."

Pearl hurried to Gladys's side and wrapped an arm around the girl's shoulders. "Are you sure, honey?" She lowered her voice. "There's no guarantee you ain't jumpin' from the fryin' pan into the fire."

"I know. But if it means keepin' Curtis, I gotta take the

chance. He's the only family I got in this world, Pearl. Givin' him up tonight nearly broke me." Gladys sat a little straighter and patted her friend's arm. "Besides, you have the best intuition I've ever seen when it comes to men. You wouldn't have brought these two up here if you didn't believe them to be honorable. If you trust them, so do I."

"Well, I guess all we have to do now is figure out a way to get you off the property without Opal catching you."

"Actually," Frank said, stepping forward, "I have an idea about that. Ever hear the story about Rahab and the Israelite spies?"

Gladys's face scrunched. "Who's Rahab?"

"A harlot, just like us," Pearl said, surprising Frank once again. She glanced his way and gave him a saucy wink, clearly enjoying having the upper hand. "She hid a pair of spies in her room, then let them down out of her window to help them escape. I'm thinkin' the professor here is plannin' on switchin' things up and having the spies lower the woman through the window. Am I right, Professor?"

Frank grinned. "That you are, Miss Pearl."

"Well then, I guess we better get busy tying the bedsheets together."

CHAPTER 11

"They're sweet when they're sleeping, aren't they?" Norman's wife, Alma, smiled at Stella over her knitting as her needles clicked quietly in the small parlor.

Alma had welcomed the baby boy into her home without batting an eye. She'd shown Stella how to change and swaddle him, and had just finished feeding him a few minutes ago, which had soothed the little lad back to sleep.

All the wrinkles smoothed from his pink face as he relaxed in Stella's arms. His bow-shaped mouth hung slightly open as his chest rose and fell in a gentle rhythm.

"I feel like I could just sit here and hold him for hours."

Alma chuckled softly. "I was like that with my first, too. Didn't want to put her down. Just wanted to hold her and nuzzle those chubby cheeks. With a toddler in the mix this time, I'm too busy to do much baby nuzzling, but I treasure the quiet moments with Millie during nursing." Her knitting paused as she looked up and met Stella's gaze. "Except the predawn feedings. Can't say I treasure those."

Stella smiled as she brushed the back of one finger along the baby's face. Like most women, she'd experienced a desire to have children of her own, but she'd forced herself to forfeit that particular dream years ago when she realized marriage wasn't in her future. Frank had changed all that, however, and dreams she'd set aside as impossible were resurrecting with surprising speed.

A quiet knock on the front door brought Stella's head up and Alma's husband out of the kitchen, where he'd been raiding the cupboards for a snack after putting his girls to bed. He shoved the remains of what looked to be a piece of jam-slathered bread into his mouth as he crossed the room, taking a moment to swallow before opening the door.

"Professor. Glad you could make it."

Stella's heart pounded as Norman opened the door and stepped aside so the newcomers could enter. The moment she spied Frank, she thanked God for bringing him through the night unscathed.

Well, perhaps not precisely unscathed. When he pulled off his hat, she noted his thick red hair standing up in ruffled disarray. Not only that, but his bow tie was askew, and the bottom button of his vest was undone. If she wasn't so sure of his trustworthiness, she might be a tad concerned over the significance of his rumpled appearance, considering where he'd been for the last hour and a half. But the way his gaze eagerly sought hers and radiated with a desire to please silenced the insecurities stirring in her breast.

"We found her, Stella." He smiled and stepped deeper into the room to admit Mr. Muir and a young lady with red-rimmed eyes and a thin carpetbag. "This is Gladys."

The girl looked as comfortable as a mouse being invited into a room full of cats. Her gaze darted to and fro as she nibbled her bottom lip. Until she caught sight of the small bundle in Stella's arms.

"Curtis?" Her voice cracked as she dropped her bag and moved toward the sofa where Stella sat.

Tears misted Stella's eyes as she rose to her feet and met Gladys halfway. "He's been fed and changed," she said, "but I'm sure he's missed his mama."

Careful to support the baby's head, Stella opened her arms, surprised at the pang that ricocheted through her heart when she transferred him over.

"Oh, my sweet boy." Gladys sobbed quietly as she curled her son close and dropped kisses on his head. "I'll never leave you again. I swear it." She glanced up, looking first to Stella, then to Alma. "Thank you for looking after him. I . . . I know you must think me a terrible person, but I didn't know what to do."

"No one thinks you are a terrible person." Stella circled an arm around Gladys's shoulders and gave her a little squeeze. "Anyone can see how much you love him. You were in an impossible position and did the best you could to protect your child. Thankfully, God led these modern wise men to your babe just as he led the magi of the past to his own Son. Things will be better now. You'll see."

Gladys peeked over her shoulder to where Mr. Muir spoke in quiet tones to Norman. "He says I can have a fresh start. That no one back east will know about Sherod's. That he and his wife will help me find honorable work and provide for Curtis." She looked back to Stella, her voice barely a whisper. "I want it to be true—I *need* it to be true—but miracles don't happen to girls like me."

Stella leaned close. "God doesn't make mistakes when it comes to handing out miracles." She smiled down at Curtis and rubbed the bottom of the blanket where his sweet little feet were cocooned. "As much as you love your son, that's how much God loves you, Gladys. More than you could ever imagine. None of us deserves to be his children. We all fall short of his standard. Yet he offers to adopt us anyway. Just like the Muirs are doing for you. You can trust them, but more than that, you can trust the God who brought them to you."

Alma came alongside, a small bag in her hands, which she held out to Gladys. "I put a couple of extra baby gowns and diapers inside. They should see you through the train ride to Cambridge."

"Thank you." Gladys took the bag in one hand, her chin trembling. "I don't know how I'll ever repay you and the professors for your kindness."

Alma pressed a hand to Gladys's back. "You'll repay us by using this opportunity to turn your life around and raise Curtis to be a man of honor."

Stella gave the babe's toes a final wiggle. "Maybe one day you'll even be in a position to extend a similar kindness to someone else in need."

Catching movement in her peripheral vision, she turned her head and spied Frank standing off by himself, trying to get his unruly hair to lay flat as he regarded his reflection in the front window. She bit back a grin.

"I'll fetch the men so we can be on our way," she volunteered before meeting Gladys's gaze again. "You'll be staying in my home tonight."

Gladys nodded. "All right."

Stella moved to join Frank. "Let me help."

He pivoted, a sheepish expression on his face. "Pearl said I had to look mussed if we didn't want Opal to get suspicious."

Stella ran her fingers through the front of Frank's hair, enjoying the feel of his wavy locks. "Pearl?"

"She . . . ah, helped us find Gladys." He cleared his throat and fidgeted as she began to straighten his bow tie. "Nothing improper occurred between us, Stella. I swear it."

"I know." She leaned close and pressed a kiss to his flaming cheek. "I trust you, Frank. Completely. Besides, you were only at that place because I insisted. It would be the height of hypocrisy for me to disparage you for doing what needed to be done to rescue Gladys."

Appreciation and a humbling bit of wonder glowed in the depths of his blue eyes. "I love you, Stella."

A smile stretched across her face to match the stretch she felt in her heart as it expanded to accept him fully into her life. "I love you, too."

She could have enjoyed that moment for hours, but their privacy shrank quickly as people gathered by the front door.

Professor Muir gazed over the heads of the others, seeking her out. "Where's Goldstein?"

"I sent him to my father so they could prepare the spare bedroom for our guest. They'll be ready for us."

The older man dipped his chin, fetched the carpetbag Gladys had left behind, then opened the door for her and her babe to pass through. Frank offered Stella his arm, and they followed the others into the coolness of the mild December night.

Nervous energy vibrated through Frank as Stella walked beside him, hugging his arm. They moved at a quick pace due to the nip in the air, and every step they took ticked like a giant watch counting down in his head.

Tonight. He'd talk to her father tonight. While Stella helped Gladys get settled. He owed Professor Barrington a declaration of his intentions. He'd kissed the man's daughter this evening. Had practically proposed. All without officially requesting her hand in marriage. He needed to—

"Thank you again for what you did tonight." Stella's quiet statement broke into his thoughts.

Kissing her?

"It was quite heroic, you know. Infiltrating the enemy's keep to rescue a damsel in distress."

Ah. That. Frank shook his head. Of course she was talking about Gladys. The young woman was walking directly ahead of them. Only a muddle-headed pigeon would be thinking about kisses at a time like this.

"I'm no hero, Stella." In truth he'd been a mess, nearly bungling the entire operation before they'd even begun. If it hadn't been for Pearl, he and Muir would have been tossed out on their backsides with a pair of black eyes as souvenirs. "I'm just an ordinary man fumbling about as best as I can."

She cast a sideways look at him, her eyes shining with admiration. "You are far from ordinary. Though I do appreciate your humble spirit."

"I don't think I can claim humility. It's more of a personal awareness of my many shortcomings."

"Spoken like a humble man." She laughed softly and snuggled a bit closer as Muir and Gladys turned a corner, several strides ahead of them.

He covered her hand with his, loving the feel of her leaning into him. Going home to Cambridge without her would be lonely indeed.

Unless . . .

"Would you consider spending the Christmas holiday in Massachusetts with me?" His pace increased slightly as the excitement of the idea took hold. "Now that the fall term is completed, your father would be free to travel. I could introduce you to my parents, show you around Harvard, and even take you on a walk down Brattle Street to show you the house where Henry Wadsworth Longfellow lived."

Bribing her with literary landmarks probably wasn't necessary, but he really wanted her to say yes, and he was willing to pull out all the stops.

"I'd have to talk to my father first," she hedged, "but it . . . it sounds lovely. I'd enjoy meeting your family."

That wasn't a no. Frank's pulse increased its tempo.

"I told Muir he could use my return ticket for Gladys, so we wouldn't need to leave right away. We could wait a few days. That is . . . if you want to. I don't want to pressure you."

Her grip on his arm tightened. "Of course I want to see your home. Meet your family. Walk the hallowed halls of Harvard." She straightened a bit and shot him a grin. "I want to know everything about you, Frank. And your home is a big piece of who you are. The truth is, I've been thinking a lot about Cambridge lately. Of what it might be like to . . . live there. With you."

He stumbled to a halt. "I thought you didn't want to leave your father."

She shrugged, her gaze falling to his shoes. "I don't. But Papa and I had a long talk about it, and he promised to come visit often. Said he wanted me to experience the same kind of happiness that he and Mama shared." Slowly, she raised her chin and looked him in the eyes. "I can't say that the idea of leaving doesn't terrify me, because it does. So when you mentioned spending Christmas with your family, I felt a bit like you were asking me to jump into a cold river all at once when I thought I'd have time to wade in little by little and get used to the water."

Frank collected both her hands in his. "I'll give you all the time you need to get used to things, Stella. If you come to Cambridge as my wife and, after a year or two, decide you hate it there, we can look at other options. I've heard rumors of a university being built in Chicago. One that intends to cater to the study of advanced mathematics. It's not Texas, but it's closer than Massachusetts." He lifted the backs of her hands to his mouth and pressed a kiss to both sets of knuckles. "Wherever we end up, I know we can make a good life together."

Her dark eyes glowed in the light of the corner streetlamp, glistening and beautiful. "I agree."

Admiration and hope radiated from her so strongly, he swore he saw visions of their future together reflected in her eyes. His chest ached in response as his gaze fell to her mouth.

Her breath caught as if she sensed his intent, but she didn't pull away. He released one of her hands and settled his palm at her waist, slowly tugging her closer. Finding her eyes once again, a thrill shot through him to discover them brimming with shy welcome. His right hand slid into the small of her back as his left secured her palm against his chest. He hadn't thought his heart could pump any harder, but the feel of her delicate fingers pressing into his coat sent his pulse oscillating at a frenzied speed that definitely surpassed the threshold of statistical significance.

When she tilted her chin upward in silent invitation, he bent his head to hers. He swore he heard a heavenly host break out in song as his lips found her mouth. The tender touch sent shock waves through him that caused him to tremble. She must have felt it, too, for a slight tremor coursed through her body. He tightened his hold in an effort to steady them both but quickly became lost in the taste of her. Mercy, but she was sweet. She kissed him back with a tenderness that stretched his heart beyond any known measure. Never had he imagined a love so abundant!

As if awakening from a dream, Frank gradually loosened his hold and leaned away from her beautiful lips. A fetching blush colored her cheeks as her lashes dipped to hide her eyes.

Unable to resist, he bent back in and placed a chaste kiss on her forehead.

"I love you, Stella."

Her blush deepened, bringing a smile both to his face and his heart.

He'd come to Texas to collect data and conduct a compatibility experiment with a woman he'd met through correspondence. What he'd found, however, defied calculation, quantification, or statistical analysis. For who could ever measure the infinite breadth of love?

Tracie Peterson is the award-winning author of over one hundred novels, both historical and contemporary. She has won the ACFW Lifetime Achievement Award and the Romantic Times Career Achievement Award. She is often referred to as the "Queen of Historical Christian Fiction," and her avid research resonates in her stories, as seen in her bestselling HEIRS OF MONTANA and ALASKAN QUEST series. Tracie considers her writing a ministry for God to share the Gospel and biblical application. She and her family make their home in Montana. Visit her website at TraciePeterson.com or on Facebook at Facebook.com/AuthorTraciePeterson.

USA Today bestselling author Misty M. Beller writes romantic mountain stories set on the 1800s frontier and woven with the truth of God's love. Raised on a farm and surrounded by family, Misty developed her love for horses, history, and adventure. These days, her husband and children provide fresh adventure every day, keeping her both grounded and crazy. She writes from her country home in South Carolina and escapes to the mountains any chance she gets. Learn more and see Misty's other books at MistyMBeller.com.

Christy Award–winning author Karen Witemeyer writes historical romances because she believes the world needs more happily-ever-afters. She is an avid cross-stitcher, tea drinker, and gospel hymn singer who makes her home in Abilene, Texas, with her heroic husband, who vanquishes laundry dragons and dirty-dish villains whenever she's on deadline. To learn more about Karen and her books and to sign up for her free newsletter featuring special giveaways and behind-the-scenes information, please visit KarenWitemeyer.com.

Sign Up for
Tracie's Newsletter

Keep up to date with Tracie's latest news
on book releases and events by signing up
for her email list at the link below.

TraciePeterson.com

FOLLOW TRACIE ON SOCIAL MEDIA

Tracie Peterson   @AuthorTraciePeterson

Sign Up for Misty's Newsletter

Keep up to date with Misty's latest news on book releases and events by signing up for her email list at the link below.

MistyMBeller.com

FOLLOW MISTY ON SOCIAL MEDIA

Misty M. Beller, Author

@MistyMBeller

Sign Up for
Karen's Newsletter

Keep up to date with Karen's latest news on
book releases and events by signing up for
her email list at the link below.

KarenWitemeyer.com

FOLLOW KAREN ON SOCIAL MEDIA

 Karen Witemeyer's Author Page

Be the first to hear about new books from Bethany House!

Stay up to date with our authors and books by signing up for our newsletters at

BethanyHouse.com/SignUp

FOLLOW US ON SOCIAL MEDIA

   @BethanyHouseFiction